XBestia

XBestia

Book One
Xenofreak Nation

by Melissa Conway

Chapter One

July 2032, New York

As protests go, the gathering in front of the Huffman Building in the Capital District was unimpressive. Most of the people attending were friends of the organizer, the head of a little-known organization called The Pure Human Society. The only media presence was a bookish, bored-looking little man from a small conservative newspaper out of New Jersey.

Bryn Vega watched as her father stepped up on an overturned orange crate and addressed the crowd of about forty people with a completely unnecessary bullhorn.

"Not long ago," Harry Vega spoke into the bullhorn to get their initial attention. He paused both for effect and to let the crowd quiet sufficiently down. "I saw a young man at the bank with an armband xenograft. Only it wasn't pig skin or rabbit fur or even snakeskin."

The woman standing next to Bryn sneered at the word 'snakeskin.' She looked at Bryn briefly and shook her head as if to say, "What's the world coming to?"

Harry Vega raised his voice and the bullhorn magnified it enough to drown out even the traffic sounds coming from busy Huffman Park Avenue.

"What I saw was an abomination. An unforgivable sin of vanity and cruelty. This—this xenofreak…" her father's face fell into a look of abject disgust as he slowly enunciated each word, "had a pelt strip with a very distinctive black and white pattern on it. It was a zebra."

A collective gasp rose from the crowd and everyone began talking. Someone shouted out, "Damned xenofreaks!" Another countered, "Xeno murderers, you mean!"

Bryn glanced over to the reporter, who still looked bored, but who was at least texting something on his holophone.

1

In a voice filled with derision, her father said, "The president of the United States has seventeen tattoos. During his campaign, he showed as much ink as possible to attract the Generation Y and Z votes."

At almost eighteen, Bryn didn't belong to a generation that she was aware of. Probably someone had already given her group a name, but since the previous gens had reached the end of the alphabet, Bryn didn't know if her group was supposed to start over from the beginning or what. She did know that the world she and the other Gen-somethings would inherit was about as messed up as it had ever been. As for the 35-year-old president, she thought it was cool that the youngest president ever had been elected in her lifetime. If she could have, she would have voted for him despite her father's opinion. The prevailing sentiment among her peers was that only a young president could possibly keep up with the times. President Frisbie's opponent had been sixty-two years old and barely knew what a holophone was, much less how to use it.

She tried to concentrate on her father, who was only getting warmed up. "Yes, we are in the midst of a depression surpassed only by the great depression of 1929. Our president, our legislature, the leaders of this once-great country are too busy digging us out of a very deep economic hole to care about the wholesale desecration of other species. Violent xenofreak outbursts, like the unprecedented attack against peaceful protesters last month in Chicago, have been ignored, left for local authorities to deal with. This country's leaders have done nothing to prevent the heinous spread of xenofreakish outrages. Every single year the ethical implications are debated in the legislature and every single year the bills that would impose restrictions on the practice of xenotransplantation are shot down."

Bryn had heard the speech several times over the last few days as her father practiced it at home. She'd made the mistake of asking him what the difference was between wearing a leather jacket and getting a xenograft, and had to listen to a forty-minute lecture peppered with comments like, "How could you be my daughter and ask such a thing?"

The next part of his speech always upset her, so she tried to tune it out, but was only partially successful.

"My wife," Harry's voice softened deliberately, and the crowd hushed and leaned forward, "was one of the very first recipients of a pig heart in 2014. The donor pig had been genetically engineered for compatibility with the human immune system, but technology at the time was unable to account for the difference in tissue aging. My wife could have lived to be eighty or so, but a domesticated pig only lives to be ten or fifteen years old. The heart began to age and my wife…" here Harry's voice broke and Bryn's eyes burned with sudden tears. He cleared his throat and continued with more strength, "My wife died. She was a hero, a pioneer for xenotransplantation—for its intended purpose—which was to save lives. And now that the xenosurgeons have perfected the process, it does save lives. But just the other day I heard tell of a four-year-old child with a congenital heart defect that was unable to get a xenodonor and do you know why?"

Bryn knew why; everyone did. The grim, expectant silence of the crowd demonstrated her father's control. They were waiting for the high point—the inciting statement that they all knew was coming. Harry Vega did not disappoint.

"Because the genetic xenoengineers make more money producing animals for the perverted lifestyles of xenofreaks! They make millions upon millions of dollars enabling these atrocities!"

Bryn's father had recruited her to help find words strong enough to convey the depth of feeling he had for the subject. He'd initially rejected the word 'atrocity' until Bryn pointed out it was oft used to describe the horrors of Auschwitz.

The word and her father's emphatic use of it did its job: the crowd burst out in a supportive cheer, the strength of which made Bryn realize the gathering had swelled to double its original size. The reporter no longer looked bored. His holophone was now aloft and recording her father's every word.

Standing among the bodies pressing forward to get a better view gave Bryn a moment of panic. She edged backwards, through the shouting, cheering throng until she stood on the fringe and could breathe again. From a more comfortable distance she was better able to assess the crowd as a whole. Most stood together reveling in the whipped frenzy of mob mentality. Several were less involved, with only the occasional, "Yeah," or a nod of the head to show solidarity. A few—no, there were exactly four of them—showed either no response to her father's words, or worse, rolled their eyes at each other in disdain.

Two of these dissenters were off to her left eating fast food hamburgers. One young woman with a black scarf draped over her head and wrapped around her neck sat on a cement retaining wall watching Bryn's father from behind mirrored sunglasses. The fourth stood about ten feet away from Bryn, a tall, broad-shouldered young man with a white scar that sliced vertically through his left eyebrow, leaving his cheek unblemished but then continuing down to mar his otherwise well-shaped lips. Bryn wondered how he'd gotten such a scar; it looked like someone had gone after him with a sword. He certainly seemed tough enough to have gotten into some kind of deadly conflict. His brown hair was pulled back into a stub of a ponytail that revealed he'd shaved his hair from the tops of his ears down. The muscles in his neck, the only part of his body she could see since he was wearing jeans and a light windbreaker, were thick and strong.

He turned and caught her staring. She looked away, feeling a blush creep over her cheeks, and looked back to where her father was still giving his speech, still putting his all into garnering supporters for his cause. Harry Vega was at the point where he once again, more ardently this time, emphasized the depth of his despair at losing his wife. In many respects, it bothered Bryn whenever he used his personal loss for professional gain. She doubted her mom would find it acceptable that her husband, a man she'd come close to divorcing before her xenoheart gave out, would martyr her for his own purposes.

But she loved her father. He meant well, even though he played the widower card more often than she'd like. And just because she didn't feel as strongly as he did about xenoaugmentation didn't mean she approved. Sure, she had a few friends who'd had stuff done; even her best friend Maria threatened to get a bovine 'tramp patch' on her lower back to spite her parents. Xenografts were as popular in this generation as plain tats were twenty years ago. The xenofreaks, though, they took it to a level both incomprehensible and frightening.

Bryn realized she'd tuned out a good portion of her father's speech. Even standing on the orange crate, he was barely elevated enough for her to see his face above the throng. Behind the yawning mouth of the bullhorn, his eyes burned with an almost evangelical fervor. She tried to concentrate on his words and the reaction of his listeners, all the while aware that every once in a while, the scarred young man glanced her way with bright blue eyes that seemed completely at odds with his severe countenance.

Chapter Two

While keeping half an eye on the target, Scott Harding pretended to listen to the buffoon on the orange crate spewing inflammatory nonsense. The target was a pretty little thing in a crisp apple green sundress; not a mark on the creamy skin of her arms and legs. The speaker, her father, had the significantly darker skin of a Latin American immigrant, and the accent to go with it. Scott idly mused that the target's mother, the dead woman with the pig heart Harry Vega had so eloquently spoken of, must have been white indeed to tone down Harry's genetic contribution to the target's skin color. Her dark blonde hair must have come from her mother, too, although Scott knew a guy from south of the border who'd been born with light hair even though his parents had black. The poor guy's dad had run a paternity test only to find out it was some kind of recessive gene. One thing was sure; the daughter of the head of the Pure Human Society didn't bleach her hair. Scott doubted her father allowed her even the smallest act of rebellion. Someone as rabidly anti-xenofreak as he was would pop an artery if his little girl so much as got her ears pierced.

Scott shifted his weight, flexing his fingers inside his pockets. Somewhere deep in the part of his brain that controlled motor function, a clutch of nanoneuronal implants aided him as he unsheathed his claws and then relaxed again. He hated having to wear a jacket on what was becoming a very warm morning, but here among the fanatical xenophobes he had to keep his alterations hidden.

He glanced over at the target and found her looking right at him. She turned away so rapidly it almost brought a smile to his lips. Almost.

He wasn't in the mood to smile; his reasons for being here didn't exactly amuse him, and his accomplices weren't being unobtrusive enough for his comfort. Padme was keeping a low enough profile, but Fiske and Barney weren't hiding their contempt very well. They actually laughed out loud when Harry Vega suggested that all xenofreaks belonged in the zoo.

Neither of them was the sharpest scalpel on the tray. They thought they were tough, but it was all attitude and most of that came from their xenoalterations. They were members, as was Scott, of a gang called the XBestias. In and of itself, membership gave a person status, but Fiske and Barney weren't qualified to handle themselves should the crowd figure out what they were. Even Scott would have a hard time hoofing it fast enough to escape this many riled-up people. He was supposed to be acting like he didn't know either of those fools, but he couldn't help shooting them a look of warning.

The target happened to intercept it and Scott was just about to mentally kick himself when he spotted her tiny smile of approval. Okay, she thought he was giving the hecklers a dirty look. Still, he shouldn't make any contact with her whatsoever, so he moved back towards the street. If for whatever reason she wanted to look at him again, she'd now have to turn 180-degrees.

Harry Vega went on and on. Scott hadn't slept well last night—if he was honest, he'd admit he hadn't slept well since he'd taken on this assignment—and he fought a persistent series of yawns. Out of the corner of his eye he saw Padme adjust her scarf. She was a mystery to him, more so than most females. Her scarf covered her alteration: a set of drooping cow ears. Rumor was she'd had it done as some sort of penance, but Scott knew different. Whatever the reason, Padme's cow ears effectively blocked her eardrums, giving the term 'earmuffs' a whole new meaning. Sometimes he spoke to her and wasn't sure if she was ignoring him or just hadn't heard what he said.

She'd gotten them from the same person they'd all gotten their xenoalterations from, the infamous Dr. Nicholas Fournier. He'd been head of surgery at Manhattan's prestigious Xenotransplantation Hospital until it was discovered he had a gruesome secret. Despite requirements that all organs and tissue removed from patients be destroyed, Dr. Fournier had been caught with a macabre collection of appendages and whatnot from a wide range of patients, some of them powerful enough to make a very big stink. He kept them in his apartment in a room dedicated to the ghoulish display, a shrine of body parts pickled in jars of formaldehyde. He'd been booted out of the hospital, of course, and his license to practice medicine had been revoked. But that didn't stop him. If anything, it freed him to pursue his more Frankensteinian perversions.

His ignoble plunge from grace served to embitter him towards the establishment, or so Scott was told. When Scott went underground to get his alteration from the good doctor, he didn't ask. Not that he actually met him. Scott had been shuttled around by a chosen few nurses, who conducted his interviews and exams, took payment and prepped him for surgery. Security was so tight they'd sedated him before moving him to Dr. Fournier's secret facility for the procedure.

Scott lifted his chin when Harry Vega began a rant against the XBestias. While in recovery after his xenotransplant, Scott had been recruited into the notorious gang by Dr. Fournier's right-hand man, known only as Lupus. Latin for wolf, the name fit perfectly, since Lupus no longer had a human face—it had been replaced with that of a grey wolf.

"Two days after I saw that zebra-defiling xenofreak scouting security at the bank, it was robbed at gunpoint by known XBestia gang members," Harry Vega said. "I have it on good authority that every person in the bank during that robbery is now dead."

Scott couldn't control the look of alarm that crossed his face, but if anyone noticed, they'd think he was as appalled as the rest of them.

No one was supposed to know about this.

As Vega went on to assert that the XBestias had somehow identified and killed each and every person who'd been in the bank that day, Scott relaxed. Vega didn't know squat.

By the time the windbag began wrapping up his interminable speech, the crowd had grown to about a hundred people. The target looked around when a television news van pulled up and Scott practically felt her eyes brush over him again. Once the news crew approached and asked Vega for an interview, the speech was over, and the throng finally began to dissipate.

The target seemed to be trying to catch her father's eye, but he didn't notice. She waved to him anyway and a thoughtful look settled over her face as she began walking up Huffman Park Avenue.

Padme jumped off the retaining wall and followed her. Fiske and Barney too fell into line a few people behind Padme. Scott went the other way, through the alley west of the Huffman Building, across a weed-choked dirt lot and through a broken chain link fence.

The gravel parking lot was one of few free places to park in the area, which is probably why Vega chose this location for his demonstration. Scott got into a nondescript white van and started the engine. In the side view mirrors, he watched as the target approached her pert little VW Hamster, which was parked across the aisle directly behind the van.

Padme caught up to her and Scott got a glimpse of one of the shy xeno's rare and dazzling smiles. The target would think Padme was all friendliness as she asked for directions, but only until she sensed Fiske and Barney closing in.

7

Chapter Three

Bryn was surprised when the girl in the scarf approached her. She'd pegged her as pro-xenofreak, but here she was, all smiles, saying in a genteel, lightly accented voice, "It was a good speech, yes?"

Bryn shrugged and tried to look pleasant even though she was on guard—and not about to cop to being Harry Vega's only daughter. Just that morning he'd warned her, "I'm ticking off some very unpredictable people, Brynnie. We need to take every precaution to keep ourselves safe."

It was just like him to instill a sense of fear in her but not give any indication how she was supposed to protect herself. Just last week a horrible news holo out of Chicago showed a clash between an animal rights group holding a peaceful demonstration and three passing xenofreaks. There were conflicting reports about who started it, but one of the xenofreaks ended the name-calling and shoving by producing a home-made mini-submachine gun and, quite casually, razing the crowd. Miraculously, no one was killed. Cops didn't catch the perpetrator, but several people got his face on holo. He had a scrolled xenograft curving around the outer portion of one eye a la Mike Tyson, in what authorities believed to be crocodile skin.

The girl in the scarf removed her sunglasses with a flourish to reveal large, amused brown eyes. With a bounce in her step, she walked to the back of Bryn's Hamster so Bryn had to spin around to keep her in view. It struck Bryn that the girl seemed to be almost aggressively trying to engage her attention.

"Do you hate us, then?" The girl asked, pulling her scarf away on one side just enough to reveal long black hair partially covering what appeared to a droopy bunny ear, or, given the rough appearance of the fur, a cow ear attached upside down. A cold ball of dread formed in Bryn's stomach.

The girl's smile faded, and her eyes shifted for a fraction of a second to somewhere over Bryn's shoulder. Bryn started to look around, but something pressed firmly into the small of her back and a low male voice said, "Don't move."

Bryn stared into the xenofreak girl's newly expressionless face as the newcomer positioned himself to stand behind her, so close she shuddered at the feel of his hips brushing against the back of her dress and stiffened when he rested his chin on her shoulder. His unshaven face pricked her bare skin and she flinched away from the rank odor of onions on his breath. "Do as we say, and you won't get hurt." Like the girl, he sounded cheerful.

Bryn's knees began to shake as he grasped her arm with his free hand and steered her toward a white van. Another man—except Bryn had already begun to think of them as less than human—sprang ahead of them. As soon as the second man reached out for the door handle at the back of the van, a burst of adrenaline sent Bryn's heart racing. She reacted without thought. Clasping her fist in her hand she shot her elbow up and back, connecting with onion-breath's nose. Ignoring the shaft of pain down her forearm, she bent forward at the waist and simultaneously lifted her knee. A hard stomp on her accoster's instep forced a grunt out of him. The xenofreak girl stepped back and held her hands up as if denying any involvement. Bryn had just enough time to suck in a breath for a scream when onion-breath's hand came from behind and awkwardly tried to cover her mouth. She was frantic now, throwing her arms out and twisting away.

She heard a distant voice yell, "Hey!" and experienced a fleeting hope that help was on the way just before something fast and hard caught her in the temple. The ground rose up to meet her face, crushing gravel into her cheek. She lay there, stunned and barely aware when she was dragged, lifted and dropped onto a hard metallic surface. The sound of the van doors slamming in finality was the last she heard before floating away into unconsciousness.

Chapter Four

If he compared the loosely structured hierarchy of the XBestias with that of the US Marines, Scott figured he'd fall somewhere between a private first class and a lance corporal. Not at the bottom of the heap exactly, but in the six months since he'd been playing henchman to the goons who reported to Lupus, it had been extremely difficult to gain their trust. Every one of the xenofreaks he'd met had some kind of serious personality flaw—which would explain why they'd chosen to basically mutilate themselves. Not that they thought of it that way.

The Warehouse was located in a primarily xenofreakish part of town, and that's where they took the target. The story was that the Warehouse had been home to a chemical manufacturer shut down by the EPA for transgressions unknown to the XBestia squatters now occupying the huge tumbledown space. It took Scott months to get used to the smell, kind of a cross between sewer gas and car exhaust that was so strong it permeated the brick walls and cement floors. The original owner had purportedly gone bankrupt and never complied with EPA orders to decontaminate the site. The building went up for auction, but no one wanted to buy it, for obvious reasons. Scott and the others had no idea what they were exposing themselves to every time they came 'home,' but until the consequences of living in such a toxic environment manifested itself, they considered the risk marginally better than living on the streets.

He drove the van through the gate of a chain link fence with battered privacy slats and left the keys in the ignition. They got out and Scott hefted the limp and unresponsive target in a fireman's carry. Another XBestia got into the van and took it away while Scott carried his boneless burden into the Warehouse, inhaling the scent of her vanilla body spray before the noxious odor inside had a chance to overpower his olfactory sense.

He took her to Exam Room Three, one of about a dozen eight-by-eight rooms along the west wall that had functioned as offices for the management of the previous occupants. Most of the exam rooms had blacked-out windows, but number three was built up against a load-bearing section of wall with no windows at all, and when not in use by the nurses, it doubled as a detention room of sorts. Exam Room Three got a lot of use.

Scott was met by Vonda the Snake, whose job history included surgical nurse and a short-lived stint in the medical ward at a correctional facility. From there, she'd been fired for insubordinately flouting the dress code. This was a euphemism for Vonda having gotten herself xenografted with, at last count, the skins of a dozen types of snake. Vonda was heavy-set, butch as they come, and even though she'd been nothing but nice, Scott secretly found her intimidating as hell.

He laid the target down on the exam table, said, "She took a punch to the temple, but I think she came to during the drive. Fiske didn't hit her hard enough to last this long. I'm pretty sure she's faking it."

Vonda gave the target a cursory examination, lifted her lids, shined a penlight into her eyes and said in her phlegmy smoker's voice, "This'll go much faster if you just open them on your own, Missy. Otherwise, I'll have to examine you further. That might involve some probing I guarantee I'll enjoy much more than you will."

The target's slack face instantly tightened, and her eyes opened, the left one not as widely as the right due to swelling. Scott noted an abrasion on her cheek and a bruise forming under the eye. The target glared when Vonda chuckled and gave Scott a pleased look. He forced an answering smile.

"What are you going to do with me?" were the first words out of the target's mouth. Vonda threaded her fingers together across her prominent belly and smiled beatifically, producing an impressive double chin. "Oh, I hear you're in for a real treat."

From the door, a gruff voice said, "That's enough."

Scott looked over at Abel, an older man who functioned as Lupus' mouthpiece and sometimes enforcer. His hairless pink pate reflected the light from the bare bulb mounted twenty feet above them, but most people didn't so much notice the baldness as the two horns that protruded from his skull. Set above his forehead in line with his eye sockets, the pointy, three-inch long dik-dik horns were the perfect complement to Abel's sunken cheeks and hollow grey eyes.

Vonda compressed her lips for a moment before turning to Scott. "If she vomits or starts raving—really raving, not faking it—come get me." She walked out with her nose in the air. Not many people got along with Abel, who didn't, as far as Scott could tell, have a good side.

Scott leaned against the wall farthest from the target as Abel entered the room and shut the door. The target had lifted herself up on her elbows, but now she sat fully up and scooted backward until her back hit the wall. She pulled her knees up under the apple green dress and wrapped her arms protectively around her legs. Scott noticed that her eyes were green, a shade or two darker than the dress.

The spurs on Abel's cowboy boots jangled ominously as he took the two strides necessary to reach the target's side. He reached out and grasped her chin, lifting it to get a better look at her face. She let him do it, a tear sliding down her cheek.

If Scott didn't know him better, he'd think Abel took the tiniest bit of pity on her. The lanky old man moved back a few feet and smiled, a movement of his lips that normally reminded one of the Grim Reaper, but now looked almost pleasant.

"Your father's a pain in the ass, did you know that?"

The target's head seemed to be frozen in the position Abel had placed it. Her mouth barely moved as she replied, "Yeah, I know that."

It wasn't the response Abel expected. He burst out laughing and swung around to look at Scott. "I heard she broke Fiske's nose. You got your work cut out for you."

Scott took that to mean he had just been appointed the target's official jailer, which in the Warehouse also meant protector. He nodded.

"Nurse Nancy will be here in a few to run her through the protocol. Don't let any of the yahoos get any ideas."

Scott nodded again. The 'yahoos' consisted of nearly every man in the place and several of the women. Their 'ideas' would involve harassment at the least and sexual assault at worst. The Warehouse was not kind to the innocent. Not that Scott had ever seen anyone here that fit that description.

After Abel left the exam room, Scott and the target stared at each other for a full minute. Her bottom lip quivered the whole time. Finally, she asked in a little girl voice, "Are you going to rape me?"

Scott didn't bother to hide his surprise. "You want me to?"

"No! God." She sniffed and ran the back of her hand under her nose. "I want you to take me home."

Scott imagined himself trying to do just that. "Me and what army?"

"My father is rich. He could pay you."

She was a terrible liar. "Your father's a mailman."

"There—there's lots of people who would help him. The Society…" her voice broke on a suppressed sob.

Scott waited until she pulled herself together before saying, "Look. I don't really feel like doing this, so if you don't mind, let's just can the chatter."

"Chatter? Chatter?" The second 'chatter' she uttered was so shrill it was almost out of Scott's range of hearing. She leaned forward, still gripping her legs. "This is just another day for you, isn't it? You kidnap people all the time."

He shrugged, getting uneasy. Vonda said to come get her if the target started raving. He was pretty sure an emotional breakdown wouldn't qualify.

Luckily, her hysteria didn't escalate. She took a deep breath and let it out. Scott looked at the door and wondered when Nurse Nancy would get here. Maybe he could hit her up for a sedative that might make the target more amenable.

She must have caught him glancing at the door, because she asked, "What's the 'protocol'? What does that mean?"

"Ask Nurse Nancy."

Even with red eyes and blotchy skin in a furious face, the target still managed to present an attractive picture. Even with the bruise, which had spread further under her eye, a thin streak of purple. She was tall, 5'8" or so, but not overly thin. Her legs, what he had seen of them anyway, looked like they belonged on an athlete—a runner maybe. Too bad she wouldn't be able to run from what was coming.

Her eyes closed. In a defeated whisper, she said, "I can't believe this is happening."

Neither can I, thought Scott. Less than a year ago he was completing Marine basic training and looking forward to serving his country in the Fourth Iraq War. Turns out his country had different plans for him.

Chapter Five

It took every ounce of self-control Bryn possessed to stay relatively calm. Her head pounded and the effort to hold back tears didn't help matters. Perched on the examination table with its stained and torn vinyl cushioning, she told herself it could be worse. She could be in a bare concrete cell chained to the wall—naked. She could be fair game for the 'yahoos' the old devil-man referred to.

She could be dead.

These xenoscum obviously had an agenda—some plan to make use of her—most likely to blackmail her father into backing off. They'd bring in a holocam, hand her a holoreader displaying the main page from some news site and tell her to read a statement. She'd cooperate fully.

There was no guarantee she'd get out of this alive, but the fact that she hadn't seen where they'd taken her was a positive sign. One glaring negative was that her jailers weren't hiding themselves from her. If they eventually set her free, she'd be able to describe everyone she'd seen.

Dead girls don't talk.

In an effort to avoid further contemplation of that terrifying possibility she focused on the young man leaning against the wall, hands still casually in his jacket pockets. He looked like he was about to break out in bored whistling any second now.

"What's your name?" she asked, not expecting him to answer.

"Scott."

A short, humorless laugh escaped her. His face showed no curiosity as to what prompted the laugh, but she told him anyway. "I thought all xenofreaks had weird names."

"Most do."

"How'd you get that scar?"

"Fight." He looked at the door again.

"So what's your graft?"

In an instant, his face changed from indifferent to coldly angry. "Why don't you shut up?"

"Because I'm scared and I'd rather not think about what you people are going to do to me," she snapped. Ever-present tears filled her eyes again. She did not want to cry in front of this cretin.

He went to the door and opened it, looking out into the dark, cavernous space she'd glimpsed while upside-down over his shoulder. Nurse Nancy must not have been anywhere in evidence because he shut the door again and sighed.

Bryn knew she'd have a better chance coming out of this alive if she connected somehow with her jailers. But these people had debased and dehumanized themselves; how was she supposed to make them sympathize with her?

This Scott guy took taciturn to a whole new level, but Bryn felt it was imperative to get him talking. She asked the first thing that came to mind.

"What the heck's that smell?"

He flashed a fleeting grin and responded, "That's just us xenofreaks."

It winked into and out of existence so quickly she almost missed it: Scott had a sense of humor. Desperately, she tried to think of something funny to say.

"Well it smells like a janitor's mop," she said. When the corner of his mouth barely twitched, she resorted to the one thing all guys found amusing: potty humor. "Or a dinosaur fart."

That did it. Scott looked at her like she'd gone insane, but he laughed. She'd wedged the chisel in the crack; too bad she didn't have time to hammer away and make it wider. A perfunctory knock on the door heralded Nurse Nancy's arrival.

She was a he.

Nurse Nancy ignored Scott and greeted Bryn with a wide smile. In a feminine twang, he said, "Having a rough day, are we?"

She nodded, struck dumb by his xenoalteration. The skin of his lower face, along his jaws and chin and above his lip, everywhere a man's beard would grow, had been replaced with soft brown fur. She tried to keep her gaze level with his, but it kept dropping.

"You want to touch it?" He leaned forward.

The last thing on God's green earth Bryn wanted to do was feel this man's face, but she couldn't afford to alienate him from the outset. Keeping her revulsion under control wasn't easy as she placed her fingertips against the fur. It wasn't as soft as she'd expected, and as soon as she realized the stiffened tufts contained remnants of past meals, she snatched her hand away.

15

Nurse Nancy didn't seem to notice. "Much better than a prickly old man beard, don't you think?"

Bryn flashed on a memory from last year during her blissful two-month relationship with the junior class president. She and Paul made out at every opportunity, and not even the best moisturizer had toned down the redness and chafing around her mouth from the sparse stubble on his chin. Paul ended up dumping her for skanky Sheila Gottfried, claiming that all Bryn's teasing drove him to it. She wondered how he would feel when he saw her picture in the news.

"Alright, my pretty," Nurse Nancy said. "I need to take some blood and get your vitals. Have you ever had a serious illness?"

For the first time, Bryn noticed the tray of medical accoutrements Nurse Nancy held. He set it on the only other piece of furniture in the room, a small end table in the corner.

"Yes? No? Maybe so?" he prompted.

Baffled, Bryn answered, "No."

Nurse Nancy continued to pepper her with questions about her medical history while he wrapped a flexible tube around her upper arm and withdrew some blood. For the life of her, Bryn couldn't think of a logical reason for what he was doing.

"Anyone in your family have cancer?"

"My great-grandmother died of pancreatic cancer."

Nurse Nancy removed the tube and the needle and pressed a cotton ball on the prick site. "Hold that."

Obediently, Bryn put her forefinger on the cotton ball while he stuck a piece of tape over it.

"How about heart disease?" he asked.

For some reason, Bryn's eyes sought out Scott's. He'd heard her father's speech. He knew about her mother. Yet there wasn't the smallest bit of sympathy on his face.

"My mom," Bryn said.

Nurse Nancy tutted, wrapped a blood pressure cuff on the same arm and rapidly squeezed the pump.

"What kind of heart disease?"

"Dilated Cardiomyopathy."

He nodded sagely, watching the dial on the cuff as he slowly released the pressure. "She die?"

"Yes."

Apparently, not everyone here knew her history. Did he even know who she was or that she was being held against her will? She'd assumed he did because he'd asked about her day, but maybe he was just referring to her swollen cheek. A brief flash of hope was squelched when he said, "Alright gorgeous, you're all set. Blood pressure's a little high, but I think that's understandable under the circumstances."

He picked up the tray with its medical instruments and finally acknowledged Scott with a hard look. "Don't mess with her."

Scott just lifted his eyebrows.

"Mr., um, Nancy?" Bryn asked. "Why did you do all this?" She indicated the tray.

"Oh, Sweetie," he shook his head, features suffused with compassion. "Cooperate and you'll be back home before you know it, I promise."

It was a non-answer, but it gave her the first hope she'd had since this nightmare began. Nurse Nancy offered her a final reassuring smile before sashaying out the door.

The tears she'd been holding back would no longer be denied, but now they were tears of relief.

Chapter Six

In basic training, there'd been a lecture or two about keeping things in perspective when in combat. Scott knew he'd have to kill people, knew those people had families, friends, lives that if Scott was lucky, he'd cut short before they cut his short. He'd been told to forget about all that; keep his distance, stay focused on the goal, which was to shoot the target. If you sympathize with a target, you'd better hope your body armor holds up.

Bryn Vega seemed to be doing everything in her power to become more than a target to him. After Nurse Nancy told her she'd be going home, Scott almost said, "Yeah, in a box," but he didn't because she began crying like her mom just died all over again.

It was one hundred-percent essential that he show no weakness. 'Bestia' was Latin for 'animal,' an apt name for a gang of animalistic criminals. Even alone in the exam room with her, he couldn't risk appearing soft in any way. She cried for ten minutes, and he bit back maybe a dozen comments his traitorous brain produced to make her feel better.

When her wet sniffles got to be too much for him, he opened one of the drawers under the exam table and handed her a paper gown. She blew her nose several times and wiped her eyes. To Scott's surprise, she left no black smears of mascara on the paper. Her lashes were really that thick.

The door opened and Barney stuck his head in. "Hey Cougar, you still combustin' tonight?"

"I'm on duty. Tell the Viscount I'll kick his ass some other time."

Barney gave a little, "heh," and focused his attention on Bryn. He started to come into the room, but Scott shoved him out, said, "Later, dude," and shut the door. As soon as he did it, he knew what she'd say.

"What is that? On your hands?" Her voice was thick from her bout of crying.

Scott had kept his hands hidden in the pockets of his jacket because he didn't want or need her questions. "None of your business."

"Is that your alteration? You got fur put on your fingers?"

"Yeah, sure," he said. Cougar fur and the claws that came with it. "Why?"

"Why'd you wear that dress today? 'Cause you like it, right?" He'd said too much. He was not ignoring her very well.

"No," she replied. "I wore it because my dad asked me to."

Bryn was sitting with her lower legs hanging over the side of the exam table. The dress had a fitted bodice and flared skirt straight out of the 1950's. Almost a poodle skirt, like the costume his sister had worn for Halloween when she was six. Bryn's dad had good taste; she looked great in the dress, but he doubted Harry Vega had picked it because it made his little girl look hot.

He blew out a frustrated breath. "Whatever."

"What does 'combusting' mean?"

His brows dropped. "Seriously?"

She looked at him expectantly, the rims of her eyes so red they clashed with the green of her irises.

"A fight. We were supposed to fight tonight."

"Why?"

His shoulders came up. "Because we want to."

Her mouth opened slightly, but she didn't pursue the line of questioning. After a moment, she asked, "How long am I going to be here?"

He knew exactly how long but wasn't about to tell her. "No idea."

"Do you know anything?"

The question and the scorn with which it was delivered was designed to get him to open up and he knew it. "I know you talk too much."

"So…what? Are you going to shut me up?"

She was getting bolder as he continued to do nothing. He wasn't a threat to her, and she was figuring that out. "If I have to. Think about whether you'd like to spend the next few hours with or without duct tape over your yap."

She turned her head to stare at the wall.

Standing there, he was just regretting having kicked Barney out without asking him to bring back a chair, when the door opened again.

This time, Abel entered.

"Lupus has money on tonight's fight, so get greased up. You better win, for the little lady's sake. Ain't no one else I trust enough to keep their grimy mitts off her, not even me."

Normally, Scott would take that as a compliment, but among the XBestia it was dubious praise. He thought about suggesting one of the tougher gays or trannies watch her, but he knew just because they wouldn't mess with her themselves, didn't mean they wouldn't enjoy currying favor with those that would.

He started to leave, but Abel stopped him. "Gimme your jacket."

Scott didn't ask why. He fumbled for the zipper pull, irritated and a little embarrassed when the pads that had replaced his fingertips hampered him. He missed having normal dexterity and sensation in his fingers.

The assistant who'd explained the procedure to him hadn't sugar-coated it.

"We will be removing your fingers from just above the knuckle and fusing the feline middle phalanx to your bone. This will allow the extensor tendons to function. You will lose significant touch sensation. The pads on a cougar's paws are for protection much like the calluses on our feet. However, since the donor cougar has been genetically engineered, it's lived its whole life in a cage and I'm sure you'll find your new 'fingers' to be— soft."

He got the zipper down, removed his jacket and handed it to Abel, who immediately passed it over to Bryn. As Scott was leaving, he heard Abel say, "Let's hide some of that glaring wholesomeness, shall we?"

Chapter Seven

Bryn was several inches shorter than Scott even with low heels, which meant his jacket was way too big. Since the jacket would serve to disguise her, it was a good thing—to heck with just covering up her 'wholesomeness'—she was all for covering up her entire body. Abel suggested she pull the hood up and cinch it tight.

"I don't want to miss this fight," he said, "so you get a little treat. Not many outsiders see our humble community and live to tell about it."

Bryn's heart had been tripping nervously ever since the devil-man had rematerialized. She didn't know his name and didn't want to. But as frightened as she was of his appearance and demeanor, she was grateful to him for confirming she was going to live through this.

He opened the door and waved her to precede him. "Stick close. I'm sure I don't have to tell you what will happen if you try to run."

Beyond Exam Room Three, the roof of the warehouse rose to maybe thirty feet. Columns supported a framework of beams and corrugated metal roofing. Diffuse afternoon sunshine came through dozens of dirty skylight domes spaced in three rows along the ceiling. Bryn estimated the size of the place to be about as big as a football field. The prevailing odor was the same chemical smell that permeated everything, but interwoven with smoke from wood, incense and cigarettes. There was food cooking somewhere, too, a pungent garlicky dish that made Bryn's empty stomach growl.

In orderly rows spanning the entire length of the place stood tents of all shapes and sizes. Most were the kind you could purchase; the camping variety, from small one-person domes to elaborate family-sized versions with more than one 'room.' Others appeared to be homemade, mishmashes of canvas cloth, rope, bricks, wood and cardboard. The poorly constructed ones stood side-by-side with the better-quality tents; there was no segregation here. Most of the tents were drab, brown or tan or camouflage. Other than a row of light green portable toilets along one wall, there was a distinct lack of color. No growing things; no potted plants or trees or brightly colored anything. The whole place, from the grey of the cement floor, to the primarily black attire of the people, was dull and dingy.

People were everywhere: hanging out in front of the tents, strolling aimlessly or with purpose, talking, laughing, smoking, eating and drinking. Some hawked wares, either from their tents or from carts or from packs on their backs. As the devil-man led Bryn down the center aisle, the widest boulevard in the place, people nodded to him or waved. A few said hello. Bryn got the impression this man commanded respect and even fear.

None of the people looked normal, of course. Bryn had seen plenty of xenoalterations, but mostly in holos—advertisements for edgier products like alcohol and hard music. She'd glimpsed them in real life on the street and in the news. Most of the denizens here had common tattoos mixed with grafts in various designs and skins—snake and fur from multiple species. A few had tails or wings or ears, like the girl who'd distracted Bryn so her cohorts could more easily subdue her.

Here, a person would stand out if their skin was unmarred, like Bryn's. She kept her hands in the pockets of Scott's jacket, trying not to think about his furry fingers having been in the same pockets only minutes before. She knew the jacket looked incongruous combined with her girly skirt, smooth tan legs and strappy sandals, but most of the people they encountered seemed strangely incurious. Probably, no one questioned devil-man.

The jacket was also quite warm. The air was stagnant; no breeze freshened the place, which meant the ambient temperature inside the warehouse on this hot July day was sweltering. Most of the people wore sleeveless shirts and shorts that showed off their grafts and did nothing to disguise their body odor. She wondered where they bathed and imagined what fun could be had with dousing the lot of them with a fire hose.

Devil-man walked with authoritative purpose, spurs jingling, and Bryn had to practically trot to keep up. They were headed for the center of the place, an open area like a town square, only much more grim. Portable chain link fence sections had been set up in the shape of an octagon and people were milling about, at least a hundred of them in a circle around the cage, mostly men. Smoke rose from multiple sources and hovered in a hazy cloud above them.

"Abel! Your boy's going down," a big man in cargo shorts and a black t-shirt called out.

Bryn's captor said, "He's not my boy."

A guy with a flat-top haircut and the rounded ears of some tan-furred animal took issue with the big man's statement. "Cougar's gonna shred the Viscount."

"Ahh, you only say that because you losers share the same donor!" The big man responded good-naturedly.

Devil-man, or Abel—Bryn assumed that was his name—kept moving towards the center. Next to the fence stood the young woman with the cow ears. Gone was the overly friendly smile and exuberant charm.

"Padme," Abel said, nodding to her. "Keep an eye on this for me, will you?" He grasped Bryn's arm and pulled her forward. As soon as he walked away, just about everyone in the vicinity turned to stare. Padme was maybe five-foot four-inches tall and petite as a child. Bryn didn't think she'd stand a chance against even one of the xenofreak men looking at them like they were prime cuts of meat, grilled and garnished and laid out for their consumption.

"Don't worry," Padme said in an undertone. "I belong to Lupus. They won't bother us out here in the open."

"Who's Lupus?" Bryn asked.

Padme's face turned to stone. As if she were speaking to a child, she enunciated, "My owner."

Bryn wanted to dispute it, wanted to assert that in America in the 21st century, no one owned anyone, but Padme's demeanor convinced her any argument would be in vain. There were a lot of things Bryn wanted to ask Padme, but standing in this most surreal environment among the noise and the smoke and the almost palpable smell of testosterone, she didn't. Instead, she concentrated on surviving each moment.

It occurred to her that her "cooperation," as Nurse Nancy put it, might simply involve not freaking out, not falling apart. She'd kept her cool and instead of keeping her locked up, Abel brought her out here to meet his people. Did he want her to see how they lived, maybe even connect with a few of them, like Padme? Go back home and tell her father that xenofreaks were human after all? The idea seemed far-fetched even to Bryn, who knew herself well enough to accept that she was naïve, perhaps more so than most girls her age. These people were certainly human, but they also embodied the worst of human traits. Abel knew it, and he had to know Bryn would see it.

Next to them, a skinny blonde kid with a studded collar around his neck lit a joint, took a deep drag and held it out to Bryn. She shook her head rapidly and stepped closer to Padme, who laughed.

"You've never smoked pot?" she asked. "I bet you're a virgin, too."

Bryn looked around to make sure no one heard. "Why don't you just wave a red flag?"

23

Padme's head tilted to the side as she studied Bryn. "I like you," she announced. "So I'm going to give you some advice. Stop taking yourself so seriously."

That's advice? Bryn thought. But Padme had said she liked her, and Bryn wasn't in a position to turn down offers of friendship at the moment. "Thanks," she muttered.

A ragged roar rose from all around. She looked across the octagon cage where the crowd had parted to reveal two muscular, barely clothed men wearing swim goggles. The older, wider of the two wore a black Speedo and was covered head-to-toe with two-inch-wide wavy grafts in a familiar, scaly diamond pattern. The taller was Scott. He wore black bike shorts, and the only mark on his body, besides his furry fingers, was a plain tattoo on his left shoulder. He was too far away for Bryn to see what it was. Both men were barefoot and were either wet or slicked down with a shiny substance. It looked as if they'd just come from the pool.

"Are they—is that grease?" Abel had told Scott to get 'greased up.'

"What? Grease?" Padme lifted one of her ears. "Kind of. Highly flammable."

"Why do they call him the Viscount?" Bryn asked, nodding at the man in the Speedo, who was strutting for the crowd.

Padme shrugged. "Probably because 'Snake' was already taken."

A man in black leather pants and matching vest over his bare chest entered the ring. He set a cone-shaped metal apparatus in the center and knelt down to fuss with it. When it burst into flames, he fell back, and the crowd roared again.

Bryn turned to Padme with wide, horrified eyes, but the cow-eared girl just snorted.

Leather Pants left the ring and the combatants entered. There were no introductions. As soon as the fence was chained together, the Viscount threw a mean uppercut to Scott's jaw.

He missed. Scott weaved away from the next few punches, faster than the older man. They stayed near the fence, away from the flames but also out of reach of the fingers that poked through the chain link. Scott jabbed with his right, connecting with the Viscount's mouth, and dodged away. When the older man came after him, Scott jumped up and kicked him in the face with his heel, snapping the Viscount's head back. Bryn wanted to look away but couldn't seem to make herself. The noise of the crowd was deafening, and they were all pressing in closer and closer. Her empty stomach cramped, and her head spun. The smell of marijuana was thick in the air. She turned and caught the blonde kid exhaling in her direction. She waved futilely at the cloud of smoke. The kid laughed and stuck his artificially elongated tongue out and waggled it suggestively at her.

She looked back into the ring just in time to see the Viscount finally land a punch. Scott was faster and had a longer reach, but the Viscount had power. When his fist connected, it sent Scott spinning into the fence right in front of Bryn. He looked at her, seemed surprised, and then dropped straight down, narrowly avoiding the Viscount's next hit, which smashed into the fence and sent moisture spraying into her face. From this angle, she clearly saw the USMC tattoo on Scott's shoulder. With a fierce yell, he rammed his shoulder into the Viscount's abdomen, forcing him backward towards the flame. The crowd howled its approval.

Chapter Eight

Scott didn't have time to contemplate why the girl he'd helped kidnap just hours before was watching the fight like any member of the community. If the Viscount landed another one of his pile-driving punches, he doubted he'd be able to contemplate anything for some time. Grappling with the Viscount was a foolish move on his part, since the older man had been known to squeeze his opponents into unconsciousness in the past. Scott hoped the element of surprise would put him off-balance long enough to get him to the flame.

It didn't.

The Viscount dug his heels into the cement floor and stopped his backward progress, bent down and wrapped his meaty arms around Scott's back. With a mighty heave, he lifted Scott's feet off the ground. Scott let go of the Viscount's middle and allowed himself to be turned upside down. The Viscount staggered towards the fire, but Scott wrapped his lower legs around the Viscount's neck and clamped down. The Viscount's scaled skin-grafts gave Scott an advantage—while Scott's body was slick as an eel's, the Viscount essentially had built-in grippers. When Scott suddenly relaxed his legs, his body weight caught the Viscount by surprise, and he slipped right through his arms. Scott had been trained in how to fall; as soon as his shoulder contacted the cement, he rolled away and sprang to his feet. The Viscount swung and missed, swung again and clipped Scott's chin.

"Slash him!" Someone screamed from the crowd. They wanted blood, but Scott wouldn't use his claws. He'd fought a lot of guys with xenoalterations that gave them an edge in the cage, like horns, or whip-like tails, and in those cases his claws came out. The Viscount had no such advantage. Scott wouldn't resort to cheating even if Lupus did lose money on this fight.

He continued to lure the Viscount around the ring, dodging his punches. The older man was getting visibly tired, but Scott could do this all day. Finally, the Viscount gave him his opening. Scott's fist shot out, connecting solidly with the Viscount's nose. Blood gushed and the crowd responded with a roar of approval. The Viscount stumbled forward and tried to grab him, but Scott danced around to his rear and kicked him behind the knee. The resulting loss of balance made it almost easy for Scott to shove him into the flame.

Scott stepped out of range as the chemical coating on the Viscount's skin caught fire with a crackling whoosh, spreading over his entire body. The crowd screamed in delight. One high-pitched scream lasted longer than the rest, however, and Scott looked over to see Bryn with her hands over her face, hysterically shrieking. Clearly, no one had explained the rules to her.

The Viscount stood with his arms outstretched to the side as the flames died out into blue-tinged nothingness. He held his right hand out for the traditional finale, and Scott clasped it and allowed himself to be pulled into the flame as well.

Through his protective eyewear, he saw Padme on the other side of the chain link fence laughing her ass off at Bryn. He almost chuckled, too, but had to hold his breath until the chemical and its harmless flames burned completely away. The crowd applauded and hooted. The ones who'd bet on him chanted his name, "Cou-gar! Cou-gar!"

He raised his arms and walked the victory walk through the crowd. No one patted him on the back or shook his hand. He and the Viscount went straight to the showers, a tiled area on the north wall that had originally been used by the chemical factory as emergency showers in case someone spilled whatever they'd been manufacturing on themselves. The water wasn't heated, but it was free—well, technically, it was stolen from the city since the Warehouse wasn't officially occupied.

Although the 'grease' itself and the flames it produced weren't harmful, after you burned it, a caustic residue was created. Scott and the Viscount soaped up thoroughly, rinsed and repeated three times, amiably rehashing the fight.

It was times like these Scott almost enjoyed being a xenofreak.

Back in his tent, he put on the same clothes he'd been wearing earlier but left his hair loose. He automatically checked his holophone for messages, then lifted a secret flap near the bottom of the tent and checked his second holophone. The hidden one was a burn phone, the fourth one he'd had since living in the Warehouse. Each time he got a message, the phone went into the storm drain or the local pond or down the toilet at the corner gas station. He never called out on it.

He was not surprised to see a message today. All it said was, "Report," which was a bit problematic for him since he was due back in Exam Room Three.

Chapter Nine

Bryn hardly noticed her surroundings when Abel took her back to the exam room. At first, she'd been outraged that Padme hadn't told her what to expect—that she'd laughed at Bryn's abject horror when the Viscount caught fire. Bryn's anger wasn't misplaced; it was just…useless. She wondered at herself for having such a stupid reaction. Padme was a xenofreak. She'd cut off her own ears and replaced them with those of a dead cow. She seemed to be perfectly comfortable being owned by a man. It shouldn't have surprised her in the slightest that Padme found her discomfort humorous.

Abel had asked Padme to accompany them, and when the three of them entered the exam room, he shut the door. Bryn went to stand as far away from him as possible on the other side of the exam table. She'd been looking forward to taking off Scott's jacket, but as soon as she did, she saw the look in Abel's eyes, and wished she'd kept it on.

He licked his lips and said conversationally, "You're sweet, aren't you?"

Drug-laced second-hand smoke may have clouded her thinking, but Bryn definitely didn't like the way he was leering at her. "I don't know about that, but I am hungry."

She regretted the admission as soon as she made it. He would send Padme to get food and then she'd be alone with him.

Sure enough, he said, "Padme…" but Padme interrupted him.

"Remember what Lupus said."

His horned head jerked around, and he gave her a dark look, but then he muttered, "Right, right. I'll just take myself out of the equation; have someone get you some chow."

Bryn tried to be cool, tried to thank him, but she choked on the words. When he left, her knees nearly buckled. She couldn't help it; she looked to Padme, who met her eyes blandly.

"You could do worse," Padme said. "He's high up in the organization. Powerful."

Bryn shook her head in disbelief. "Are you kidding me? That's gross! He's an old man. He's—"

Padme shushed her with a loud, "Chht! These walls are thin, and you don't want to insult him. God, are you for real?"

"Am I for real? Am I for real? Yes, I'm real and you and all the rest of the freakshows here are one big nightmare!"

Padme laughed. "Feel free to pinch yourself all you want. It never worked for me."

Bryn sagged against the exam table and then decided to climb back up on it. Leaning back against the wall made some of the dizziness subside, but she floated on a strange, narcotic cloud for some time. It was impossible to guess how many minutes had passed, but sometime later, she asked, "What did you mean when you said pinching yourself never worked for you?"

Padme crossed her arms over her narrow chest. "Not every xenofreak is into self-mutilation."

Bryn closed her eyes. "That doesn't make sense."

"No, I suppose it doesn't. Not to a spoiled American brat like you."

With great effort, Bryn opened her eyes to give Padme what she hoped would be a withering glare, but Padme had a hand to one of her ears and an almost vulnerable expression on her face.

"Tell me," Bryn said.

Padme made a 'tch' sound and said in her accented English, "Yes, why not? I was the only child of wealthy parents. They were traditional, but wanted me to have a good education, so I was allowed to go to college abroad. They were killed in an automobile accident and my loving uncle tried to force me to honor an arranged marriage. It happens all the time in Pakistan. Instead of obeying, I attempted to run away with my lover, a student from India on scholarship. Such scandal! Such shame upon my family. Can you guess what happened?"

Padme's words were heavily tinged with sarcasm. It was clear to Bryn that this was the older girl's compact version of events.

"I have no idea."

"Have you never said the words, 'holy cow'?"

Bryn frowned. "What does that...oh."

"Yes...oh. In India, among the Hindu people—my former lover's people—cows are sacred. My uncle is nothing if not imaginative. I had already ruined myself, so there was nothing to be done but to exact his vengeance upon me. Like you, I was kidnapped. Then I was drugged and taken to the Bestia Butcher's lair to have this done." She gestured to one ear.

"That's awful. But why did you stay?"

Padme's smile was bleak. "Where else would I go? My uncle ensured that I will inherit nothing from my parent's estate. I am not an American citizen. If I'm caught, I will be deported to Pakistan. Xenofreaks are not tolerated there."

Bryn hardly knew what to say. She'd completely misjudged Padme, who was a victim like herself.

Padme scoffed and said, "Look at you. Are we BFF's now?"

The scorn stung, but Bryn understood it better. She was about to inform Padme that yes, under different circumstances they probably could have been friends, but someone banged on the door. Padme opened it and Scott entered. In one hand he clutched two fast food bags and in the other he balanced a drink holder with three sodas. Slung over his back was what looked like a rolled-up sleeping bag. Without greeting either Bryn or Padme, he set the meal at the end of the exam table and began rummaging inside one of the bags.

He handed Bryn a hamburger and some fries. She barely peeled the wrapper off the hamburger before shoving it into her mouth.

"I see you're not a vegetarian," Padme commented, accepting her own hamburger from Scott.

Through a mouth jammed with food, Bryn said, "Nope, I'm a card-carrying carnivore."

"I hardly understand your logic in hating us," Padme said. "How is raising an animal for food and clothing any different from what the xenos are doing? In the biolabs, they are raised in healthy environments, which is more than can be said about the average food production farm."

"I never said I hated you."

"Your father does, and you certainly looked supportive at the rally."

Bryn didn't bother denying Padme's accusation. Her father did hate them, and Bryn had been there to support him. "Family is complicated. You should know that better than anyone."

When Scott raised an inquisitive eyebrow, Padme said quickly to Bryn, "I can't believe how fast you ate that."

Bryn briefly considered licking the wrapper then looked at Scott suspiciously. "It wasn't my last meal, was it?" And then, unaccountably, she began to giggle.

Scott leaned closer to Padme. "Did Nurse Nancy give her something?"

Padme shook her head. "I think she got a contact high out there."

"Is that why I feel so funny?" Bryn asked. "Funny, funny, funny. That's a funny word."

"Lightweight," Scott muttered.

"You know what's really funny?" Bryn reached out and put a hand on Scott's arm. "That I got kidnapped today. Isn't that funny?"

"Hilarious." He shrugged her hand away. "Eat your fries."

Bryn's merriment disappeared as fast as it had arisen. She finished her meal in silence, enjoying the salty goodness of the French fries, even though they were cold and there weren't enough squishy ones.

When Padme swallowed her last bite, Bryn watched her gather up the wrappers and napkin. She shoved it all into one of the bags and said to Scott, "Have fun." Bryn didn't expect her to say goodbye, and she didn't.

When the door closed behind her, Scott began unrolling his sleeping bag in front of it.

"What time is it?"

"Around four."

"Are you going to sleep?"

"I'm going to sit. Unless you want me up there on the exam table with you."

Unbidden, the memory of Scott's lean, muscular body popped into her head. "Of course not," she murmured and then remembered his tattoo. "Were you in the Marines?"

"For about ten seconds."

"Why'd you—"

"How about you stop asking questions? There's magazines here if you need to do something." He opened one of the drawers under the exam table, selected one for himself and sat cross-legged on his sleeping bag. When Bryn flipped through the stack in the drawer, she found only back issues of Xeno Design Quarterly.

She didn't know how much longer they planned to keep her here, but every time her mind went idle, she started to freak out, so she pulled a few magazines from the stack and settled down to read them. An hour later, she looked up from a mind-numbingly boring scientific article explaining nanoneuron technology and asked, "What's 'grease' made of?"

Scott shut his magazine. "I don't know."

Oh, that's right, she thought, he doesn't know anything.

He surprised her by elaborating. "One of our bioengineers discovered it, though. The flames barely even get warm, but they burn out real fast. I guess he wanted to market it, but no one could find a use for it."

"Oh."

Instead of ignoring her further and going back to his magazine, he said, "Um, so what did you mean when you said Padme should know more than anyone that family is complicated?"

31

Bryn narrowed her eyes at him. "Why should I tell you? *She* obviously didn't."

Chapter Ten

Scott already knew the gist of what had happened to Padme, although she'd never told him herself. He'd been attempting from the get-go to win her over, but she didn't trust anyone, least of all men, and from what he heard, she had good reason. But she was the key to getting in deeper with Lupus, a task that thus far, Scott had failed to accomplish. Sure, Abel trusted him as far as that sick psycho trusted just about anyone, but at this rate, Scott was years away from reaching the inner circle.

And he didn't have nearly that long.

Bryn was waiting for his answer. He tried to think of something charming to say, something that would tempt her into giving up what Padme had said about her family. Not that Padme had necessarily told her anything useful; told her the truth even. Still, even mentioning to Padme that Bryn had told him what she said could give him the 'in' he needed.

He decided on the sympathy angle. "Padme's had a hard time of it."

Bryn's face softened slightly. "That's an understatement."

"Did she tell you everything?"

Bryn nodded. Scott wanted to grab her by the shoulders and shake it out of her. Maybe he should try a different tack.

"I heard she deserved it though."

"What? No one deserves that! What's wrong with you? Oh, sorry, I forgot, you're the one who got furry fingers. Ooo, big man, with your furry fingers thinking Padme should get cow ears because her uncle's a dickhead."

Scott restrained the urge to show her his claws—barely. New plan: tell Padme Bryn had told him anyway. Not like Bryn was ever going to talk to Padme again to refute it.

He subsided into silence, content with his decision. Bryn suddenly gasped and he looked up.

Her face was contorted, like she'd seen a ghost.

"What now?" he asked.

She'd begun to breathe hard and her eyes darted in all directions. Was she having a latent reaction to the pot?

"Tell me the truth," she said in a tortured whisper. The whites of her eyes showed all around. "What are they going to do to me?"

Oh, shit, he thought. Nurse Nancy was due any second now, and Scott had just begun to think clueless Bryn wasn't going to figure it out until after the fact. Now he had to calm her down or it could get very ugly, very fast in this little room.

In a firm voice, he said, "They are going to return you to your father, alive."

Tears spilled out of her eyes and her chin quivered. "They kidnapped Padme, too."

The lie was on the tip of his tongue, despicable. But he didn't have to use it. Before he could tell her that everything would be alright, a knock sounded on the door, like a toll bell ringing. It was the catalyst that set Bryn off into abject hysterics.

"No!" she screamed, scrambling to her feet atop the exam table.

Scott barely had time to get out of the way before the door swung open. Nurse Nancy tromped in, followed by Nurse Vonda. This wasn't the first time Scott had seen the two burly nurses subdue a patient, but it was the first time he felt absolutely sick about it.

Chapter Eleven

When she was five years old, after a series of unrelenting sore throats, Bryn's tonsils had been removed. She remembered bits and pieces of the event despite a sedative-induced fog: the reassuring hand-squeeze from her mother as she was wheeled down the hospital corridor, the smiles of the nurses and surgeon, the kind eyes of the masked anesthesiologist as he put something over her nose and mouth and asked her to count backwards.

When she came out of her drug-induced fog this time, she knew there would be no unlimited ice cream or cartoons and video games all day. She opened her eyes to the dark interior of a vehicle. The steady hum of an engine and constant bouncing motion told her they were moving. Right away she remembered this wasn't the first time she'd awakened. There'd been a grey room somewhere and masked people, and restraints on her arms and legs. Each time she'd come to, she weakly protested against the pain. She'd been scared, angry, and then nothing.

The motion stopped and sometime later, not long, she thought, she heard doors opening. A fresh breeze, the first she'd felt in some time, cooled her hot face. Silent, shadowy figures appeared on either side of her. The dimly lit studded metal ceiling of the vehicle seemed to slide disorientingly over her until the night sky appeared and she realized the figures had pulled her out. She tried to move her head, but it was weighed down somehow. The sound of slamming doors was followed by the revving of the engine. She breathed in a wave of exhaust fumes as the vehicle departed.

"Hello?" she tried to call out, but her throat constricted. She swallowed a few times to lubricate it, but her mouth was too dry. Moving her hands, she found them unbound at last.

Realization dawned. They'd released her. She drew a shuddering breath and felt the sting of tears but didn't pause to indulge them. Hands shaking, she reached up to her head. It was wrapped in thick layers of what felt like gauze. She lowered her hands to whatever she was resting on and carefully levered herself into a sitting position.

She was on a sidewalk on a deserted street in the dark space between two orange streetlights. They'd dumped her, stretcher and all. Slowly, she moved first one leg and then the other off the side of the stretcher. Her clothes and shoes were gone, but they'd dressed her in a hospital gown and paper booties. Dizzy and nauseous, she slid to her feet.

Bryn wanted to run but was physically incapable of more than keeping herself upright. Turning her head was a challenge, so she twisted her torso to look up the street and then down. One way looked more promising than the other; a large, well-lit building beaconed. Walking unaided was out of the question, however, so she gritted her teeth and began pushing the stretcher.

It was a long, slow journey, but soon after she began, a lighted sign came into view and spurred her on: Middleborough Hospital. The shuffling of her feet had long since worn the paper booties away when she reached the emergency room entrance. A man in blue scrubs came through the sliding glass doors and glanced her way.

"Help me," she said.

Chapter Twelve

Everyone in the Warehouse was on high alert. Dozens of squatters were packing their things and moving on in anticipation of the retaliation that was sure to occur, and probably soon. Like everyone else living there, Scott knew the police looked the other way when they cruised down the sprawling block that was home to the Warehouse and its tumbledown outbuildings. They did so not out of kindness towards the xenofreakish people, but because Lupus ensured it was worth their while to give the block a wide berth. But the big news of the day had everyone fidgeting nervously, wondering when the raids would begin and how bad it would go for them.

Scott watched a Holonews Worldwide broadcast from Abel's office, which was powered, like the exam rooms, with a portable gas generator. The reporter was young but remained unflustered even when the swirling wind out in front of Middleborough Hospital blew her shoulder length blond hair into her face. She removed a strand that had gotten stuck in her lipstick and began her report:

"It has been confirmed by the FBI that the daughter of Harry Vega, the director of a New York-based anti-xenofreak organization known as The Pure Human Society, who mysteriously disappeared two weeks ago, has been found alive. Although no one has agreed to speak with us in an official capacity, our sources tell us the FBI had no leads on the case and had received no demands from seventeen-year-old Bryn Vega's captors. She disappeared in broad daylight after the latest in a string of rallies by her father to gain supporters for his cause: regulating xenoalteration in the Legislature. Our sources say the girl was dropped off a block away from Middleborough Hospital, where she was admitted and examined and is in protective custody as we speak. No word on her condition, although witnesses described her as disoriented, with nearly her entire head swathed in bandages."

So it was something on her head, Scott thought. He hoped it wasn't her face, and not for the first time felt helpless and frustrated. With Abel in the room, he kept his face blank and appeared to be unmoved by the holocast. Abel, however, was jubilant.

"Now everyone will think twice before messing with us," he said with a guttural chuckle. "I can't wait for the big reveal. I heard Dr. Fournier outdid himself on this one."

Scott nodded, thinking, you're insane. The general populace already did think twice before messing with xenofreaks. As far as Scott was concerned, this act of stupidity would accomplish exactly nothing towards inspiring fear and respect, and it was more likely to fuel Harry Vega's fire than shut him up. Once Bryn told her story of how she'd been kidnapped by the XBestia gang, and once they examined Dr. Fournier's handiwork, swift retribution could be expected from the authorities. A few were responsible, but many would pay, and Scott doubted the flak would be contained within the city of New York.

"People are leaving." He jerked his head towards the door. "Even Paddy packed up his hotdog stand and took off. Shirley said she and her girls are going to lay low until this blows over. She's got two strikes."

Abel threw his hands into the air. "Let 'em leave! Damned place is too crowded anyway."

Scott nodded. "Exam Room Three's been sanitized and the word's out." Everyone knew what would happen if they talked. It was said that Lupus' wolf face disguised one of the ten most wanted criminals on the FBI's list, and he'd certainly proven himself to be vicious enough to qualify since he'd been in charge of Dr. Fournier's operation.

Abel shut off the holovision and stood. He reached for the stained and battered cowboy hat he wore in public and settled it over his horns. "My wife has chemotherapy this morning."

Coming from just about anyone else, the statement would elicit sympathy, but Abel made it sound like an inconvenience and an excuse to leave at the same time.

Scott asked, "What should we do if the cops come?"

Abel looked annoyed. "Run. Walk. Sit on your tuchus. I don't care; just keep your mouth shut."

Scott preceded him out the door and watched as he locked the office and set the alarm, a necessary precaution to prevent theft from the Warehouse folks, some of whom had proven desperate enough in the past to risk severe retribution to fuel their expensive habits. The alarm wouldn't stop the police from breaking down the door, but they wouldn't find information linking this branch of the facility to Dr. Fournier, much less anything leading them to his location. Scott knew because he'd already searched for it.

Abel took the one elevator in the Warehouse leading down to a very small underground parking lot with four large spots used exclusively by him and Lupus and for the vans that transported patients. Scott made his way to his tent. More and more xenos were leaving; it was starting to look like a mass exodus. As he approached Padme's tent, he saw beyond the unzipped opening that she, too, was packing.

He'd tried to talk to her after Bryn was carted off, tried to use what he'd learned to get her to open up to him, but if anything, it backfired. Padme had muttered, "Stupid girl," and walked away. She hadn't spoken to him since, and he didn't push it. The last thing he wanted was to give the impression that he was chasing after Lupus' woman.

But today's events gave him an opportunity to casually approach her and he wasn't going to pass that up. He didn't go so far as to invite himself into her tent, however. Standing a few feet from the entrance, he said, "You leaving?"

Padme pressed her lips together in an approximation of a smile. "Obviously."

"Well, I heard there's room at Montenegro House." It was a battered women's shelter.

She tossed her rucksack over her shoulder. "They require residents to attend counseling sessions and to have a green card. I have a place to go, thank you."

He wondered if she was going to be allowed to stay with Lupus but didn't dare ask.

"Well," he said in a deliberately casual tone, "If I don't see you again, good luck."

"Scott," she said.

He turned, surprised she'd used his real name. She didn't say anything right away, like she was deciding if she should. Finally, she began walking backwards. "You seem like a decent guy...which is why they don't trust you."

A cold knot formed in his gut as she spun on her heel and disappeared from view. He'd worked hard for 'their' trust, done things that he never would have imagined himself capable of doing—all to gain their slippery trust. If his basic decency showed through, it was because the one thing he couldn't do convincingly was pretend he enjoyed it. That's why he kept his face as inscrutable as possible at all times—so they'd expect him to show no emotion no matter what was going on.

Padme's words were intended as a warning, but Scott didn't have time to contemplate them. Someone ran towards him, shouting, "They're coming!" Before Scott could even react, a loud, bright series of flash-bangs sounded all around and smoke began belching out of multiple grenades from every entrance along the perimeter of the Warehouse. Armed and armored figures poured in, gas masks covering their faces. Scott hoped none of the panicked xenos fired on them, or there'd be a bloodbath. Just in case, he lay flat on the ground and waited.

The acrid green smoke that burned his eyes and nasal passages had dispersed evenly by the time a team of two agents ordered him to his feet at gunpoint. Scott stood, arms raised, and allowed himself to be frisked, bagged and tagged. He was forced to stand with one of several guarded groups of frightened xenos, hands bound behind his back with a specially made zip-tie. They'd been told to stand quietly, but Barney was making his way over to talk to Scott, who refused to meet his eyes.

"Psst! Cougar!" Barney said. "Hey Cougar!"

Out of the corner of his mouth, Scott said, "Shut it, dumbass!"

"You!" One of the agents said, pointing right at him. "Come with me."

Scott gave Barney a dirty look and snarled, "You're dead," before trudging forward, the picture of unwilling cooperation. The agent said loudly, "We've been looking for you, Cougar," before grabbing his arm and manhandling him out the door. As soon as they stepped into the sunshine, the agent said quietly, "It'll be a bit of a wait." He tucked Scott into the back of an unmarked car and shut the door.

It had been a multi-agency raid. Scott watched as xeno after xeno was escorted into police or FBI or ATF vans. Most of those that hadn't fled the Warehouse in time were tweakers or alcoholics; the lowest members of the community, too high or drunk to appreciate the danger. Scott didn't see Padme among the captives—maybe she'd gotten away.

He hoped not.

Chapter Thirteen

Bryn's adjustable mattress allowed her to sit upright, a position she favored so she could avoid the discomfort of laying her head down. The doctors and nurses had removed the bandages and told her what they saw but refused to allow her a mirror so she could see for herself. They also forbid her from touching her new 'hair.'

"You don't want to accidently get stuck with one of the quills," said Dr. Lauren, the young resident assigned to her case. Dr. Lauren's brown hair was pulled back into a perky ponytail, something Bryn would never be able to do again.

She was so wrung out from her ordeal she couldn't even cry. Dr. Lauren told her father that she was in shock, told him she'd made a referral for someone from the psych ward to come talk to her, as if talking would somehow make everything all right. As if anything would.

Bryn spent almost an hour answering the questions two XIA agents fired at her. She'd never even heard of the XIA, which, she was told, stood for Xeno Intelligence Agency. She told them everything she could remember, but got the strange impression there wasn't much they didn't already know.

Her father stood outside her door, engaged in an intense conversation with the head of Middleborough Hospital's neurology department. Bryn had a private room with a guard stationed outside. She'd eaten as much of the bland hospital lunch as her stomach could stand, and now waited to hear the verdict: what would be done about the porcupine pelt that had replaced her hair?

She'd loved her hair. It wasn't her father's thick black or her mother's thin blonde, but somewhere in between. It wasn't unruly like her best friend Maria's curls, nor stick-straight like her other friend, Kim's. Bryn could coax her hair into curls or blow it out straight.

Past tense.

She tried not to think of her scalp and hair lying in a bloody wad in some landfill. She also tried not to think of the poor porcupine that had been genetically engineered, raised in a lab and killed so that her captors could send her father a message: Look what we can do.

Bryn had asked Dr. Lauren what her options were and had been devastated at the response.

"Cadaver hair is one option," Dr. Lauren had replied, clinically objective. "That would of course involve taking anti-rejection drugs for the rest of your life, and there'd be no guarantee it would work. We could also remove the xenograft and use your own skin to rebuild your scalp."

"My own skin? From where?"

"Your thighs or your back."

"I'd be bald," Bryn said.

"Yes. But there are wigs made out of human hair for chemotherapy patients that are quite good."

Bryn remembered when she was six, before her great-grandmother died. Gram fought the cancer to gain some time even though it was the incurable kind. She'd been brave and cheerful despite the chemo that made her sick and made her hair fall out. She'd purchased synthetic wigs in several styles and colors, some of them quite bold and sassy, like the bright red bob she wore to the Fourth of July picnic.

Bryn was not brave like Gram. She didn't want everyone knowing her hair was really a wig. But there was no way the hospital staff could keep this out of the media. Word would get out; pictures would be taken in secret or leaked from her file. She'd already had to pose for snapshots.

Her father came back into the room, followed by Dr. Lauren and the neurology guy, Dr. Brunswick, plus two other people Bryn didn't know.

"Honey," her father began, and she knew from his tone that the news wasn't good. "Dr. Brunswick has serious reservations about…well, about what would happen if we removed the—the—graft."

"If?" Bryn asked in a small voice.

Harry Vega looked helplessly at the covey of doctors standing behind him. Dr. Brunswick squared his jaw and stepped forward. "Miss Vega, when we scanned your brain, we found that whoever did this to you also implanted nanoneurons, which are programmed to stimulate the brain in specific ways depending on what the graft is. Nanoneurons can never be removed, but they can usually be disabled—reprogrammed to do nothing. In this instance, however, we don't know what program they used; it's unreadable to our scanners. This means it could be dangerous to remove the graft. If the nanoneurons can't perform their intended function, there's no telling what will happen."

Bryn stared back at the doctors' concerned faces and at her father's tortured one.

"I want a mirror," she said. "Now."

Chapter Fourteen

Scott had been in jail once before, in San Diego, his first day of leave after twelve weeks of intensive Marine Corp boot camp training. He and his buddies had gone out to burn off some excess energy playing volleyball on a beach populated with southern California hotties. When it got dark, they visited a tattoo parlor, snuck into a Pacific Beach bar and got into a fight, in that order. The fight gave him two things: his scar and a one-way ticket to the downtown jail.

The San Diego jail had been in an eleven-story building and smelled like bleach. Scott had gotten rudimentary medical care for his knife wound and sat in the drunk tank with his friends even though out of the three of them, he was the only sober one.

The xenofreaks, including Scott, that were rounded up in the Warehouse raid were taken to Rikers Island. Scott's cell smelled like Pine Sol tainted with urine and vomit. He wasn't surprised when he was processed like all the rest, denied bail and transferred to a Federal facility in an old building with thick layers of paint on the walls. He waited for his day in court, chafing at the necessary delay—any special treatment would look suspicious. As it was, his day came around faster than it should have, but all Scott felt by then was relief.

The officer that escorted him to his arraignment had no idea who he was. Scott wanted to slash him when he said in a suggestive voice, "The cons are going to love those soft little paws once we get you declawed, Puss-puss."

Shasta Fox, Scott's handler, was waiting for him in the box-sized virtual courtroom. He hadn't seen her since the day of Bryn's abduction when she'd arranged to bump into him at the fast food place a block away from the Warehouse. She'd gotten her hair cut since then and the short, spiked style did nothing to soften the dark skin of her aging face. On the wall were three holovision monitors labeled "Presiding Judge," "Prosecutor," and "Defense Attorney." The monitors for the judge and defense attorney were blank, but a pre-recorded holo was playing on the one from the prosecutor's office, explaining Scott's rights and the legal process.

They ignored it. A holocam was pointed at them, but the blinking red light indicated it wasn't on. Still, Shasta spoke quietly with barely moving lips.

"We lost her."

No shit, Scott thought. "What happened?"

"They disabled the tracking devices."

"How?"

It was a dumb question; a frustrated knee-jerk reaction kind of question in the face of the obvious. He'd sprinkled the micro-transmitters Shasta had slipped him onto Bryn's hamburger and watched her unknowingly consume them. If the XIA had any inkling Fournier's people could disable the supposedly undetectable, foolproof tracking devices, they wouldn't have let Fournier take her. They'd gambled and Bryn had lost. Scott didn't wait for Shasta to answer.

"What about the reconnaissance satellite and video surveillance?" he asked.

Shasta gave him a quick, impatient shake of her head. It was another useless question. If anything had worked, Bryn would have been rescued before they'd mutilated her, and Fournier and his goons would be standing where Scott was now.

He'd done his part and there was nothing he could do about the rest of the team's failure, but that didn't mean he could shrug it off. He had his own reasons for hating the paranoid, psychopathic doctor, reasons Shasta had used to recruit him when she sought him out in that San Diego jail.

The camera light went green and a uniformed bailiff appeared on the judge's screen. The bailiff announced, "All rise for the Honorable Judge Pricilla Adams." There were no chairs in the room; Scott and Shasta were already standing when the background screen came to life and the bland face of Judge Adams popped up in front of it. Simultaneously, the prosecutor's holographic face appeared. His only introduction was a line of 3D text that scrolled through the air in front of him, reading, "Marcus Quick, Assistant District Attorney."

Shasta straightened her shoulders and said, "Shasta Fox for the defendant."

After Quick read the criminal complaint against Scott, Judge Adams perked up.

"Mr. Harding, these are serious charges," she said. "Do you understand them as they've been presented?"

"Yes, Your Honor," Scott said.

"And how do you plead?"

"Not guilty."

Shasta switched her holopad to 2D and handed it to him as the judge launched into a lecture about high-profile trials and media coverage. He tuned everything out in order to concentrate on the typed paragraphs on the holopad. His assignment was far from over.

There'd been two agents prior to Scott who'd insinuated themselves into the Warehouse community. Both had disappeared. Scott didn't know much about the first agent; just that his name was Eduardo Quinones and he'd been a Green Beret. The agent immediately preceding Scott had been forty years old, an eminently qualified, decorated former detective from San Francisco with years of undercover experience. He had a wife and two kids. Voice stress analysis of his last communication before his disappearance showed extreme duress, and the XIA analysts determined it was probably a relayed message from Lupus or even Dr. Fournier himself. The agent had called on his burn phone and said simply, "Records can't be expunged."

The fact was: the agents' records *had* been expunged. Deep-cover standard procedure is to thoroughly erase and replace with false identities and criminal records, and yet that cryptic message suggested their true histories had somehow been accessed despite the best efforts of the XIA computer forensicians. This prompted a search for new recruits, candidates who had no affiliation with any law enforcement agency and therefore no records, no old news items, nothing lurking on the net that could get them killed. Preferably someone with no family—not because they wouldn't be missed if they disappeared—but because family could be used by the enemy as leverage. Someone young, smart and good in a fight.

By the time Judge Adams banged her gavel, Scott had memorized his orders.

Chapter Fifteen

The scar, one long, thin pink line joining Bryn's skin to the pelt, was almost undetectable now. The intern who'd removed the stitches hadn't been very tactful when he'd examined Fournier's handiwork. He'd pursed his lips in a light whistle, a glint of undisguised admiration in his eyes.

That trip back to the hospital was the only time Bryn had left the house since she'd identified three of her four kidnappers in a series of lineups. She'd lost her job at the daycare center, of course. They'd replaced her after she'd been gone two days, out of necessity, and had respectfully declined to rehire her now that her head was essentially a dangerous weapon. Bryn was disappointed but understood. She couldn't imagine cuddling with a child ever again.

She'd hidden in her room, ignoring calls from friends and strangers alike. The media had been aggressive and unrelenting in their efforts to get an interview with her, a recent photo, anything. They'd camped out in front of Harry Vega's modest house, an oppressive presence that made Bryn wanted to run out and throw flaming bags of poo at them. Among the news vehicles hogging up the street parking and thrilling their neighbors was an unmarked sedan with at least one XIA agent inside at any given moment, watching.

It was too little, too late, but Bryn's new holopsychiatrist continually urged her to focus not on what was done and irreversible, but on the future. Bryn tried, but no matter how many ways she envisioned that future, her girlish hopes for a happily ever after were just—gone. So what if there was someone out there for everyone? Someone who would love her despite her artificial deformity, despite the fact that her dubious fifteen minutes of fame would be resurrected every time someone recognized her? The real question was: could she love someone who could love a freak?

Her face had been plastered all over the news, local, national and world. It seemed like every 'before' photo ever taken of her found its way onto the net. Holos Bryn hadn't even known existed were posted on Holo Tube by supposed friends and school mates: Bryn with her hair in an updo at the

Homecoming Dance, laughing and sipping sparkling cider, Bryn setting a school record in the 200-metre dash with her ponytail streaming out behind her, Bryn wearing a perky knit cap in a snowball fight at a popular sledding hill. She watched them over and over, wallowing in the miserable knowledge she'd never experience that kind of normalcy again.

Sometimes she found sites that weren't so kind. More than one wannabe cartoonist had satirized her. One depicted her with a live porcupine perched on her head bossing her around; one superimposed her face over that of Pinhead from the old Hellraiser movies. The ignorant, hurtful comments below the cartoons were much worse. They called her 'Porcubryn' and 'Porcubrain.' They said she got what she deserved and that her father was the new Hitler.

He'd taken a leave of absence from work, ostensibly to care for her, but he'd spent the majority of his time fielding calls in his capacity as the head of the Pure Human Society. These calls had changed drastically from those he'd gotten before the kidnapping. Those were often from people looking for help and answers. Now they were from people offering to help—people who had political power, money or both.

Bryn was fine with all that. She didn't really understand the politics behind it, but the more time her father spent wooing supporters, the less time he spent awkwardly attempting to console his daughter. If she heard one more analogy about making the best of a bad situation, she'd throw up.

Alone in her bedroom, she'd read up on the XBestias and Dr. Fournier. There weren't any recent holos of him, just old photos from before he went off the grid. He looked the epitome of the average Joe: medium height, short dark hair, not fat, not thin. Like Ted Bundy, he was not unattractive, and had a reputation as a personable guy. Also like Bundy, he'd reportedly used his modest charisma to fool people into trusting him.

She'd spent some of her self-imposed isolation learning everything she could about porcupines. Given the dark brown color of the wooly undercoat and the yellowish quills, she figured her donor had been a common North American type, the kind she'd only ever seen before dead on the side of the road. Dr. Fournier had harvested the pelt carefully, as far as Bryn could tell, removing it from the donor's shoulders on down so that when he attached it to her scalp, shorter quills formed her bangs and graduated to longer length in the back. It sickened her that he took such obvious pride in his work even when striking back at an enemy. The last thing she wanted to feel was gratitude, but the pelt, as hair, was esthetically pleasing in its own horrible way. Like everyone kept telling her, it could have been so much worse.

It would have been so much better if the quills didn't poke her unmercifully. She didn't just look like a pincushion, she felt like one. Her neck and shoulders were a bloody mess. She'd begun wearing her leather jacket at all times just to protect her skin. The quills had taken their toll on her hands, too, especially during the phase of healing that itched. She wore her mother's leather driving gloves until the urge to scratch faded and she no longer reached up automatically only to get a painful stab.

She read that a porcupine's quills were used as a defense: when frightened, tiny muscles in the porcupine's skin raised the quills, which then fell out easily if another animal came into contact with them. Bryn found that her quills were firmly entrenched even when she disturbed them. Her first instinct had been to pull them all out, but when she tried, it hurt like hell. As soon as she got up the courage to go out in public, she planned to head to the nearest hair salon and pay extra to get the ends snipped off each and every spine.

A knock sounded on her bedroom door and she automatically called, "Come in," expecting her dad. Maria peeked in with a hopeful, apologetic look on her face.

"Happy birthday," she said tentatively. She held up a wrapped box.

Bryn was mortified her father hadn't warned her, hadn't given her enough time to cover her head or change her clothes. She sat there on the bed in her grungy nightgown and leather jacket, speechless.

"Don't be mad at your dad. We've been working on him all week and he finally caved because we showed up with gifts and begged him to let us in."

"We?" Bryn asked weakly.

Maria pushed the door open and Bryn saw Kim grinning over her shoulder. "Those reporters are nosy, did you know that? Told 'em my name was Sally Forth."

Maria raised her hand. "Anita Man."

There was nothing else to do. Bryn couldn't hide in her room forever. "Nice to meet you."

Kim was the less diplomatic of Bryn's two best friends. She walked partially around the bed to get a good look at Bryn's head from all angles.

"It looks awesome!"

"What?" Bryn felt like laughing and crying at the same time.

Maria sat on the bed and put her hand on Bryn's arm. "It does. It's totally you."

Chapter Sixteen

There were seven people seated around the conference room table and one guard standing outside the door. Padme and Barney, both wearing businesslike suits for the occasion, sat next to their court-appointed counsel. Scott, dressed in jeans and a long-sleeved dress shirt, sat by Shasta, with Marcus Quick on his other side. The Assistant District Attorney had spent the last ten minutes trying to persuade defense counsel that it was in their clients' best interest to cooperate in the investigation. He was having very little luck.

"I want the location of Fournier's lab. This is your one chance at leniency, and it expires in the next ten minutes," he said. "I'll leave you to discuss it."

He signaled the guard and left the room. Across the table, Padme and Barney's shared attorney began whispering to them behind her hand. Padme didn't bother to lift her ear to hear.

To keep up appearances, Shasta, too, leaned over to speak quietly to Scott.

"She's not going for it," she said, referring to Padme and the deal they never expected her to take. "Are you ready?"

He shook his head, like he was rejecting whatever she said to him, but responded, "Yep."

Under the table, she passed him the key to his handcuffs and pushed her chair back. "You're going to regret this." Her voice rang loudly enough for all to hear. She stood, turned her back on him, and moved toward the door, calling out, "Guard!"

The guard entered on cue, stun gun drawn. Scott was instantly up with his arm around Shasta's neck, claws at her throat. The other attorney screamed and ducked under the table as Barney leapt to his feet. The guard swung around and fired, his one charge sinking into Barney's chest and incapacitating him with a high-voltage jolt. Padme scrambled out of the way, around the table behind Scott, who threw Shasta to the floor and laid the guard out with one punch.

The guard's body blocked the door open and Scott leaned out to look up and down the hallway. No one in sight, as planned. To Shasta, he growled, "Which way is out?"

She was good; her terrified victim imitation would have fooled him if he didn't know it was an act. "Right," she said. "Turn right. But you'll never get away."

He bent and snatched her ID from where it was clipped to her shirt. "Purse," he snapped. Shasta handed him her purse, hand shaking.

He turned to Padme. "Coming?"

She looked flabbergasted but nodded.

He rolled the guard's body into the conference room and the door shut and automatically locked. Almost immediately they heard muffled banging and shouting from inside. They turned right down the corridor, unimpeded. Ten yards away was a door marked 'Exit.' Scott swiped Shasta's ID through the card reader and opened the door onto a parking lot.

"That was too easy," he said, looking all around.

"I agree." Padme squinted in the unaccustomed sunshine. There were people in the distance, but no one noticed the fugitives as they walked quickly away from the building.

Scott rummaged in Shasta's purse and pulled out her keypad. "Damn it. Password."

"Here." Padme grabbed it, snapped the back off and poked around inside, still walking. Scott had been counting on this. Late model Toyota keypads were notoriously easy to hack into and Padme had shown herself in the past to be handy in a technological pinch.

She turned the keypad and tapped some numbers with her thumbs. Several cars down, a black Camry II beeped. She looked up at Scott and grinned.

He drove.

"I'll bet you a million bucks we're being tracked," he said as he turned out of the parking lot onto the street.

"It seems likely. How did you get out of your handcuffs?"

Scott raised his right hand and extended his forefinger claw. "Picked it."

"We should ditch the car and split up," she said.

He nodded, even though the plan was for him to stick to her like glue. "Where'd you want me to drop you?"

She didn't answer, so he glanced at her. She was looking at him with a mixture of distrust and something else. Pity maybe? Whatever it was, he didn't like it. She'd already given him notice that he wasn't trusted. Nothing about their 'escape' had rung true. There was only one thing he could think of that might erase that look from her face.

He turned onto a residential street and parked. Shasta's wallet quite conveniently had several hundred dollars cash in it. He handed Padme half, slipped Shasta's phone into his pocket and without a word got out of the car and started walking. Every step took him further and further away from his duty. He didn't look back until he got to the end of the block.

She was right behind him.

Chapter Seventeen

It only took Bryn about ten attempts to change the subject before Kim stopped trying to discuss the kidnapping. Not that Bryn didn't necessarily want to talk about it—she couldn't.

"It's an ongoing investigation," she parroted Mr. Quick, the stiff, prissy prosecutor who'd met with her and her father several times. "I'm not allowed to say anything."

Kim finally got the message and the girls dug out Bryn's yearbook and began rehashing their senior year highlights. Bryn knew it was supposed to cheer her up, so she did her best to laugh in all the right places, but she couldn't shake a pervasive, disassociated feeling, like the girl in the yearbook was someone else. Like there was an acrylic bubble separating her from the past.

Maria reached for another of the birthday chocolates she'd brought and said, "Oh! Did you hear about Paul?"

"Do I want to?" Bryn asked.

Paul, the ex. She'd thought about him when she'd touched Nurse Nancy's fur beard. Would she ever be able to think of Paul again without remembering that grimy exam room and the stench of the Warehouse? Without thinking about how shocked Scott's face looked when she'd begun screaming?

"Sheila's pregnant," Kim blurted.

That made Bryn laugh, the first genuine one she'd produced in weeks. "Oh, my gosh, that's exactly perfect. Are they getting married?"

"Are you kidding? He's going around telling everyone he's having a paternity test done. What a jerk." Maria had never liked him, which had been a sore subject between she and Bryn even a year later, but not now. Bryn found she no longer cared the smallest bit what happened to Paul.

The bedroom door suddenly opened, and her father barged in. He always knocked, so right away she knew something was wrong. Without any preamble, he said, "Turn on the holovision."

She reached for the remote and at her father's direction, tuned her small H.V. to a local news channel. Whatever he'd wanted to show her had ended and now a commercial for an electric Harley Davidson motorcycle was playing, so he took the remote out of her hand and began switching channels.

"There," he said. An older man sat at a news desk with a recent picture of Bryn superimposed behind him. She'd never seen the shot before; none of the 'after' pictures of her were supposed to have been released. It showed her resting her chin in her gloved hands with a pensive look on her face and a faraway look in her eyes, porcupine quills sticking out of her head every-which-way.

"Where'd they get that picture?" she asked.

"Just listen."

The newscaster was saying something about the case. "...in broad daylight and forced to undergo a xenotransplant. Three of the four wanted kidnappers were in custody until this morning when two of them, Scott Harding and Padme Lango," the picture behind him changed to side-by-side mug shots, "assaulted a security guard and escaped just hours ago from a low-security federal facility. Police are advising the public to take extreme caution and to consider the pair armed and dangerous."

Bryn was outraged, but not so much that she didn't notice a couple of shocking details.

"That's not Scott! And Padme has cow ears!" The photos were close enough likenesses, but the one that was supposed to be Scott looked like a hardened criminal a decade his senior and the one of "Padme" had perfect, shell-like human ears. Bryn looked at her father and stated emphatically, "They have the wrong pictures."

Harry Vega clapped his hands together and turned to Bryn's friends. "I'm afraid we're going to have to cut the party short."

Maria got off the bed and said, "Wow, girl, this reeks."

"Yeah, are the cops stupid, or what?" Kim said.

After they'd gone, Bryn expected her father to come back into her room so they could discuss the turn of events, but after a few minutes she heard his low voice coming from the kitchen. She assumed he was calling the XIA to let them know they'd made some kind of terrible mistake. Either they'd captured the wrong people in the first place, or someone in the records department screwed up.

Thoughts spinning, she picked up the box of birthday chocolates Maria had given her and wandered down the hall with the intention of leaving it on the counter for her father. Just as she was about to round the corner into the kitchen, she heard him say, "…and donations coming in. You'll get your money."

It wasn't what he said, but the harsh way he said it that made her pause and listen.

"It'll have to be next week after the check clears the bank. I'll meet you—" He stopped and then said in a defensive tone, "Okay, okay…fine."

Bryn heard the little beep that indicated he'd ended the call. She walked into the kitchen and asked, "What was that all about?"

Her dad jumped and put a hand to his heart. "How much did you hear?"

She frowned. He looked not only guilty, but almost frightened. Slowly, she said, "You owe someone money…?"

He set the holophone in its charger and took a few deep breaths before responding. "It's politics. Sometimes you have to grease the wheels to get anything done."

"You're bribing someone? With PHS money? Can you do that?"

He sighed. "Technically, no, Sweetheart. Essentially what I'm doing is wrong, especially given that the money was donated and PHS is a non-profit organization. It's hard for me to think of it as embezzlement, though, when it's so very necessary to the cause. These guys—you know, the legislators—are all on the take these days, even though it's considered legal. They only listen to their caucuses, the groups who fund their elections who are in turn funded by big business. Caucuses influence the way they vote, caucuses even write the damned bills for them!"

Bryn recognized that he was getting worked up for one of his lectures, so she interrupted. "What about the photos?"

"I had to take that, Brynnie. It was—oh, the mug shots. Um, yeah, let me call Agent Smart. Heh, 'Agent Smart,' that kills me."

Bryn had no idea why her father thought Agent Smart's name was so amusing, but she did wonder what he'd started to say about the photos. He picked up the holophone again just as it occurred to her: the picture of her on the newscast—the one with her porcupine hair in all its glory—had been taken right here in the kitchen. It had flashed by so quickly she hadn't picked up on it at the time, but now she realized the background had been familiar.

Her father was the only other person who'd been in the house since the kidnapping. He'd taken that picture when she wasn't looking and released it to the media.

Chapter Eighteen

They needed to disguise themselves quickly and the best way to do that was the last thing Scott wanted to attempt: home invasion. All the houses in this neighborhood looked alike; older two-story brownstones built right up next to each other. They had no side yards to speak of, no garages and most of the front yards were taken up by huge old oak trees.

Padme shot down the first two houses he picked. One had a couple of neat rows of well-tended planters in the front yard with brightly blooming roses. By the door, a flagpole proudly displayed a faded American flag. "Retired couple," she said. "They're most likely home right now."

He started down the walkway of the next house, but she threw her arm out to block him and nodded towards small porch overhang. "Camera."

She approved of the third house, with its sparse grass and no cars parked out front. They walked up the steps and knocked. Padme gestured to the doorknob and said, "Pick it."

Scott couldn't admit he had no idea how to pick a lock, not with his claws or anything else.

"It'd take too long," he said.

He looked around furtively before picking up a decorative stone that had an embedded brass plate engraved with the word, "Welcome." He had every intention of using it to break the narrow window next to the door, but by its light weight he could tell it wasn't a real rock. Underneath, a lone key lay on the concrete.

He flashed Padme a triumphant grin.

"Luck smiles upon us," she said drily.

Inside, the place was tidy enough, but a thick layer of dust on nearly every surface suggested the occupant wasn't terribly concerned with housekeeping. One of the back bedrooms told them why. It was empty except for large black bars mounted parallel to the ceiling and floor on each wall.

"Cool," Scott said. The setup was a holoroom, an expensive hobby for serious hard-core gamers, which explained the unused look to the rest of the place.

"We should hurry," Padme said, reaching past Scott to shut the holoroom door.

"What, are you afraid I'm going to geek out?"

"No, I'm afraid I will."

The other room was the bedroom, and they rummaged through the closets and drawers to select from their unwitting host's clothing. Scott went into the bathroom and stripped down completely. He knew their clothes weren't bugged, but Padme didn't, so he had to keep up appearances.

He dumped the hamper out on the bathroom floor and tossed his stuff in, shoes and all, before squeamishly pulling on the newest-looking pair of the dude's tighty-whities he could find. The jeans were short and too snug, but the pullover hoodie fit okay. The dude's footwear was ridiculous; wherever he was, he must be wearing his only good shoes, assuming he owned any. Scott had to choose between a beat-up pair of work boots or some grungy tennis shoes. He'd picked the boots so Padme wouldn't have to clomp around in them, hoping as he slipped them on that he wouldn't come away from this with a nasty case of foot fungus.

He saw an actual pair of glasses sitting on the sink and put them on, but took them off again when they blurred his vision too much to ignore. When he went back into the bedroom, Padme had changed into jeans as well. They were large on her, but she'd rolled the legs into cuffs and found a belt somewhere. She, too, was wearing a hoodie that she'd pulled up to conceal her ears. She put her clothes and shoes into the hamper as well, stuffed the occupant's own clothing on top and then fastidiously washed her hands.

By unspoken agreement, they were trying to leave as small a footprint as possible in this man's home. The longer it took him to realize he'd been invaded, the more of a lead Scott and Padme would gain. Or so she'd think.

"Here," she said, handing him a baseball cap.

He had to adjust the strap to make it bigger and the hat had a rather embarrassing video game logo on it, but it hid his distinctive haircut well enough.

"Let's get out of here." He led the way down the hall but came to an abrupt halt two steps into the living room.

"What the hell are you doing in my house?" The speaker was Caucasian, about thirty years old with a receding hairline and weak chin. He had something in his right hand, but since he wasn't pointing it at them, Scott assumed it wasn't a weapon. The poor guy looked terrified.

"We're not going to hurt you," Padme said. "We just needed to borrow some clothes."

The man's eyes flicked back and forth between Scott and Padme. "You're those xenos who escaped."

Scott was slightly encouraged that the man used the term 'xenos' instead of xenofreaks. He took a chance and asked, "You a brother?"

The guy hesitated, but said, "Not XBestia." He lifted his shirt to reveal a porcine graft on his thin white belly, the least expensive kind of xenoalteration available. It was a Celtic emblem or logo of some sort—not one of the symbols representing a rival gang to the XBestias. Scott figured the graft probably meant something in whatever online hologame the guy participated in.

Dr. Fournier no longer did porcine grafts, but he wasn't the only game in town by a long shot. Demand for genetic engineers and xenotransplantation surgeons had been high when the technology first surfaced. Schools and training facilities had sprung up everywhere, but eventually the job market was glutted. Desperate out-of-work engineers and surgeons began providing underground non-organ grafting and transplantation services to the unique new xenofreak demographic.

The practice became mainstream when the lead singer of the UK bang-metal band Stank Afterlife appeared onstage with a functional pair of snowy albatross wings attached to his back. He couldn't fly, of course, but the xenosurgeon did such a good job rearranging his muscles and tendons that with the help of the nanoneuronal implants in his cerebellum to aid in motor control, the singer had nearly full range of motion in his new feathered appendages.

"We were just leaving," Padme said. "We didn't steal anything except the clothing."

A calculating look passed over their host's face. He lifted his arm and opened his hand. A set of keys rested there.

"Look," he said. "I won't report this for an hour. That's how long my lunch is. But you gotta take my piece of shit car and dump it in a river or set it on fire, okay? The tranny is on its last legs and I'd rather get the insurance than get it fixed."

Chapter Nineteen

Bryn did what she always did when she was angry with her father. She took the family photo album off its place on the hearth and closeted herself away with it. Her mother had put the album together with old-fashioned photograph prints. The cover was a cross-stitched pattern of hearts and flowers. Bryn ran her fingers over the faded needlework, remembering how happy she'd been when her mother allowed her to stitch an entire flower all on her own. She'd been four or five at the time.

The photographs covered Bryn's whole life, from her parent's wedding where you could barely see the bump under Miranda Vega's homemade wedding dress, to the last week of her mother's life, when they'd waited so desperately for a human donor organ to replace the failing pig heart. Bryn didn't often look at those later photos because as much as the pictures of her mother smiling and happy and living her life made her sad, the ones of her mother gaunt and yellow with fear in her eyes broke her heart.

Today, maybe because of her own recent brush with death, she flipped to the end of the album and looked at every shot of her mom's battle, from the momentous weeks after she survived one of the first bioengineered xenotransplants in history, to her last days.

Pictured were several old friends of the family who no longer came around. Her mom's best friend Carla had taken most of the photos towards the end and had been the one who shuttled Bryn from school to the hospital, where Bryn would sit quietly and do her homework or read. Her father was rarely there. Carla hadn't hidden her anger with Harry Vega very well. Bryn recalled one particular argument between them where her father had justified his absence by yelling at Carla right there in the hospital hallway.

"I have to work," he'd shouted. "We're drowning in medical bills! They gave her a goddamned pig heart for free, but are they taking responsibility now that it's crapped out? No. We're on our own. The only thing I have to look forward to is the life insurance."

He'd apologized for saying it, of course. He was always remorseful. Her mom told her the stress had gotten the best of her dad and that Bryn shouldn't hold it against him. That he was absent because he needed to be strong and he couldn't be when confronted by Miranda's impending death. It was her mom's way; making the best of things.

"It's easier for him to bury himself in work," she'd said.

"But he's never here," Bryn had cried.

Her mother had patted her hand. If Bryn had it to do over again, she wouldn't have complained, wouldn't have added to her mother's burden. "He'll be there for you when it counts," Miranda Vega had said. "Right now, he's letting you have all my time."

It hadn't rung true. Bryn had been young, but she knew excuses when she heard them. Her mother was too good a person to allow Bryn to think badly of her father. The man who would be left to raise her alone.

She pulled a tissue from the box on the end table blew her nose. She started to close the album when a photograph caught her eye. One of the nurses posing next to her mom's bed looked familiar—not familiar from the past, but alarm-bells kind of familiar. Bryn looked more closely and then gasped as recognition dawned. The woman in the picture was younger, thinner, and significantly more pleasant looking, but it was definitely Nurse Vonda.

She didn't have time to ponder the implications; her father knocked and opened the door without waiting for her to invite him in.

"Honey, I'm sorry your birthday is so sucky this year," he said, as if 'sucky' were a strong enough adjective. "I got you a present. I know you had your eye on these, and I know I told you they were too expensive, but under the circumstances, I thought they might cheer you up."

He held out a small box from a jewelry store in the mall. A few months ago, he'd needed to get his watch repaired, or he wouldn't have gone within a hundred yards of the mall, with or without Bryn. She remembered expressing mild interest in a pair of silver drop earrings while they'd waited. Inside the box, the earrings sparkled against the black velvet lining. She swallowed back tears. Her dad had always been clueless about gift giving. He was often thoughtless, but not deliberately hurtful. The earrings would have been perfect a month ago, but if she put them on now, they'd be completely hidden behind fur and quills.

"Thanks, Dad." It was her standard answer.

"Well, you're very welcome, Honey. Listen…now that the graft has pretty much healed and you've had a chance to get used to it, I think it's time to hit back."

Bryn looked at her father like he'd spoken in an alien tongue, but he forged ahead without noticing.

"I've hired a marketing director for The Pure Human Society, and he wants to strike while the iron is hot. If we wait too long, we'll lose momentum. Media interest has already started to fade. Did you notice we only have a few die-hard crews still outside?"

Bryn hadn't so much as peeked out the blinds this entire time for fear someone would snap a shot of her. She shook her head at her father, dreading to hear more.

He said, "Manny, the marketing guy, is as good as they get. He's already got you scheduled for appearances on two major morning news shows. You've always wanted to meet Hannah MacManus, right?"

Bryn knew who Hannah MacManus was, but had never expressed interest in actually meeting her. As she listened to her father rattle on, she finally understood the phrase, 'through the looking glass.'

"I don't want to," she interrupted him.

"What?"

"I'm not going to do any of that."

He stared at her uncomprehendingly for a moment before clenching his jaw and speaking through his teeth. "Yes, you will. This is essential to everything I'm trying to accomplish. You're the victim here, Sweetie, but you don't have to lie down and take it. You can be a voice for all the other victims out there."

"No," she said in a small voice. "I just want to be left alone."

"That's the depression talking. I thought you were getting better. The psychiatrist is helping, right? Or maybe we should talk to the doctors about medication. Until then, if you really need more time, I can ask Manny to reschedule. But no more than a week, tops."

A germ of an idea was spreading in Bryn's mind; a terrible confluence of what she'd assumed were separate, and coincidental, events that had one thing in common—her father.

After they'd mutilated her, when she'd surfaced briefly from her drug-induced fog, she'd heard a snippet of conversation. She'd told neither the XIA agents nor her father what she'd heard because it hadn't made any sense and she'd convinced herself she'd hallucinated it. Now it came back to haunt her.

Someone, and from the deep, barely feminine voice, Bryn suspected it was Nurse Vonda, had said, "He asked for something subtle."

A man's voice had responded authoritatively, "Subtle won't cut it. He needs public outcry, or no one will give a damn—is she awake?"

She'd faded out again almost immediately, but somehow the words stayed with her.

Her father was waiting for her to say something. She did, but not what he expected. "Why didn't you do anything to protect me at the rally?"

"What?"

"Why was I there all by myself? Why was I allowed to walk back to my car alone when you knew I was in danger?"

Her father's face froze except for tiny twitches around his mouth and eyes, as if he was struggling to control multiple emotions. "I was planning on setting something up after the rally, but it's not like we could afford to hire a bodyguard. I feel awful enough about everything without you trying to make me feel worse."

He'd turned it around, like he turned everything around. If she screamed at him, threw accusations at him, she would lose. He would have an answer for everything, and his strategy would be to deny everything. It was not a battle she was equipped to win. There was only one possible way for her to get to the truth. He may outgun her in the lying department, but she had an advantage—she rarely lied, and he wouldn't expect it.

She sniffed pathetically and rubbed a hand under her nose. "I'm sorry, Daddy."

His tense body relaxed like a puppet whose strings had been cut. "Oh, Baby Girl, I know I'm asking a lot of you."

She forced a tremulous smile and lifted her chin. "I've decided I will do it after all. I'll help you, but there's a catch. I want you to tell me the truth."

He started to say something, but she held up a hand and continued resolutely, "I'd do anything for you, and for Mom. And…just so we're clear…I already know. They told me when they kidnapped me, but I need to hear it from you. I need to know why you did it."

Her father looked like she'd slapped him, but as he searched her face to verify the meaning of her words, she didn't give her own fake honesty a chance to waver. She reached over to the photo album, turned it around and tapped her finger on Nurse Vonda. He leaned down to look and couldn't hide the flash of recognition and guilt that swept over his face.

"She was your contact, wasn't she?" Bryn asked.

He sat on the bed, defeat in every line of his body.

"They could have saved your mom, you know," he said, low and slow. "The corporation who gave her the pig heart."

"Why didn't they then?"

"They paid for everything the first go-around, when she agreed to be their lab rat. Then they abandoned her when the heart failed. Said they wouldn't fund another one. Said we were on our own, that we had health insurance. But back then, insurance only covered human donors, not another porcine one, even though by that time there were so many bioengineered pigs out there we could have juggled the damned things. But human hearts? Not so many, and none that matched. That area of science, anti-rejection medicine, hadn't advanced, still hasn't."

"What does that have to do with me?" she asked.

"Your mom never should have done it. I fought her every step of the way. You know how I feel about xenoalteration in any form. It's unnatural, especially when stem cell regenerative cloning would use human cells, pure human cells, to accomplish even more—if only the conservatives would get off their ethical high-horses and allow it. There are bioengineers who've already made amazing advances in the area, but they're crippled by the world-wide ban on embryo use."

She was struck dumb by his words, by a revelation so earth-shattering, she stopped breathing and wondered if she had the fortitude to begin again. He didn't have to say another word; she already knew the depths to which he'd sunk to further his cause. That he'd used her as a pawn was bad enough, but that he'd done it hand-in-hand with a monster like Dr. Fournier was the ultimate betrayal.

An unnatural calm suffused her soul. "You want to make human cloning legal?"

Her father let out a frustrated growl. "I'm not alone. In the last decade, cancers and autoimmune diseases have skyrocketed. Health insurance premiums are second only to the mortgage in the average household budget. Quality of care is in the toilet. If the United States doesn't take a stand, there won't be anything left to stand for."

"The legislation," she said dully. "The Pure Human Society is a front."

"No. Everything I've said about regulating the practice of xenoalteration has been true. It needs to be made safer for the poor fools who choose that lifestyle."

"I didn't choose it."

He grabbed her hands and squeezed painfully. "But you understand, don't you? You see why I had to make the ultimate sacrifice…my beautiful daughter. Think what will happen once the legislation passes and grant money becomes available! Research facilities will break the speed barrier to compete for the money. In a couple of years, I guarantee they'll be able to grow new hair for you from your own cells."

Bryn's shaky nod went off to one side, but she managed to keep a look of agreement on her face even though tears began streaming down her cheeks. Her heart was breaking, not only from the betrayal, but because what she'd always mistaken in her father for fervent zeal was in reality something much more dangerous.

"So you'll do it?" He, too, had tears in his eyes. "All we lacked was public support, and that's where you come in. You'll be the anti-xenofreak poster child, and once we have their attention, we can change the message."

Bryn was having a harder and harder time maintaining her composure. The rage and hurt rose in waves, and every time she beat it down, it rose again more strongly. Her goal now, for the short term, was to get her father out of her bedroom.

She gulped a breath of air and said, "I'm on board, Dad. Just—can I be alone for a while? I really need to think."

He made an aborted motion like he was going to hug her but didn't want to deal with the quills. "I'm so, so sorry, Baby. Sorry that I didn't trust you enough to let you know what—what needed to be done."

If he didn't leave, she was going to explode in a fiery ball of hate and fury and that couldn't happen. She no longer knew what he was capable of. It was vital that she keep her true feelings under control if she wanted to get out of this in one piece. He'd had her kidnapped and mutilated. What else would he do to secure her compliance if she didn't go along with him now? She recalled his words, "Maybe we should talk to the doctors about medication."

She choked out one last word, "Okay."

When he left, she took her pillow with her into the closet, shut the door and despite the quills, managed to muffle her sobs. When she emerged an hour later with a tentative plan of action, she hid the shredded pillow and picked up each and every feather.

Chapter Twenty

Scott wanted to drive, but Padme pointed out that anyone looking in would see his hands on the steering wheel.

"You should have found a pair of gloves," she said.

"In July? That'd be just as conspicuous."

"We are both wearing our hoods up. Is that not conspicuous? We radiate conspicuosity."

Scott didn't think 'conspicuosity' was a word but didn't argue.

She drove. The car was, indeed, a clunker, a gasoline-powered monstrosity that probably cost its owner a bundle every year in green tax. If they did as he asked and destroyed it, he'd be able to put a down payment on a modest electric version. Instead, because there was no way they trusted the guy not to call the police immediately after they walked out the door, Padme parked the car four blocks away, near a corner convenience store.

Scott picked up some snacks in order to break one of Shasta's twenties while Padme selected a small bottle of antacids and two sodas. There was an old television behind the counter blaring a news report. In the worst timing possible, they'd come in just as their mug shots were plastered across the screen. Scott sensed Padme tense up next to him, but since the cable networks only broadcast in holo, the picture on the television was blurry and the color off just enough to make the photographs resemble almost anyone fitting their general descriptions. Except for the fact that the woman who was supposed to be Padme had normal ears. He hoped she wouldn't notice.

Their good luck held out. There were no other customers in the store and the guy behind the counter, in typical New York fashion, showed no curiosity whatsoever. They stayed calm, paid for their stuff and walked out casually.

Half a block away, they sat on a bus stop bench. Padme opened her medicine bottle, penetrated the safety seal with her fingernail and handed Scott four blue capsules and one of the sodas.

"No thanks," he said. "I have an iron stomach."

"I'm not suggesting your anxiety level is producing excess stomach acid," Padme said. She held her hand out until Scott accepted the pills. "The new class of proton-pump inhibitors will cripple any micro-transmitters we may have consumed in jail."

Scott's cultivated neutral expression helped him disguise his shock. He tried not to sound as avidly curious as he was. "What does that mean?"

"Routine countermeasure. The FBI and CIA, and probably the XIA now, as well, can track our whereabouts with microscopic devices that transmit infinitesimally small radio pulses undetectable to normal receivers. They have no power source, but instead use acid from the host's gastrointestinal track to run, like battery acid. Ingenious, really, but not infallible. The key is that unless you happen to be in possession of one of the feds' special receivers, they are undetectable, so the host is never aware of them to attempt countermeasures. Dr. Fournier, however, is the most paranoid person I've ever met."

Scott looked at the capsules in his hand suspiciously. "So the antacid will disable the transmitters?"

"No, just weaken them enough so the radio pulses can only be picked up when we're close to a receiver. Mostly, they're located on cell towers, so easily avoided."

"Wow," he said. Unbidden, the memory of Bryn being subdued by nurses Vonda and Nancy came to mind. They'd given her a shot of something that calmed her significantly and then coaxed her to swallow some pills. They'd initiated Dr. Fournier's 'countermeasures' right in front of Scott and he'd been none the wiser.

When they got on the bus, the driver didn't so much as glance their way. There weren't very many passengers this time of day, and the few that were on the bus were either snoozing or had their heads buried in holoreaders. They rode that bus, took the subway and then got on a few other buses until debarking on Coney Island.

After Poppy, a powerful category four hurricane that dealt Long Island a direct blow in 2020, the already seedy Coney Island underwent a drastic change for the worse. Poppy didn't discriminate. She wiped out public housing and rich communities alike. Tourist attractions that had been there for more than a century were flattened. Many businesses were destroyed, and others moved elsewhere as the neighborhoods failed to regenerate. The stadium that housed the popular Brooklyn Cyclones had collapsed from the flooding, and the city, beleaguered with the cost of reinstating basic services everywhere, had temporarily condemned it. Temporary had become permanent, at least until funding sources manifested, and in this economy, that wasn't likely any time soon. The XBestia gang moved in.

"They will look for us here," Padme said. They were standing on an intact section of the boardwalk south of the stadium, looking out at the ocean.

Scott made a scoffing sound. "Probably won't have to. As soon as they offer a reward, we're done."

"I know a place we can stay. For now."

He gave her a thoughtful look. "We?"

She shrugged. "You can accompany me or not."

"Why don't you stay with Lupus?"

"He would not allow me to endanger him. When he deems it safe, he will find me."

It was cooler along the shore, so their hoods weren't so out of place. Despite the island's deservedly bad reputation, people were safe enough in broad daylight and still came to the beach. Four teenagers were playing volleyball and a family of six was building a sandcastle nearby. Scott walked with Padme quite a ways before she turned toward an unprepossessing burger joint. The words 'Bluto's Last Stand' were spray-painted in graffiti urban art on the weatherworn exterior. A wooden sign with a grimacing, bearded cartoon character holding a blackboard stood near the door. The special of the day, a Bluto Burger and fries, was printed on the blackboard in white chalk.

Despite the laws prohibiting smoking in public establishments, the dark interior reeked of tobacco. The place was nearly empty; the only customers sat at the bar drinking even though it was just past mid-day. He suspected the two rough-looking men were xeno and probably XBestia, but didn't spot any obvious alterations. The only waitress hollered out to them to take a seat. Padme chose a booth along the west wall. Scott expected the table to be sticky and wasn't disappointed.

The waitress scurried over and wiped the table down with a rag that looked and smelled like she'd found it wrapped around a garbage truck axle. She was a tiny thing with streaked blonde hair and a pointy nose. Her nametag read, 'Mouse.'

"Sorry 'bout that," she said, pulling two menus out from under her arm. Before she set them down, she took a closer look at their faces and said quietly, "You folks look a little out of place. There's a café a few blocks down that's probably more your style."

Padme lowered her hood and asked, "Is Phaco cooking today?"

Mouse didn't miss a beat. "Yep. He's got a pot of chili on. Hot stuff."

"I will take the special. No onions. Will you tell him Pad is here?"

"Sure thing." Mouse lifted her eyebrows at Scott.

"Chili sounds good," he said. "And a Coke, please."

Mouse spun on her heel and disappeared behind a swinging door next to the bar.

Less than a minute later, the door swung open again and a black man with a huge belly trotted out. "Padme! I heard you was in jail. Dey let you out?"

Padme put a finger to her lips. When the man reached their table, she said, "I need a place to stay, Phaco."

Scott studied the big man's xenoalteration with interest. His lower jaw jutted forward naturally, placing his bottom teeth in front of the top. He'd had his lower canines and probably the tooth next to them replaced with thick, protruding tooth-like objects that pointed up and slightly outward, ending at just beyond his wide nostrils.

"Da back room is all yours. Won't be quiet, but it's safe. Who's your friend?"

"This is Cougar. He helped me escape. In the spirit of full disclosure, we're wanted."

"Well, dat makes more sense den da judge givin' an XBestia bail." His eyebrows dropped into a frown. "Lupus okay wif you and Cougar…" he jerked his thumb, presumably toward the back room.

"Lupus knows I would never cheat. Avoiding torture and death is a good incentive for faithfulness."

Phaco laughed. "Dat true."

He wiped a hand on his filthy apron and held it out to Scott. It was a perfunctory shake, like Phaco was putting him on notice that he was tolerated for Padme's sake and no other. He was talkative, though, even if his alteration made diction a challenge.

"I was born wif dis underbite. Coulda got it fixed, but it just wouldn't be me, ya know? Dese here," he ran a forefinger up and down one of the protrusions, "are the bottom tusks off a warthog, phacochoerus africanus. Dat why dey call me Phaco."

"Very intimidating," Scott said sincerely.

"Dat what I was goin' for," Phaco replied. Then he winked. "But I'm really a big softie. Ask Padme."

"It's true," Padme confirmed.

"I din't hear no mention of claws on da news," Phaco said. "Dey functional?"

Scott didn't like to, but he felt obligated to demonstrate. He curved his fingers inward and extended his claws. Phaco set his tongue against his upper lip between the tusks and let loose with a low whistle.

"Doc do good work." He reached out and tweaked one of Padme's ears. "Now I gonna go make you da best damn burger you ever had, you little cannibal."

It was the first time Scott ever heard Padme laugh.

Phaco disappeared behind the swinging door and soon after, Mouse reappeared at their table. Without a word, she set a glass of water in front of Padme and gave Scott his chili and Coke. After she left, Scott commented, "Not so friendly anymore."

Padme quirked one side of her mouth and sipped her water.

Surreptitiously, he watched Mouse. She went behind the bar and generously topped off her customers' drinks. Scott heard the phrase 'on the house,' but couldn't pick up the rest of what she was saying. She leaned her skinny elbows on the bar and seemed to be earnestly explaining something to the two xenos. One of them turned and stared in Scott and Padme's direction.

Phaco delivered Padme's hamburger himself and chatted for a few more minutes before going back into his kitchen. At that point, the two xenos at the bar stood up. Instead of heading for the exit, they sauntered over to the booth.

Before they could say or do anything, Padme spoke. "Do either of you gentlemen happen to know who I am?"

The taller of the two, with shaved head and a spiderweb tattoo on his throat, cracked his knuckles. "We hear you two like to mess with little girls." His breath was fetid with whiskey and something sour. Scott leaned away from the odor and let Padme handle the situation.

She held up her arm and pulled back the sleeve. A roundish patch of scars, both raised and dimpled, marred her forearm. Scott recognized it as a healed bite-mark; one that would have been a vicious injury to produce such a scar. He'd seen photographs of the very same mark—on a series of corpses allegedly dispatched by the top XBestia enforcer.

"This was a gift from Lupus," Padme said coldly. "When you see his brand on a person who is not dead, my advice is to run, not walk, in the opposite direction."

"Lupus?" The shorter of the two asked. He shot a look over his shoulder at Mouse, who began wiping down the bar as if she hadn't been avidly watching to see what would happen.

"And," Padme continued. "It would be best if you forgot you ever met such a person."

Both men began nodding, quite agreeable now. They backed away, and when they left, they were walking, but it looked to Scott like they wanted to take Padme's advice and run.

Scott took a bite of his chili. It was delicious, but as Mouse had warned, very spicy. He took a long sip of his Coke and spluttered, "Hot!"

Chapter Twenty-one

It was a good thing her father slept like a hibernating bear every night. As long as Bryn avoided the squeaky floorboards scattered throughout the old house, it was no problem packing her car. The little Hamster didn't hold much, but she took only what she needed, plus her mother's photo album and a few other keepsakes. Tucked at the back of the album, she found the Christmas cards from Carla she'd stashed away each year. After her mother passed, Carla tried to stay in touch, but her father discouraged it. Bryn accidently discovered that first Christmas card unopened in the trash, so she made a point of sorting through the holiday mail each year before her father got to it.

The address on the envelope changed every couple of years and it seemed to Bryn that the handwriting got sloppier, too. The message had over time remained the same, however. "You will always have a place to stay if you need it."

Bryn needed it.

Technically, and ironically, she'd turned eighteen that day, so she wasn't running away. After what he'd done, her father didn't deserve any sort of goodbye other than a terse note letting him know she hadn't been kidnapped again. But then, he'd know that already, given his role in her first abduction.

Bryn had finally peeked out the window. The news vans had gone for the night, but the XIA agents were parked right out front. She didn't make the mistake of thinking she could run for it—this wasn't holovision—she wouldn't be able to shake them no matter what she did, and pitting her compact car against their souped-up sedan would make for one ridiculous chase.

She'd found a lightweight beige cashmere scarf among those of her mother's things she'd been allowed to keep. It covered her head pretty well, except for the odd quill poking through. Looking at her reflection in the mirror, she flashed on Padme the first time she'd seen her. She, too, had worn a scarf to hide her alteration. Bryn had assumed from her appearance that Padme was a modest Middle Eastern young woman. At one point in the Pakistani girl's life, that had probably been true.

Bryn's father slept on the opposite side of the house from the garage. She pressed the garage door button, wincing as it went through its rumbling, grinding process. After the door was fully up, she listened for a moment. Her father's snores reverberated down the hall. She flipped on the light, went past her car and down the dark driveway to the agent's car. The woman in the driver's seat rolled down the window.

"Hi, Agent Yang," Bryn said.

"Is everything okay?"

"Not really. Today was my eighteenth birthday."

Yang's left eyebrow lifted slightly. "Happy Birthday."

"Thank you. So…I'm an adult now. Legally, I can do whatever I want." Bryn didn't phrase it as a question. She was determined not to sound like she was asking for permission.

Yang tilted her head but said nothing.

Bryn licked her lips and wished she hadn't. It gave her nervousness away. She stood up straight and spoke firmly to counteract it. "I'm going to leave my father's house. I'm not going to tell him I'm leaving. I don't want you to tell him I'm leaving, and I no longer want your protection. Is that clear?"

Yang looked over to the passenger seat at an agent Bryn had never met. They exchanged a few hushed words before she turned back.

"It's not that simple, Bryn. Why do you want to leave?"

Bryn sighed. "That's between me and my father. I'm going to get into my car now and drive away. I'd prefer it if you didn't follow me, but obviously I can't stop you. I mean it, though, about my dad. Don't tell him where I am. If you do, I'll just take off again."

She didn't wait for Yang to summon up an argument or pepper her with more questions. She stalked back up the driveway and got into her car. Halfway down the lane, she caught sight of headlights in her rearview mirror. They stayed there all the way to Brooklyn.

Bryn wasn't familiar with the demographics of Brooklyn's neighborhoods, so she wasn't prepared for Carla's home to be located on a rundown block of three-story apartment buildings. She drove around for twenty minutes looking for a parking space, which, at two in the morning, were nonexistent. Finally, Agent Yang pulled up alongside and motioned for her to roll down her window.

"There's a pay-to-park structure six blocks away," Yang said. "We'll give you a ride back from there. Even if you find a spot on the street, a sweet little car like that all packed with stuff is going to be stripped by morning or flat-out gone. I assume your dad was handling the car insurance?"

Bryn was upset enough without Yang dealing that last low blow. There were a lot of things her dad had paid for. Her salary had been adequate for her needs; make the car payment, buy electri-gas for the car and purchase a few luxuries now and then. In point of fact, her holophone had already been shut off and this month's car payment was due, and she had no idea how she would pay it.

There was nothing else to do. She was tired, emotionally wrung out, and had a headache from crying. She didn't know if Carla even lived here anymore and she didn't have a plan B. With a defeated wave of her hand, she indicated to Yang that she would follow.

Once the Hamster was parked safely, Bryn got into the back of the sedan and resignedly gave Yang Carla's address. It wasn't like they wouldn't find it out anyway. To her immense relief, the agents didn't cross-examine her during the ride. They double-parked to drop her off and as she walked away through the dimly lit, narrow lanes, the sedan inched forward to keep her in sight. Despite her determination to make this fledgling attempt at independence her only attempt, it was reassuring to know they were there.

She located Carla's building, but when she pressed the buzzer to her apartment, there was no response. Bryn depressed the button every thirty seconds for about five minutes before sitting on the steps in utter dejection. Carla either wasn't home, was a heavier sleeper than even her father, or the buzzer wasn't working.

It was a warm enough night to sit outside and wallow in miserable reflection, especially since she was wearing her leather jacket and the scarf covered her head and shoulders. While she waited, every word her father said this afternoon paraded across her consciousness. She tried to find some error of judgment on her part; some redeeming word or phrase that her abhorrence had obscured. Instead, her anger reignited.

The muted sound of a car door alerted her, and she looked in the direction of the street. A dark-clothed figure walked toward Bryn along the sidewalk, trailed by another figure—Bryn was pretty sure the second figure was Agent Yang. The first person was also female; Bryn saw her glance over her shoulder at Yang and begin walking faster. By the time the pool of light at the entrance to the apartment building revealed the woman to be Carla, Yang was only a few yards behind.

Bryn stood up and Carla gasped in surprise. She reacted by jumping back to put both Bryn and Yang in her line of sight. Her arm shot forth from her pocket, a wicked-looking pistol in her grip. Before Yang did something stupid, Bryn exclaimed, "Aunt Carla!"

Yang responded by holding her hands up and walking on past like she hadn't been deliberately tailing her.

Carla said, "Bryn? Is that you?" Then she laughed self-consciously and tucked the pistol away. "Gawd, I almost shot you! I thought—oh, never mind. Sweetie, come here!"

Instead of allowing Carla to fold her into a hug, Bryn removed the scarf from her head, or tried to since it got stuck and only came halfway off. It was enough for Carla to see what had become of her.

"Oh, Brynnie." Carla's voice held a wealth of sadness, but no surprise. Like everyone else, she would know all about Bryn's misfortunes from the news. "Let's get you inside."

Carla's apartment was midway down on the third floor. Bryn didn't think the shabby chic décor was deliberately shabby, but it was cozy and clean. She sat on the faux-suede tan couch and let Carla untangle the scarf from her quills while she poured her heart out.

"That son-of-a-bitch," Carla muttered when Bryn told her what her father had done. "He was never right in the head. I tried to tell Miranda, but she couldn't see the bad in people."

"I was hoping I could stay with you until I got on my feet," Bryn said.

Carla sprang off the couch and said, "Of course! Even if I hadn't promised your mom I'd take care of you, I'd be thrilled to have you. The sofa pulls out into a bed."

She removed her overcoat and hung it on a wooden coat rack by the door. Underneath was a uniform consisting of a short maroon dress with a white mini apron over it. Her hair was cut in a shoulder-length shag that flattered her petite form and features. Bryn remembered being nearly as tall as Carla as a child; now she towered over the older woman.

"I've got some sweats that might fit you until we can get your car moved," Carla said. "I have a spot assigned to me but haven't used it since I lost my license. It might upset whoever's been parking there, but who cares?" She crossed the room and bounced back down on the couch. Bryn caught a whiff of alcohol, and cigarette smoke emanated from her clothes and hair. A network of fine wrinkles surrounded Carla's brown eyes and a few deeper lines intersected the contour of her upper lip. For some reason, the lip lines reminded Bryn of Scott's scar.

"It's late. You're probably exhausted," Carla said. Bryn thought that no matter how hard life had been for her mother's best friend, she seemed as kind and loving as ever.

She pointed to the nametag on Carla's uniform. "Mouse?"

Carla's lips curved in a mischievous smile. She pulled the front of her dress partially down. In short white fur on the top inside curve of her left breast was a small xenograft in the shape of a mouse.

Chapter Twenty-two

After the confrontation with the two drunken xenos, Scott and Padme decided it would be best to stay hidden. The back room at Bluto's was nicer than Scott expected. He'd imagined a smelly broom closet, but it was a sizable space with a desk, couch and two armchairs. Phaco was running the place while Bluto, the man who owned the restaurant and bar, did time for assault. From the décor in the back room and throughout the establishment, Scott surmised that Bluto's favorite pastime was hunting. Framed photos of a big, bearded man in camouflage fatigues dotted the walls. In each shot, the man had a rifle in one hand and the carcass of some dead animal in the other.

Padme sat at the desk, where Phaco had given her access to the old-fashioned company computer. Scott settled into one of the oversized armchairs and watched idly as she tapped on the keyboard.

After a while, she said, "Abel's been arrested."

"Has he?"

Abel's full name was Abel Wiener, a retired forklift operator from New Jersey. The XIA had more than enough evidence to charge him with crimes that would lock him up for the rest of his life. They'd left him alone because he'd been Scott's 'direct supervisor' within the XBestia organization. His arrest was a calculated move to get Scott a 'promotion.' Scott considered it a long shot, but Shasta felt differently.

"We've fished a lot of dead XBestia lieutenants out of the river lately," she'd said. "There's plenty of room for upward mobility."

Scott thought Shasta was putting an overly optimistic spin on it. Moving up was essential but given the rate at which Lupus went through underlings, significantly more dangerous.

Padme looked up from the keyboard. "Tomorrow you should head for the stadium. Most of the displaced Warehouse folk are there now."

Scott inhaled deeply and let it out in an audible sigh. "Not sure I should stick around. I got a friend in Seattle who might put me up." He forced a short laugh. "I'm running out of places to go where the cops aren't looking for me."

She tapped some more keys and in a surprisingly short amount of time, said, "Looks like you have a warrant out of San Diego in addition to the one here."

Scott nodded.

The Marine Corp probably wouldn't have kicked him out for his San Diego arrest considering he'd only been defending himself, but Shasta and the XIA got him dishonorably discharged and had his police record doctored to implicate him in several burglaries. They didn't need to expunge anything from his past that would indicate who he really worked for, but he did need a background befitting a true badass. It nagged at him that the XIA didn't seem to equate his faked criminal background with the other agents' expunged ones. All he could hope for was that the computer forensicians did a better job making stuff up than they did erasing it.

"I wouldn't recommend leaving town until Lupus clears it," Padme said.

"Yeah, I guess. But I'm not much use to him at the moment."

"Perhaps you should alter your appearance." He knew she meant change his facial features surgically.

"No money. I used every cent I had to get this done." He held up his hands.

"Why did you do it?" Padme had never asked about his alteration before and she didn't sound particularly interested now, but he'd rehearsed his answer in his head so many times he responded almost without thought.

"To ditch my fingerprints."

He'd been printed only twice in his life; before entering the Marines and when he'd been booked into the San Diego jail, so his answer was patently untrue. He'd gotten the alteration for two reasons: because the first two XIA agents to go in had gotten fake alterations and subsequently disappeared, and because a xenograft appeared to provide protection against a tentatively identified and deadly pathogen. The XIA suspected Fournier of dabbling in biological warfare and Scott's primary objective was to learn more about it.

"You sacrificed your sense of touch," Padme said thoughtfully, rubbing the edge of one of her cow ears with her fingertips. "And I my hearing."

"I can feel," Scott said, "but it's like I'm wearing gloves."

"And I can hear, but not as well I used to."

"You ever feel like…" he paused to get his wording right, since he'd be a fool not to take this opportunity to broach a subject that was integral to his mission, "…the nanoneurons are, I don't know, messing with you?"

"What makes you think I have them?" she asked. "My alteration doesn't do anything. The ears just sit there."

"Oh." He hid his disappointment by leaning forward and studying the antler arrangement holding up the glass-top of the coffee table.

She took the bait, though. "Do you think your nanoneurons are malfunctioning?"

He shrugged. Something in her voice, a keener-than-usual interest, warned him to tread lightly here. The truth was: his nanoneurons didn't bother him a bit. He felt nothing, but the XIA didn't like the fact that they'd never been able to hack the program that ran Dr. Fournier's nanoneuronic system.

He decided to back off. "Probably just being paranoid."

"If it bothers you, why did you choose a functional alteration?"

"So I'd always have a weapon at hand," he replied.

"Is that a joke?"

"Why? Is it funny?" He was irritated with himself now, and with Padme. She was like a nesting doll with infinite layers. Every time he thought he might get somewhere with her, she redirected the flow of conversation, usually to find out something about him.

They didn't talk after that. Scott hadn't slept well in jail. He lay down on the couch and without intending to, fell asleep. Music and noise from the bar woke him some time later. He sat up groggily and looked for Padme, who wasn't in the room. His right nostril was completely stuffed up, so he stumbled over to the desk for a tissue and blew his nose. He took a moment to check if Padme had left the old computer unlocked; she had, but when he tried to trace her Internet movements, he found she'd erased her trail.

When she came back with a tray of food and drinks, he was playing a game of Scorpion Solitaire.

"What level is that?" she asked, nodding at the computer screen.

"Four."

She shook her head. "That game is luck of the draw. The odds of winning level four are one game in fifty. I don't understand why anyone would play something you lose over and over again."

Scott had played four games and lost each one. "Can't win 'em all, but there's no shame in trying." It was something his father used to say.

"Here." She set a plate in front of him. "I got you the special because you don't need any more chili."

He frowned down at the hamburger and fries. "Why not?"

She tilted her head towards the couch, where he'd been napping all afternoon. "I don't think your digestive system needs any more stimulation."

"Oh." He felt a blush warm his cheeks.

"You also talk in your sleep."

Scott froze with his lips an inch from his straw and lifted his eyes to where she stood on the other side of the desk.

She smiled, not kindly, but like a child with a secret. "You were, apparently, dreaming of our Bryn."

He had no recollection whatsoever of any dream he may have had—usually he only remembered them if he woke in the midst of one. Padme didn't seem suspicious, so he probably hadn't said anything incriminating, but she did seem to be slyly intimating that he'd spoken inappropriately.

"So?" he said. "She's hot."

"She was. Past tense. Now she's untouchable."

He'd been irritated with her earlier; now he suppressed a flash of anger. He stuffed a French fry in his mouth and resumed playing the unwinnable game of solitaire, ignoring her as she stood there watching him. She finally took her food over to the couch.

After the meal, they briefly discussed sleeping arrangements. She would take the couch and he'd make do with one of the chairs. Given that he'd already gotten a significant amount of sleep, he told her he'd probably occupy himself with computer games until he got tired. She flipped the overhead light switch off, leaving only a small, low-watt desk lamp for Scott. When she closed her eyes, she seemed unconcerned that he might return the favor and watch her as she slept.

Eventually the noise from the bar died down. At around 3:00 a.m., Phaco knocked gently before coming in and telling Scott he was locking up for the night. Scott, still sitting at the desk, went back to his losing solitaire streak, head beginning to nod. That was the last thing he remembered before waking suddenly in the dimly lit room, instantly alert.

He sensed someone in the room, but the proximity of the lamp put everything but the desk in shadow. Padme shifted on the couch and moaned—Scott knew pain when he heard it—and the dark bulk on the couch was too big to be Padme alone. He started to get up, claws fully extended, when the man on top of Padme lifted his head. Glittering human eyes stared malevolently out of an inhuman face.

Scott had no idea how Dr. Fournier had transplanted a wolf face onto a human one. He had to have accounted for several significant differences in skull structure, and yet he managed to make Lupus look very wolf-like. Lupus' voice was naturally low and gravelly, furthering the impression when he spoke. Now his throat produced an uncannily accurate growl and his canine ears went back as he pinned Scott with his gaze.

Scott wanted nothing more than to leap across the room and take the pseudo-wolf on, but he sat slowly back down and resheathed his claws.

Lupus stood. Scott estimated his height to be about six-foot-four-inches tall. He was a big man, but not particularly muscular. It was hard to guess his age, but going by the style of jeans he preferred, he was older than Padme by at least a decade. Those jeans were unbuttoned and partially unzipped. Scott knew Lupus was completely lacking in morals; still, he had a hard time believing the man would attempt to have sex with Padme while Scott was in the room.

Lupus' face was unreadable, of course, but his body language as he refastened his pants was cocky enough to tell Scott it had been some kind of show, possibly to stake his claim over Padme. As if Scott needed a demonstration of Lupus' domination over the girl to warn him off her. The truth was, Scott wouldn't have been interested in her even if she weren't so very off-limits. The circumstances that led her here may not have been her fault, but she'd become toxic in the process.

Padme sat up and adjusted her displaced clothing, ignored by Lupus, whose focus was all on Scott.

"Abel has been eliminated," Lupus said.

Scott knew better than to voice his question, "In jail?" Abel had been a marked man the moment he'd been arrested. Probably, if Scott and Padme hadn't 'escaped,' there would have been an eventual attempt on their lives from inside, as well.

Lupus reached into his pocket and withdrew something that jangled metallically. He tossed a ring of keys to Scott.

"Abel's office at the stadium," he said. "It's yours."

Chapter Twenty-three

Bryn slept on Carla's lumpy pull-out bed, with a musty-smelling quilt for a cover and a couch cushion with a spare pillowcase over it for a pillow. She'd apologized in advance for any damage her quills might cause, and sure enough, in the middle of the night she woke to find they'd pierced the cushion in several spots. After that, she slept fitfully, plagued by nightmares of being chased by some nebulous menace that may or may not have been her father.

By morning, the vignettes floating through her slumber had mellowed significantly; she drifted awake from a disturbingly erotic dream involving Scott and his furry fingers. Her new scalp felt funny, tight, like the skin had contracted. She reached up to discover the majority of her quills were flat to her head. Unbidden, a sentence from an article she'd read on porcupines came to her, "During coitus, porcupine skin tightens, perhaps involuntarily, to hold the quills down so the animals don't injure each other."

She sat up, wiped the sleep from her eyes, and glanced into the kitchenette, where Carla was quietly adding grounds to a small coffee maker.

"Oh, hey, sorry if I woke you," Carla said. The halogen light from the ceiling cast dark shadows under her eyes. "I don't sleep much. Bluto says I should have gotten owl feathers for a graft."

"Who's Bluto?"

"My boyfriend. He's in prison for assault, but that was trumped-up. He was just protecting his livelihood, you know? He owns a restaurant on Coney Island—I work there. Anyway, he put all his money into buying the place and fixing it up and then some jerk comes along and tries to burn it down. Not like the cops care what happens out there anymore."

"What time is it?" Bryn's quills were relaxing as the physical effects of the dream on her body faded.

"Almost ten. You were wiped. I tried to stay in my room, but I needed my caffeine fix. Want some coffee?"

Bryn shook her head. She'd been uneasy ever since Carla revealed she was, in essence, a xenofreak. If the older woman thought it would seal some kind of bond with her houseguest, she was mistaken. If anything, Bryn felt less affinity for her mother's best friend than ever before. She didn't know if life had changed her or if Carla had always been so brash and brassy; it wasn't something Bryn would have picked up on as a child.

"Are you hungry?" Carla opened the refrigerator. "I can scramble some eggs."

Bryn's stomach rebelled at the very thought of eating anything even though she hadn't eaten since lunch the day before. By now, her father would know she was gone, and she figured for sure the XIA agents would tell him where. She didn't know exactly how he would react, other than being very angry, and the anticipation heightened her already high anxiety.

"You don't have to feed me," she said. "I'll figure something out."

Carla came into the living room and sat on the edge of the pull-out. Bryn couldn't decide if she seemed younger or older without makeup. Carla looked her sternly in the eye and said, "You're not a burden. Okay?"

Bryn let out a little laugh. "Okay. I just feel like I need to get my butt out there and find a job, like, yesterday."

"I don't suppose there's any life insurance money left?"

Bryn's already stressed-out stomach performed a remarkable flip-flop. "What?"

Carla took a breath. "Your dad probably spent it, but I know for a fact you were the beneficiary of your mom's policy. We both worked for the same company when she got sick, and I remember her fighting with him to keep up on the premiums after she couldn't work anymore."

This was news to Bryn. Hesitantly, she said, "He must have spent it. I had no idea there was ever any money."

Carla narrowed her eyes and jumped up to cross the room. Against the far wall sat a china cabinet that looked to be worth more than the curios Carla had on display on its shelves. She opened a set of doors in the bottom half of the unit and pulled out a cardboard box full of files. After a few minutes of riffling and muttering, she exclaimed, "Ah-ha!"

She brought a file back with her and sat with it in her lap. Bryn saw the title written in neat black letters on the tab, 'Milladay Institute of Technology.' She hadn't thought about it in years, but her mother had been a counselor at the school. It was where she'd met Bryn's dad; he'd been a student, several years younger than her and off-limits. Over the years, he'd told Bryn the story of how he'd persisted in his pursuit of Miranda McKim until he'd worn down her resistance, not only to their age difference, but to the danger of losing her job.

Carla had a different story to relate. She started talking as she thumbed through the documents in the file. "Your dad was a menace from the moment your mom met him. Honestly, she should have known better—she was a trained psychologist for crissakes! She should have seen him for what he was: a sociopath, and seen his behavior for what it was: stalking. But he was good, I'll give him that. Very suave, always said the right thing, romantic to a fault. And it paid off because she married him six months to the day after he showed up in her office for counseling. You know why he was there that day? Cheating on a test. Which he denied. Big red flag if you ask me…oh, here it is."

Carla read silently for a moment. "Alright, the life insurance company was called Provincial Mutual. Their offices are on West Trill Street. Do you want to stop by before I go to work this afternoon?"

Bryn opened her mouth to answer, but a loud, authoritative knock on the door stopped her. Her poor stomach reacted by cramping into a hard, painful ball. She met Carla's eyes with a frightened look.

"Quick!" Carla hissed. "Get dressed!"

Bryn scrambled off the pull-out and frantically stripped off the borrowed sweat clothes while Carla went to the door and looked out the peephole. Carla rushed back to Bryn and whispered, "It's your dad. He's got some lady with him, and a cop. This doesn't look good."

In her underwear, Bryn tiptoed to the door as another knock sounded.

"Bryn!" Harry Vega shouted. "We know you're in there!"

Bryn pressed her cheek to the door and peered out. Her dad's distorted face was closest to the door, but behind him was an unknown police officer and, of all people, Dr. Finnegan. Bryn's holo-psychiatrist was a real person after all. Every despairing word Bryn had said to the doctor came flooding back to her. She'd given them plenty of ammunition to use against her.

She looked frantically around the small apartment, feeling like a trapped animal. To Carla, she said quietly, "He's got my psychiatrist with him. This is some kind of intervention and I'm guessing I'm going to end up with a snug white jacket before it's over."

"Over my dead body," Carla muttered. "Finish getting dressed. I'll stall them while you go down the fire escape."

She went to the door and spoke through it. "Who's there?"

Bryn pulled on her jeans as her father said, "Open the door, Carla. I've got an emergency warrant for a 72-hour psychiatric observation. Bryn is suicidal and you're endangering her life by hiding her."

Carla said loudly, "Who are you? What are you talking about?" Then she flapped her hands at Bryn to hurry.

Bryn finished dressing and slung her mother's scarf over her head, but stopped cold when her father said, "Tell her I had her car towed. She's got nowhere to go."

As if to make up for her father's callous statement, Dr. Finnegan said, "Bryn, dear, we just want what's best for you. We'll sit down and have a nice long chat."

She'd barely finished speaking when the police officer banged on the door. "Police, Ma'am. Open up."

"Shit, shit, shit," Carla muttered. She ran into her bedroom on silent feet and returned with her purse, pulling out a wad of cash. "Here, take my tips from last night." She also shoved the little gun Bryn had seen last night into Bryn's hands. "You have to take the gun, too, because if I get caught with it, I'm history."

Bryn didn't have time to protest. Carla pushed her to the larger of the two windows in the apartment and opened it. Bryn stuffed the cash and the gun in the pocket of her leather jacket and climbed out.

"Go to Coney Island to Bluto's place," Carla said. "Catch Bus 79 two blocks east of us. It's just about to arrive, so run. I'll meet you there when I come in for work."

Bryn descended the fire escape, trying not to let the heels of her boots clang on the iron grid and expecting at any moment to be caught. She was astonished that Agent Yang or one of the other XIA agents wasn't waiting for her at the bottom. It occurred to her that just because she couldn't see them didn't mean they couldn't see her.

When her feet hit the sidewalk, she took off. If there was one thing Bryn was good at, it was running.

Chapter Twenty-four

Lupus had hung around long enough to give Scott a specific task before leaving with Padme. That's why Scott was confused when he woke up and saw Padme sitting across from him in the chair. He wondered what time it was; he must have overslept. There was no window in the room to allow daylight in, so other than the desk lamp, it still seemed dark. Padme had her usual scarf over her head, and her face was in the shadows.

Scott sat up and sheepishly rubbed the stubble on his chin. "Did I talk in my sleep again?"

Then he noticed the gun.

She turned her head so he could see her face. With evident relish in her tone, Bryn said, "This is better than all the therapy in the world."

Scott didn't for a minute believe Bryn was capable of shooting him. He decided to bide his time, let her point the dainty little gun at him and talk until she felt better. Then he'd wait until she was distracted, wait until the barrel was pointing elsewhere, and rush her.

"How'd you get in?"

"Door was open."

It was just like Lupus to break in and then leave without locking up. "What do you want?"

"I want my hair back."

"Look, I'm sorry you-"

"Shut up." She kept the gun steadily directed at his midsection while she reached up to remove the scarf with her free hand. It got caught on a few of the porcupine quills that covered her head, but after a moment she worked it free and the scarf fell to her shoulders.

He tried to hide his astonishment. Gone was the wholesome beauty. In her place was a dark, punk, pissed-off pixie in a leather jacket. Before, she was pretty. Now, her green eyes under the fringe of sharp quills had a hard edge, like she'd kicked her own innocence to the curb. She was beautiful. He almost told her so, but bit back the words. She did not want to hear it.

85

"You aren't sorry," she snarled. "You don't look sorry, you don't sound sorry. I'm not an idiot."

"No one said you were an idiot."

She made a belligerent face at him. "No one cared."

He realized by 'no one,' she meant him. "I had no choice. I do what I'm told. I'm an XBestia."

She gestured to her head. "I guess this makes me one, too."

"Oh, yeah, sure," Scott said. "That and drug smuggling, arms trafficking, a little extortion now and then."

"You forgot kidnapping."

"I didn't forget. Name a crime, the XBestia dabble in it. I know you won't believe this, but I didn't want to hurt you."

She burst out in a derisive laugh. "Oh, lordy. Are you breaking up with me, Scott?"

He sighed. "Why are you here, anyway?"

She shook her head and the quills rustled quietly. Her expression went from caustic to distressed as her gaze drifted away. He considered making his move for the gun, but her eyes snapped back to his face. "I'm here because a series of bizarre events led me here. I've never been a terribly philosophical person, but it sure looks like someone up there wants me to get my revenge."

"So you're gonna kill me?" He kept his tone light.

"Maybe I'll just kidnap you and pay someone to mess up your head."

"I didn't pay anyone to hurt you," he said.

"No. My dad did."

Scott didn't bother to hide his surprise.

She said, "You didn't know. I guess that makes sense. You're just a…lackey."

He didn't respond and she continued. "I meant what I said. I want my hair back. Everyone knows the Bestia Butcher keeps trophies from his patients. If he kept my—my scalp, I want it back."

Scott shook his head. "Even if he did, it's probably floating in a jar of formaldehyde. They won't be able to reattach it."

"I don't care. I just don't want him to have it. I don't want it to be on display, like a—like a two-headed snake. Every time he looks at it, he remembers what he did to me."

He couldn't help it: an incredulous laugh escaped. "What do you expect me to do? Even if I knew where he was, I'd be a dead man if I told you."

She lifted the gun. "Maybe you're a dead man if you don't."

"A little advice, Bryn? Next time you threaten someone's life, don't use the word 'maybe.'"

He saw her swallow nervously. She was arguing with herself internally; trying to work herself up to sound more convincing and having a hard time of it. He was ready to go for the gun, but if she tensed up and accidently squeezed the trigger, he didn't want it to be pointing at him. What she said next nearly blew him away.

"I want to join the XBestias."

Chapter Twenty-five

Bryn didn't, really. She wanted to pretend to join so she could talk to Dr. Fournier and maybe take back some of her dignity. It was an impulsive decision, but the more she thought about it, the more it made a perverse kind of sense.

"It's not a freaking social club," Scott said. "Maybe you look like one of us now, but you're not cut out for it, trust me. Most of us are ex-cons and technically homeless. It's not the mafia, where there are rules. We're more like a street gang with no honor code and a shitload of infighting. You'd have to protect yourself, and frankly, I could have disarmed you by now if I wanted."

"Then why didn't you?"

He half-stood suddenly and his hand jerked out to clamp down on her wrist, forcing her to point the gun away from him. He twisted sharply, claws grazing her skin, and with a gasp of pain, she let go. Carla's gun thudded onto the carpet.

"Because I said I didn't want to hurt you," he said.

He was bent in a crouch facing her but straightened up and pulled her to her feet. With only inches separating them, Bryn looked up into his face. He stared back, his blue eyes hard and bright as polished agate. Her breath came faster, and she told herself it was the shock of him overpowering her so easily. The fact that her quills had gone flat against her skull meant nothing.

"I don't have anywhere else to go." She cursed the tearful sound of her voice but refused to break eye contact.

"Little girl, I am not your friend."

She should be frightened. She should be trying to scratch his eyes out. Scott had helped kidnap her, had guarded her while she was held captive, and…he let them take her away. He said he wasn't her friend and yet that very honesty was telling her something different. Her own father had betrayed her in the most devastating way imaginable. Right now, she should be seriously doubting her ability to judge anyone's character, much less her former kidnapper. But all she wanted was to get closer to him, and when his eyes dropped to her lips, she thought she was about to get her wish.

Instead, he clenched his jaw and stepped away, bending to retrieve the gun. He lifted the back of his hoodie and tucked the gun into his waistband.

"My friend Carla is an XBestia," Bryn said. "That's her gun."

"Okay," he replied, like it made zero difference.

"She told me to meet her here. I ditched a bunch of XIA agents."

That got his attention. "You? I doubt it. They're probably outside right now, thanks a lot. You know they're looking for me, right?"

"They're looking for someone who looks like you. They've got the wrong mug shot."

"Oh, yeah?"

He didn't sound surprised, so Bryn figured he already knew. He probably saw it in the news and thought it was a great stroke of luck. But he also didn't sound overly worried about the agents she had to agree probably were out there. He was, to use an old-fashioned phrase, an awfully cool customer for a man on the run.

A timid knock sounded on the door and they both froze. "Phaco? Are you in there?"

It was Carla. She looked around the edge of the door and instantly assessed the situation.

"What are you still doing here?" Her short legs got her across the room faster than Bryn might have expected. She went straight up to Scott and slapped him in the face. "You son-of-a-bitch! Look what you did to her!"

Before he could react, she ran to Bryn and made that aborted hug move Bryn was beginning to expect from everyone. "Oh, honey, I'm sorry. Phaco said they'd be gone before morning. I was so worried when I didn't see you outside! Did this bastard hurt you?"

Bryn looked over at Scott, who stood there with the pink imprint of Carla's hand on his cheek. He made no move to retaliate and didn't even look angry. If he were really as big a creep as he tried to make out, he'd be livid. The XBestia in general may be a heinous lot, but this XBestia in particular was an enigma. Like he'd gone bad out of necessity, as Bryn was contemplating doing.

"I'm okay, Carla. He's been a perfect gentleman."

A fleeting look of annoyance crossed Scott's face.

Carla said, "Huh. You don't have Stockholm syndrome, do you?"

"What?" Bryn asked.

"It's where a captive falls in love with their captor." Carla glared at Scott with tight lips and slitted eyes.

Bryn forced a laugh that even she had to admit sounded phony. "That's ridiculous."

Scott finally spoke up. "I wasn't her captor. Like Bryn said before you got here, I'm just a lackey. You want to take the matter up with Lupus if you got complaints."

"Maybe I'll take it up with Fournier," Carla snapped.

Scott snorted. "Oh, yeah. I'd like to see you find someone to carry that message."

He was walking towards the door as he said it. With a sinking heart at her own foolishness, Bryn realized she might actually run after him if he crooked his furry finger. Pathetic. Carla's words about Stockholm syndrome really hit home. Bryn knew it was bass-ackwards, but if she was honest with herself, she had to admit she was attracted to Scott. Maybe it was genetic; her mom picked a bad boy. Or maybe it had more to do with the way Scott looked at her. Instead of sneering in disgust at the porcupine quills, he was almost…admiring. All those despairing days thinking no one would ever love her seemed to melt away when he looked at her.

He opened the door, and with a pang of regret, Bryn resigned herself to never seeing him again. He stopped short, though, when Carla said, "I'll deliver the message myself."

Chapter Twenty-six

Scott had to proceed very carefully here. If Bryn's friend Carla, or Mouse the waitress, as he knew her, really did know how to get to Fournier, he'd be derelict in his duties if he didn't follow that lead. However, along with the slap in the face that still stung, she'd set those drunken goons on him and Padme last night—it was obvious she was highly protective of Bryn. If he showed any interest in her alleged knowledge of Fournier's whereabouts, it would either invite her suspicion or she'd clam up just to spite him. Plus, she had to know how dangerous the knowledge itself was and was probably regretting her outburst at this very moment.

He thought fast. There was only one thing he could do to foster Mouse's goodwill and possibly find out what she knew. Bryn may talk like she hated him, but her body language after he'd disarmed her said otherwise. She'd had no idea what she was saying when she'd asked to become an XBestia, but if she meant it, she'd only go off and eventually get herself killed, or worse. At least this way, he could protect her while potentially benefitting at the same time.

She was standing next to Mouse with an almost forlorn look on her face. "You coming?" he asked, like it was his intention to take her with him all along.

"What?"

"You can stay here and wait for the XIA to make their move, or you can come with me." He turned to Mouse. "You know where the Bungholes are?"

Warily, she nodded. After hurricane Poppy destroyed the stadium, the city installed prefabricated temporary housing on the baseball field for those among the displaced with nowhere decent to stay. The bungalows, or Bungholes, as they were nicknamed, were one-room structures with no electricity and no plumbing. It didn't take long for the cheap, short-term solution to make a mockery of the word 'decent.' Separate sanitary facilities were inadequate to handle the volume of human waste, so many of the inhabitants resorted to make-shift toilets inside the structures. Rats and cockroaches took advantage of the lack of refrigeration and running water, creating an insurmountable infestation. The city eventually routed out everyone who hadn't already abandoned the place and pasted condemned notices on each unit, after which the Bungholes became infested once more—with the XBestia.

"We'll be in number nine," Scott said. He raised his eyebrows at Bryn. She took a hesitant step towards him, but Mouse said, "Wait."

She went to the desk and retrieved a flashlight from one of the drawers. "If you walk out the front door, you might not get very far. I know a secret way out. Bluto said Fournier has them in all his buildings."

Mouse went to the corner of the room and opened a closet door. She shoved a couple of hanging coats aside and kicked the back panel in the lower left corner. It magically swung open to reveal a dark space. "Follow me. Watch your step."

Scott went last, squeezing into the narrow space and pulling the back of the closet into place behind him. The bodies of the two women blocked the flashlight's beam, leaving very little for him to see by as he slowly moved ahead. The ground appeared to be bare concrete that slanted down for about six feet before becoming a steep staircase. He negotiated the steps sideways, his chest and back scraping the moist, rough walls as it led down into the ground. The air was dank and cold. At the bottom was a ninety-degree turn where the already low ceiling dropped two feet or so. He bent nearly double, but at least this part of the tunnel was wide enough for him to walk forward.

Directly in front of him, Bryn suddenly produced a series of short, sharp shrieks and shuffle-hopped backwards until he had to place his hands on her backside to keep her from crashing into him. Mouse turned the flashlight on her as she dropped to her knees and frantically slapped at the front of her jacket. "Is it on me?"

With the increase in illumination, Scott saw several webs lacing the walls, nests both abandoned and occupied. "Theridiidae," he said. "Common house spider. It's probably long gone."

Bryn swiveled her head to glower up at him. "If you say it was more scared of me than I was of it…"

The words had been next in line to come out of his mouth.

"You're tens of thousands of times bigger than it," he said instead, trying to inject reason against her phobia. "Would you be scared of Godzilla?"

Mouse waved the flashlight around. "Come on. Suck it up, Brynnie. Xenos eat spiders for breakfast. It's not far."

Bryn got her feet under her, but he noticed her quills seemed to have puffed up around her head. He made an effort not to brush up against her.

The tunnel ended in a shaft with a tall aluminum ladder propped against the wall. At the top, Mouse crawled onto a slab and stood facing a panel similar to the one at Bluto's end of the tunnel. Instead of kicking the lower corner, she banged a fist against the top left corner. A gap appeared, but whatever was inside the closet prevented it from opening inward. Mouse leaned against it and shoved until she was able to reach inside and do some rearranging of the crowded broom closet in order to get to the door handle. She opened it a crack and peered out before stepping over a janitor's bucket into the space beyond.

Once they were all standing in the dark hallway of a building that looked vacant, Mouse aimed the flashlight to the left and whispered, "This way. Keep quiet; I'm not sure who's squatting here, but they raid our dumpster and mug our clients on a regular basis."

At the end of the hallway was a large open space that appeared to have once been a waiting room adjacent to the building's reception area. The floor-to-ceiling windows along one wall had all been broken out at some point and were boarded up. Light from outside shone in through the gaps between boards, enough to see by. The front door had also been glass and was set in the center of that wall. Scott reached for the handle, but the door in its intact metal frame was locked.

He stepped back and eyed it. Someone had taken the trouble to bolt two-by-fours to the metal to hold composite wood planks in place. Those were only nailed on, however, so if they couldn't find a better exit, he'd have to locate something to use as a lever to pry the boards off.

"Is this the only door?" he asked.

"Shhh!" Mouse said. "Trust me, we do not want to go wandering around in here. Just open it!"

"Yes, ma'am," he muttered. He headed back down the hall to look in the broom closet. It would have been too lucky to find a pry bar or a tire iron, but there was a broom with a hollow metal handle. On the way back, he glanced through the reception 'window.' The room beyond was filled with what looked like coffins set in a row, five of them.

He started to tell Mouse he'd solved the door problem when he noticed she'd gone very still. He followed the direction of her gaze and immediately moved in front of Bryn, who clung to the back of his hoodie.

There were five of them, not surprisingly. Four men and a young woman who'd appeared from the hall on the opposite side of the reception area. The man in front was short, bald, and had the palest skin Scott had ever seen—so pale he could make out the blue tracing of the man's veins along the sides of his face. His white hands clutched the edges of a floor-length wool cloak, inch-long fingernails filed to a point.

"Nosferatu," Mouse said in a derisive tone. "Shouldn't you be sleeping?"

"'Ello, delicious," the man in front, clearly the leader, drawled in a Cockney accent. His upper lip curled when he talked, revealing a set of yellowed, vampire-like fangs. He flicked the tip of his tongue against his lower lip before leaning to the side to address Scott. "Is that your wife? What a lovely throat."

His black-garbed minions began to fan out, surrounding the three of them, all except the young woman, who hung back in the shadows of the hallway. Scott felt Bryn's cold hands slip under the back of his hoodie. She gently pulled the gun from his waistband. He slid his hands down the length of the broom and held it up defensively.

Nosferatu laughed. "You gonna sweep us under the rug, Mate? That, I'd like to see."

Minion number one produced a switchblade and number two a billy club. The third man was huge, fully a head taller and fifty pounds heavier than Scott. He stood there with a look that said, 'I don't need no stinkin' weapon." Scott considered the man with the knife the most dangerous, so he hefted the broom briefly to test its balance before raising it like a lance and hurling it, brush-end first, into the man's face. Billy club guy let out a disconcerting war cry before charging forward, arm raised to strike.

"Get down!" Scott shoved Bryn out of the way. There was very little likelihood Scott would win against three experienced opponents. He'd begun learning how to fight from a young age, and even though by seventeen he'd won his first junior extreme-fighting championship, he'd come to realize that the learning never stopped. He'd studied offensive and defensive maneuvers from just about every discipline there was. In a real fight, the moves he'd learned on the street—the dirtiest, most effective ones—were the ones he usually fell back on.

Billy club guy went down with a kick to the groin, but strong guy was right behind him and the broom had only delayed knife guy for a few precious seconds. Scott's claws came out, but they weren't much use against fully clothed opponents. He risked ripping them out at the nail bed if they got caught in tough fabric like jeans or leather. He ducked a sluggish punch from strong guy, but the big man backed him into the boarded-up windows and with a deep-throated chuckle, body-slammed him. Scott's head struck the metal frame with a ringing sound that reverberated through his skull. He lifted his knee, targeting the groin again, but strong guy had already backed off. Scott barely ducked the ham-sized fist that came at him, gratified when it clanged into the same metal frame his head had struck moments before. Knife guy moved in, elbow raised back; the four-inch serrated switchblade pointed right at Scott's midsection. Strong guy got in the way, though, by thrusting his other forearm under Scott's chin and pinning him to the boards by the throat. Both of Scott's arms were still free. He could barely see past Strong guy's arm, but when knife guy struck, he still managed to deflect it with a simple karate chop to the wrist. The blade penetrated the board next to his abdomen with a *thunk*.

Scott had been forced onto his tiptoes with Strong guy's face inches away—the big man was chortling wetly through teeth that looked like they hadn't seen a toothbrush in years. Scott was almost glad he couldn't breathe; the guy's breath would probably wilt a stalk of garlic. As his vision began to fade, he reached around the beefy arm at his throat and raked his claws down the side of his opponent's face.

Strong guy let out a rather girly shriek and fell back, giving Scott time to take a much-needed breath of air. But knife guy tugged the switchblade out of the board and pulled his arm back for a second attempt.

"Stop or I'll blow his head off!" Bryn yelled.

Startled, Scott and his two combatants spared a glance in her direction. She held the gun in a steady hand, aim dead center of Nosferatu's chest.

With a convincing smirk, she said, "It's not a wooden stake, but I bet a bullet through the heart will slow you down."

Chapter Twenty-seven

Despite her terror, Bryn was experiencing exceptional clarity of thought. She hadn't acted as soon as she should have, but the situation was controllable because she had the gun. The man at the lethal end of it wanted everyone to think of him as inhuman or he wouldn't be living his life as a modern-day vampire. It made it easier for her to accept the fact that she might have to squeeze the trigger. If the thugs started pounding on Scott again, she was determined to overcome her fear and shoot the pasty-faced Nosferatu in the leg and then attempt to pick off Scott's opponents one by one.

With bravado she didn't feel, she waved the gun briefly in the direction of the door. "Open it."

Getting Nosferatu to walk over to unlock the door also placed his men in her line of sight. Scott, breathing heavily, rotated his shoulders and stretched his neck briefly as he moved to join her. Bryn gratefully relinquished the gun to him and hid her shaking hands in her pockets. He examined it, flicked a little switch on the side of the snub-nosed firearm and said, "Safety's off."

Nosferatu reached into an inside pocket of his cloak. Scott said casually, "A lot of people don't have much respect for the accuracy of these short-barrel handguns, but I know you won't make that mistake."

Nosferatu hesitated. When he pulled his hand out, he held a set of keys. With the door open, Scott gestured for Bryn and Carla to precede him. When she stepped outside, the bright sunlight lanced into her eyes and blinded her. She wondered what it would do to Nosferatu. Just as Scott appeared in the doorway, she heard, "Wait!"

It was the girl. She appeared next to Scott and said, "Help me!"

Bryn could no longer see inside the dark interior, but she did see Scott raise the gun. At first, she thought he suspected the ghoulish-looking girl was trying to trick him, but then she noticed he wasn't aiming at her, but past her, presumably at the four wanna-be vampires.

"I want to go home," the girl cried. Bryn saw her face more clearly now. She was young, not more than fourteen years old. Scott only nodded, holding the door so the girl could run out—right into Carla's waiting arms.

Before he let the door swing shut, Scott said coldly, "The first one of you steps outside gets a bullet in the brain."

They were facing a dusty, deserted street, one of many all across Coney Island. The buildings that were still standing looked like something out of a post-apocalyptic movie, and Bryn wouldn't be surprised if their next encounter was with a bunch of flesh-eating zombies. Carla led them west and then south, through an alley that came out on a stretch of old boardwalk. The girl clutched her hand the entire way.

"Okay, I think no one's following us," Carla said before turning to the girl. "What's your name, Sweetheart?"

"Abezinga," the girl replied. "I mean…Ellie."

She was thin, the unnatural kind of thin that came from starvation. She wore a short, tattered black dress that looked like it had been taken off the corpse of a flapper from the 1920's. Fishnet stockings didn't hide the bruises on her legs, and her feet clumped around in huge combat boots. Her eyes were sunk deep into her face, framed by dark half-circles underneath. Behind those eyes was a blankness that said nothing and everything about the things Ellie had seen and done—and had done to her.

Carla spoke gently. "There isn't a police station here anymore and the subway collapsed. We'll have to take the bus."

Ellie stiffened up and shuddered all over her body as tears spilled down her cheeks. Her breath came in great, gasping sobs. Carla wrapped her arms around the girl. Over her head she said, "I'll meet you in number nine later," referring to the bungalow Scott had mentioned. "Go."

Bryn reached out a hand but didn't touch Ellie's fragile shoulder. She exchanged a sympathetic look with Carla and continued with Scott down the boardwalk. When the sounds of the girl's heart-wrenching sobs had faded to nothing, Scott said, "You should cover your head."

She pulled her scarf absently into place. The beauty of the day, the blue sea and bright sun, barely intruded on her consciousness. So much had happened in the last 24-hours, but her thoughts were disjointed. Nothing specific presented itself for her to contemplate. Instead, her mind replayed random events, like a collage of memories. Her father's burning eyes as he told her about his plans. The white mouse nestled in Carla's cleavage. Ellie's face as she remembered her real name. Scott's furry fingers caressing her in the dream. And his voice when he said he'd shoot those men if they came after them.

Bryn wouldn't have been able to articulate how she felt if someone tried to torture it out of her. Like a pendulum without a plotted course, her thoughts swung wildly back and forth. She wished everything were normal, but that was impossible. She wanted her life back—the exact life she'd had before her father had betrayed her—again, impossible. Her choices were limited to bad and worse, and for the life of her she couldn't say if home was the better of the two options, or if the path she was set upon—becoming an XBestia and trusting Scott to protect her—was more acceptable. And that was really the crux of it all: trust. Her father had lost hers forever, and Scott had done less than nothing to earn it. Bryn wasn't sure how to live in a world without trust. She wasn't sure how to go on when every fork in the road was unacceptable.

For now, all she could do was put one foot in front of the other.

They walked past a hotdog stand just opening for business and the savory smell brought her to an abrupt halt. "I need food. I can't think straight."

Scott obliged her by buying each of them a dog smothered in toppings and a couple of cold sodas. By the time they reached the former ball field with its row upon row of falling down bungalows, she'd eaten every bite, never once considering how many calories she was consuming. He unlocked the door of number nine and seemed cautious as he entered. There was no electricity and only one window, covered in aluminum foil to block out the light. Someone had mounted a series of eight battery-powered LED lights on the low ceiling, however, and Scott went down the length of the place tapping the lights to turn them on. The one-room structure was cleaner than Bryn expected after seeing, and smelling, the refuse outside. It reminded her of the inside of an R.V. with the narrow bunk beds at one end and compact bench and table combination at the other. Cupboards lined the walls. It appeared to be empty, but when Scott went poking around, he found linens in one cupboard and a manila folder in another.

"Here," he said, tossing sheets, blankets and two plastic-wrapped pillows to Bryn. "Make yourself useful."

Bryn assumed they were to occupy the bunk beds that night, so she was content to make them up while he sat at the table and read whatever was inside the folder. Once she'd finished, she lay down on the bottom bunk. Scott looked up from his reading and said, "Don't get comfortable."

As if the quills would allow it. "Why not?"

"We've got a job to do."

Chapter Twenty-eight

Scott didn't want to take Bryn with him, but he'd seen the eyes watching them from the other bunghole units as they'd made their way to number nine. If he left without her, he doubted she'd enjoy the time waiting for him to return. She was already turning out to be a huge liability. But then again, she had done an admirable job back there with the gun, except for not knowing how to use it properly and waiting until he'd gotten his head knocked around before bringing it into play. And the short encounter with Mouse had given him more of a potential lead into Fournier's whereabouts than anything he'd accomplished thus far. Mouse wouldn't have loosened up without Bryn's obvious attachment to him.

That very attachment might be problematic though. He couldn't decide whether he should encourage it or keep his distance. Professionally speaking, there were arguments both for and against. Personally speaking, he found he liked the idea far more than he probably should.

He finished reading Abel's notes on the job. They were written in a combination of English and Yiddish, a special 'code' Abel developed to thwart snoopers. It was how Scott had ingratiated himself with Abel in the first place. The XIA knew about Abel's code, knew his grandmother had been an Orthodox Jew. Scott had taken an immersion course in the language and pretended to have had a Jewish neighbor lady that babysat him as a kid. Abel's one big weakness had been his beloved 'Bubbe.'

It was strange to think of him as dead. The man had been a big part of Scott's life for the last six months. Scott wasn't mourning his loss—opportunistic sadists never impressed him much—but Abel had been a character. Any second now, Scott expected to hear those jangling spurs and that on-again off-again southern accent interspersed with the occasional "Oy!"

There were no decorations in this, one of Abel's 'satellite' offices. Nothing personal, nothing revealing its former occupant's personality except a utilitarian clock near the door. It was time to go.

"Alright, listen up," he said. Bryn swung her legs around and sat up a little hunched over so her head didn't hit the upper bunk. She rested her elbows on her knees and her chin in her hand and gave him her full attention.

He took a breath and launched into his explanation before the nagging doubts made him nix the whole thing. "The job we got to do should be pretty simple, but there's about a million things that could go wrong."

"Is it legal?"

He stared at her until she flapped her hands and said, "Okay, okay. I get it. We're going to break the law. Go on."

The doubts weren't just nagging now; they were setting off klaxon alarms. But he couldn't just leave her here. And the job shouldn't get messy. It was really a simple pick-up and delivery, other than the unusual form of transportation. "The most important thing for you to remember is to keep your mouth shut. You just follow along and do as I say, and we'll be fine."

He stood, pulled the gun from its spot in his waistband and examined it. Mouse's firearm was fully loaded but looked like it could use a good cleaning. Not that he was complaining. He was just glad she hadn't asked for it back.

He took Bryn back out to the boardwalk and they walked until he saw a white, jacked-up truck hauling two Wavecruisers on a double trailer. He waved at the driver, Fiske, who began backing the trailer onto the beach toward the ocean until waves lapped at the trailer tires. A few beachgoers stopped to watch, but most ignored it.

"Is he supposed to be doing that?" Bryn asked. She immediately corrected herself with, "No, don't give me that look again. I'm sorry." She made a zipping motion over her mouth.

The passenger in the truck got out and walked up to them. He was blonde, dressed in board shorts and a Hawaiian shirt with a black backpack over his shoulders. In a thick Australian accent, he asked, "Where's Abel?"

"Dead," Scott said.

"And you are?" The man's age was indeterminate; Scott thought maybe forty to fifty years old, but his tanned skin was so damaged from sun exposure it was almost as leathery as the crocodile graft on the side of his face.

"Cougar." Scott was the new Abel, but he wasn't the boss of this operation. Neither, he was certain, was this man.

"Ahhh," the man said. "I heard a' you. The fighter. Got them claws, right?"

Scott didn't hesitate to show them now; this was proving ground.

"Nice." The man didn't reach out for a handshake. "Dundee's the name." His eyes, flat and dead as his reptilian choice of donor, slid to Bryn. "Who's the Sheila?"

"My apprentice."

Dundee's eyes came to life with sudden interest. "Sign me up for training duty."

"Pincushion duty's more like it," Scott said.

Bryn pointed to her quills and said sternly, "I could put your eye out with one of these babies at twenty paces."

Scott wanted to hide his head in his hands.

Dundee's mouth hung open for a split second before he exploded in laughter that bent him double and had him clutching his midsection. It went on for some time before he finally slapped his thigh and wiped away a tear. "Hoo, that was a good one. I know a bit about porcupines, Beautiful, and they don't shoot nothin'. If yer not interested in the Dundee, that's fine by me. I can take no for an answer. What's yer name?"

Dundee's joviality didn't fool Scott for an instant. He knew the guy's reputation from sources within the XBestia and the XIA. There were a lot of disturbed xenofreaks out there, but this one was a genuine psychopath. He was surprised Lupus would send one of his most vicious lieutenants for a job that was supposed to be easy. Scott would have been happy to have never crossed Dundee's path, much less expose Bryn to him. He hoped she wouldn't use her real name, and was pleased when she said, "Porky."

Dundee shook his head once to object. "Doesn't do you justice."

Eager to stay on track and put the job behind him, Scott said, "Let's do this."

Dundee strode off to help Fiske unwinch the Wavecruisers from the trailer. Bryn grasped Scott's arm and said urgently, "Do you know who that is?"

"Yeah," he said, and the word 'duh' was implied.

Bryn went on like he hadn't responded. "I saw him on the news. It's that guy who shot up all those people! He's, like, crazy!"

Scott stepped around to block her from Dundee's view. He gripped her upper arms and hissed, "Shut up. Jesus, this was a bad idea. Look—go back to Bluto's-"

Dundee interrupted him with a sharp whistle. Scott turned and immediately saw the problem. An all-terrain police vehicle had driven onto the boardwalk in the distance, something that never happened around here anymore. It occurred to him that Mouse had taken Ellie to the nearest precinct—the cruiser was probably looking for Nosferatu and his crew.

Fiske jumped in the truck and pulled forward, leaving the two Wavecruisers bobbing in the mild Coney Island surf. Dundee, standing thigh deep in the water, pushed his cruiser to face perpendicular to the shore. Scott said, "Come on," and pulled Bryn by the hand to the other one. It was a warm enough day, but the water was cold, and he was soon soaked up to his waist. He'd never ridden this kind of watercraft in his life, but he followed Dundee's example and wrestled the cruiser around. With Bryn's help from the other side, he pushed it out past the waves. He climbed on and stared at the control panel as Dundee started his engine with a gurgling roar.

Bryn straddled the seat behind him and reached around to a compartment in front of the cushion. She pulled out a plastic key on a lanyard, attached it to Scott's wrist and stuck the key in the ignition. In his ear, she said, "Push the red button and turn the key at the same time."

The waves had pushed them back toward shore and they were almost parallel to the beach again. Bryn hopped off and straightened the cruiser out. As she was getting back on, he scooted back, pulled the lanyard from his wrist, and gestured that she should drive. With a wide grin that lit up her face, she took the handlebars.

Dundee on the other cruiser was idling in deeper water. Through the wind in his ears, Scott heard Dundee's challenging whoop as they shot past and Bryn sent a wall of spray in his direction. Scott held onto her leather jacket at the waist and leaned to one side to avoid her quills. Every dip and bump threatened to poke out one of his eyes or throw him from the cruiser altogether, but he decided after the first two minutes that someday he'd own one of these babies. Dundee caught up and maneuvered himself in the lead so Bryn could follow.

They headed out into the open ocean.

Chapter Twenty-nine

Bryn had only ridden a Wavecruiser once before, as a passenger, but Scott didn't know that and even her limited experience was obviously more than his. The cruisers weren't difficult to drive, especially these heavier, three-seater SUV-types. She'd ridden on the back of Maria's cousin Jorge's cruiser last summer on a lake in Connecticut.

Right away she realized there was a big difference between the chop on a lake and the swells in the ocean. While chop might produce a rhythmic bounce against the cruiser's hull, navigating the swells was like riding up hills and down valleys. Luckily, the swells today weren't huge, but after about half an hour of subtle highs and lows, they did make her regret eating that hotdog.

They weren't the only ones on the water by a long shot, but up ahead, she saw a white boat that Dundee seemed to be aiming for. Bryn didn't know how big it was, but if pressed, she'd feel comfortable calling it a yacht. As it came into better focus, she spotted several people in skimpy attire lounging around on its deck with drinks in their hands. The name on the side of the boat was Le Gros Poisson, which, she knew from high school French class, meant The Big Fish.

Dundee slowed up and she followed suit. Now she could hear laughter and music floating across the water. She doubted they were there to join the party.

Dundee whistled and waved and almost immediately two men manned the winches at the side of the yacht to lower a hot pink inflatable recreational boat. It was big—big enough to support its cargo—a plain wooden crate about the size of a baby's crib. Bryn eyed it suspiciously. It was probably full of enough drugs to put her in prison for the rest of her life for just being on the same ocean with it. As Dundee unfastened the winch lines, she kept expecting something bad to happen, like for the Coast Guard to arrive, guns blazing. But the sea was calm, and the partiers seemed oblivious as Dundee fed a rope through the tow loop at the front of the inflatable. He tossed one end to Scott, who in turn tied it to the back of their Wavecruiser.

Bryn followed Dundee back to the beach, towing the cargo behind her with her heart in her throat the entire way. Gone was the enjoyment of the ride; she'd had fun skimming the waves on the way there, but solemnly coasted those same waves on the way back. Scott didn't say a word the whole trip. It never occurred to her to ask what was in the crate. She didn't want to know.

It was late afternoon when the coast came into view. They were far enough offshore for Bryn to see a few stragglers enjoying the last of the sunshine before the neighborhood got too dark to be safe. She also saw a dune buggy that seemed to be keeping up with their progress as they hugged the coastline.

"Is that who's picking up the cargo?" she asked.

"Nope," Scott said.

"Then who are they?"

"Cops, maybe. Bad guys, probably." He sounded resigned. "How much electrigas do we have?"

"Enough to make it to shore."

Dundee slowed until they caught up to him. "Friends o' yers?" he called.

"Not me," Scott replied.

They'd almost reached their launch point. Bryn saw the white truck with its double trailer waiting for them, saw the driver get out and stand on the sand with what could only be a rifle in his hands. There was no way they'd get there before the dune buggy, not at the speed they were maintaining to keep the cargo steady. She glanced back and reassessed their ETA when she noticed the cargo was still upright, but it was moving. The box was shaking and swaying and there was some kind of noise, like a miniature donkey braying, coming from inside.

She opened her mouth to alert Scott, but his attention was fixed on dry land. The dune buggy had arrived and four armed men wearing ski masks and black vests poured out of it. She looked back at the cargo again. The ocean swells were increasing as they closed in on the shore. The box was lashed down but seemed to be listing alarmingly to one side.

"Scott!" she cried.

He finally turned and noticed the precariously tilted inflatable, but the scene on the beach was just as critical. Facing down the barrels of four guns convinced the driver of the white truck to surrender. One man stayed to guard him while the other three splashed into the surf, weapons at the ready. Bryn saw Dundee reach behind his head and tug at something partially protruding from his backpack.

"What do we do?" she asked.

"All they want is the cargo," Scott said. "Don't resist."

"Tell Dundee that."

The Aussie had pulled a weapon from his backpack and wore a demented grin on his face.

"I would not recommend it!" The closest of the armed men shouted from behind the sight of his weapon, which was trained on Dundee. "You're outgunned."

As soon as he spoke, Bryn recognized his voice. She'd seen and heard him speak several times at the same rallies as her father. He was the commander of the Animal Rights Army, a militant, partisan group of vegans that had taken credit for a string of terrorist acts, from torching a pig farmer's house to releasing into the wild a thousand-plus turkeys slated for Thanksgiving tables. Despite his violent occupation, he'd always been nice to her.

"Kareem?" she called.

It was not her intention to distract him, but when he responded to his name by turning his head towards her, Dundee opened fire. Bryn only had time to see Kareem take a hit that knocked him backwards before Scott shoved her out of the way for the second time that day. She was taken completely unawares and fell awkwardly face-first into the water.

He'd shoved her—saved her—by placing the Wavecruiser between her and the gunfight.

Expecting a bullet in the back at any moment, she swam down in the murky water until her fingers touched sand. The muted sounds of shouting and gunfire reached her as she tried to gain even more distance by swimming underwater towards the inflatable. When she thought her lungs would explode, she surfaced to quickly catch her breath before diving once more.

By the time she made it to shelter on the far side of the inflatable, the gunfire had stopped. She heard nothing but the waves and the plaintive cries of the crated animal. She was desperate to find out what happened to Scott, but too afraid to look. The question of whether the ARA soldiers had fired in her direction was answered when she noticed the inflatable was sinking rapidly. The noises from the crate increased in volume as water began flooding it. She tried to touch bottom, but it was just out of reach. There was no way she alone could prevent the poor creature trapped in the crate from drowning.

Suddenly, the inflatable began moving away from her toward the shore. Someone was hauling it in. She knew she risked getting shot, but the pitiful cries from inside the crate spurred her to push from behind. When she got her feet under her, she had more leverage. Soon the waves carried the cargo into shallower water until it scraped bottom.

Bryn took a steadying breath and stepped out with her hands raised high.

Chapter Thirty

After shoving Bryn, Scott had dived off the Wavecruiser on the opposite side, towards Dundee. Before he even hit the water, he saw a bloom of red appear on the shoulder of the xeno's shirt. He'd swum under Dundee's cruiser, prepared to haul him to the surface when he fell, but that never happened. Instead, Dundee turned the cruiser and hunkered down behind the seat with his knees on the running board. With the break in the gunfire the attackers began dragging their injured lead man to safety between the truck and the jeep.

Treading water, Scott had seen Bryn surface for air, relieved that she was safe and heading for cover behind the inflatable. Dundee, bleeding heavily and in obvious pain, seemed to finally realize the odds were not in his favor. He sent Scott a black look and muttered, "It's no good to them dead."

When he'd swung his semi-automatic rifle in the direction of the inflatable, Scott realized his intention: kill the cargo. But Bryn was there. Scott reacted without thought, hoisting himself up out of the water with one hand on the running board and punching Dundee in the injured shoulder with the other. Scott wasn't fast enough to prevent the shot that hit the inflatable, but with a low moan, Dundee slumped over the seat.

Scott climbed onto the running board behind him and reached for Mouse's gun, but it must have fallen out of his waistband while he was underwater. He pulled the rifle from Dundee's slack hand. He couldn't see the armed men, but knew they were there. The distressed sounds of the animal in the crate echoed over the water. He saw Bryn now, behind the inflatable. She was trying to push it to shore.

With an expletive on his lips, he'd taken a chance and stood with the gun held high. No one shot him, which was encouragement enough to fling it toward shore. He dove into the water, swam to the other Wavecruiser and climbed on. Still no gunshots—they were waiting to see what he would do. If he tried to run for it, he doubted he'd get far. He straightened the cruiser's handlebars and accelerated. Happily, the watercraft wasn't difficult to maneuver. There was no need to go slow anymore; on the contrary. The tow rope snapped taut and the sinking cargo offered significantly more resistance, but within seconds he'd driven the cruiser right up onto the sand.

Once there, he'd jumped off and grabbed the rope. Even though two of the men joined him in hauling the cargo in, he assumed he was still in someone's gun sights. The inflatable was barely afloat when the waves began to help bring it in.

When Bryn appeared, the leader of the armed men, the one she'd called 'Kareem,' walked into view. There was no sign of injury, but his vest was unfastened—Scott saw it was bullet-proof. Even so, a shot to the chest from a high-powered rifle would cause more than superficial damage.

Kareem pulled off his ski mask, wincing as the movement produced pain. "Bryn?" he asked. "Is that you?"

Bryn lowered her hands, went straight to the crate and peered into one of the air holes. "Oh, my God!" she gasped, directing eloquent, accusing eyes Scott's way. "It's a baby panda!"

Scott sighed. "She's not a baby, just a juvenile."

Bryn drilled into him with those eyes. "Why didn't you tell me?"

"Shut it!" Kareem snapped, staring at Bryn's quills. "I don't know what you're mixed up in, girl, but right now I need you to step away from our little friend there."

He directed his two men to lift the crate. Scott knew the young panda weighed around a hundred pounds. Add in the weight of the crate and the fact that the panda was shifting around inside attempting to escape, and the men would need help. He looked at Kareem and spread his hands. Kareem nodded. Scott took one corner and they hefted the cargo out of the sand and loaded it onto the white truck. Kareem signaled one of the men, who immediately got in and drove off in the XBestia's truck.

Scott saw Fiske then, trussed up in the sand with duct tape. The fourth man was on the far side of the dune buggy watching the show through his gun sight. He shouted, "Hey, Kareem!" and pointed.

Everyone turned. Dundee was a speck in the distance on the water.

Scott heard sirens. Even in Coney Island no-man's land, cops would eventually respond to an emergency call about a gun battle on the beach. The whole thing had lasted less than ten minutes.

Kareem opened the back door of the dune buggy and gingerly got in. "Let's go." His men obediently hopped aboard, and the wheels sent sand flying.

Bryn looked surprised that Kareem left so abruptly, like she expected him to stop and offer her some words of wisdom. Scott grabbed her arm. "Come on."

She dug her heels in the sand. "What about him?"

Fiske was rolling around, attempting to talk through the tape across his mouth.

"He's the guy who punched you when you were kidnapped."

Her eyebrows shot up. "Oh."

Without another word of protest, she joined him on the boardwalk as they walked away from the scene like any other xenofreaks out for a stroll in the early twilight.

Chapter Thirty-one

They went back to the bungalow and Bryn sat on the bench at the little table. Her hands shook from a combination of muscle strain from piloting the Wavecruiser and residual adrenaline. Scott retrieved a holophone from inside a cupboard and powered it up.

"You can't stay here," he said.

She knew he was going to say that. The 'easy job' had gone horribly awry, through no fault of hers. Still, she'd been a liability. She wasn't surprised he would have second thoughts about helping her. It had never been clear why he'd agreed to in the first place.

"I have money," she said.

It wasn't true. Aside from the sixty-two dollars in Carla's tips in her pocket, she had around fifteen dollars in the bank. But if what Carla said was true, there was a slim chance a life insurance check was waiting for her at the offices of Provincial Mutual.

Scott set the phone down and began texting something with clumsy paw pads. He responded absently, "That's not going to protect you when my boss comes looking for answers."

"I just need to get to Trill Street."

Without looking up from the phone, he pointed to the door.

She stood, sick inside. "So that's it?"

He avoided her gaze, focused instead on the holophone. After a moment he asked, "What do you want from me?"

She had no idea. "Apparently I want you to be something you're not."

He laughed as if her words were funny. The last thing she wanted to do was walk out the door, but he seemed immovable on the subject. The holophone had his complete attention. He was done with her.

She got slowly to her feet, toes squishing in her boots. She was wet and miserable and dying for a shower. Carla had said she would meet them back here at the bungalow, but she would have come and gone by now. XIA agents were likely still out looking for her, so Bluto's was off-limits, as was

Carla's house. Maybe the cash in her pocket would get her a cheap motel room. One night to decide where to go.

She took a reluctant step toward the door. Scott let out a frustrated groan and for a moment she thought he'd reconsidered. But he was still involved with his texting. He typed something and waited and then groaned again before snapping the holophone shut and giving Bryn an inscrutable look.

"Alright," he said. It sounded like he was conceding to something.

"What's alright?" she asked.

"I am officially your babysitter."

"Huh?"

"Nothing. You said you needed to get to Trill Street?"

He'd done a miraculous about-face. Bryn decided not to question her good fortune. "It's an insurance company. They won't be open now."

"Tomorrow then. Right now, we need to vacate the premises before I have to answer some hard questions about a certain panda."

He tucked the holophone in his pocket, opened the door and waved for her to precede him. She thumped down the steps. Instead of heading back out to the beach, they began weaving their way through the bungalows. She didn't think it possible, but the place got seedier the further in they went. Like the Warehouse, people were out and about, all xenofreaks, all watching. Fires were everywhere now that the sun was down, burning in garbage cans and makeshift fire pits, lighting their way. Bryn wanted to stop and stand next to one until her clothes steamed dry, but Scott hurried on.

She saw a streetlight and thought they were headed in that direction, but Scott veered away toward a bonfire at the far edge of the field in the space where two bungalows had once been. They merely skirted it however; just close enough for him to toss something into the blaze.

"What was that?" she asked, but he didn't answer, and she was forced to break into a trot to keep up. On the street, they walked for a few blocks before catching a bus. The driver had a xenograft on his forearm, which made sense in this neighborhood. It was warm inside the bus. She sat next to Scott, he with his hood up and she with her scarf, looking out the window, but all she saw was their reflections.

"Scott?" She didn't turn from the window. There was no one else on the bus, and they were far enough back that the driver couldn't hear their conversation.

"Yeah?"

"I—I know you said you do what you're told, but…didn't it bother you that Fournier almost got an actual panda?"

Scott shifted in his seat, his thigh brushing hers. "What makes a panda any different from any other animal?"

The words seemed insensitive, but something in his tone made her think he didn't mean them that way.

"Well for one, they're an endangered species," she said.

He snorted. "Do you know how much money has been funneled into supposed panda conservation? It's big business."

"That's not the panda's fault."

"I guess not," he conceded. "But that money could have been put to better use saving animals that aren't so cute and cuddly."

"Like the cougar?" she asked, and immediately regretted it. She turned and put her hand on his arm. "I'm sorry."

But he said, "It's not illegal to hunt cougars, except maybe in California."

"You know a lot about animals."

His lips tightened and she got the distinct impression he was irritated with himself. It was becoming apparent to Bryn that he didn't want her to get to know him. Which only made her more determined to find the proverbial chink in his armor.

Chapter Thirty-two

They switched buses once before disembarking on a dark, quiet residential street. Scott scanned the numbers on the houses and began walking, Bryn shivering in the cool evening air by his side. Two blocks from the bus stop, he started up the steep, cracked driveway of an older, one-story house. As he'd been advised when he'd contacted Shasta at the bungalow, the door was open.

"Whose house is this?" Bryn whispered as they entered.

Scot shut the door and locked it before switching on a nearby lamp. They were standing in a small, sparsely furnished living room with a white carpet. "Don't worry. It's safe."

"I don't care if it's safe. I just care whether the owners are going to be pissed that we're here."

"It belongs to friends of mine. You want to take a shower and put on clean clothes or what?"

He saw from her face that she very much did want those things, and for some reason, it brought a smile to his lips that he couldn't hide.

"What's so funny?" she asked.

"You. Come on."

Scott had never been to any of the XIA safe houses, but he'd been told they were all similar. This house had one bedroom and one bath. There hadn't been a holovision in the living room, but he was happy to see one on a stand at the foot of the queen-sized bed. He went straight to the dresser and found clothes there, in a variety of sizes, just as Shasta had promised in her text.

"Take her there and let her get cleaned up for crissakes!" she'd said.

He'd argued with her—hadn't wanted to risk the cover he'd worked so long and hard for, but Shasta was adamant. He was surprised she'd jumped so easily on his suggestion to court Mouse's favor through Bryn, given that getting usable information out of Mouse would be a long shot. Then again, Bryn did pose a problem to the XIA. Scott wasn't the only one who felt responsible for what happened to her. Shasta had been very interested to learn that Bryn blamed her father for arranging the kidnapping in the first place. For the time being, Scott was to avoid contact with Lupus and Padme and follow the new leads.

Lupus would probably have something to say about that, but Scott, as he'd mentioned to Bryn, did as he was told.

"There's a washer and dryer around here somewhere. These should do for now," he handed Bryn a bundle of clothing and ignored her perplexed look.

"Are you sure your friends won't mind?" she asked.

He grabbed her shoulders from behind, careful of the quills, and turned her toward the bathroom. "You want first shower, or do you want a cold shower after I use all the hot?"

She disappeared behind the bathroom door. It was chilly in the house, so he found the thermostat in the hallway and set it to seventy degrees. The house had a secure, old-fashioned land-line telephone in the kitchen. He called Shasta.

"All set?" she asked.

"Yeah."

"Pizza's coming."

"Good. What about the panda?"

"The ARA has it stashed at a farm upstate. I'm sending the coordinates in case you need them."

"Word on how they knew?"

"None."

"Dundee?"

"A blood-spattered Wavecruiser turned up at Bensonhurst Park. Fingerprints belong to one Duane Walker, native of Sydney, Australia. No body. No witnesses saw him come ashore—that have come forward, anyway."

"Can they tell from the blood if he's the carrier?"

"In the lab now."

"Do they know what to look for yet?"

"It's been tentatively identified as a typhoid mutation, completely resistant to antibiotics. Still can't convince the frickin' CDC that it might be airborne."

Scott had seen holos of security tapes from the bank that had been robbed by a group of XBestias. According to Abel, they'd done it without Lupus' sanction, but that was irrelevant. Abel only knew one of the perpetrators: Dundee. The holos showed the xenos lining the patrons and employees of the bank up, while Dundee forced the manager to open the safe. There was limited physical contact between the xenos and the hostages and no resistance. Cooperation had been coerced through intimidation; big guns and a lot of shouting in the hostage's faces. Within seventy-two hours, all seventeen victims had gotten sick and died. Until today, the XIA had only unconfirmed reports of the whereabouts of the perpetrators. They knew none of the xenos seemed to be affected by the pathogen. Scott's report on Dundee's robust health prior to his gunshot wound now confirmed it. One or more of those xenos appeared to be a carrier. If the typhoid mutation was indeed airborne, the XIA feared another Typhoid Mary was on the loose, but on a potentially more deadly scale. Since then, isolated non-xenos all over the city had turned up in the morgue with the infection, but none of them were linked to any other deaths—they caught it but didn't spread it themselves.

Fournier's role in all of this was uncertain. It was known that in addition to his increasingly audacious xenoalterations, he had experimented with cloning and cross-species in vitro fertilization. He had a monstrous God complex. Scott wanted nothing more than to topple him from on high.

"Fiske?" he asked Shasta.

"Rikers."

"Nosferatu?"

"Creepy bastard. Beat cops rounded him and his crew up. It'll be high-profile. The girl was snatched on her way home from school."

"How'd they get to Abel in Rikers?" he asked.

"That was a heart attack. Yang got him into the interview room and the guy went nuts. You never saw anyone so scared. Didn't seem natural."

Scott had a half-formed question at the back of his mind about Bluto's, but he heard Bryn call, "Scott?" To Shasta, he said, "Gotta go, boss."

"Burn phone's in the pizza box," she said. Then, uncharacteristically, "Take care of her."

"I will." He placed the handset in the charger and went back to the bedroom.

The bathroom door was cracked, and flowery-smelling steam curled out towards the ceiling. He heard Bryn cursing. "You okay in there?"

"No." She sounded tearful.

"Uh...anything I can do?"

She came out wearing the clothes he'd given her, black stretch pants and a long, soft sweater. Or she was partially wearing the sweater—it had gotten hopelessly stuck on her quills and only one eye was visible through the neck hole.

It took a monumental effort not to smile. "Sit."

He stood over her, easing the sweater away from a few stubborn quills, self-conscious now that she was clean. He must smell like a wet dog in comparison. The quills seemed to want to cooperate with him as he worked; they lay down close to her skull and made the job easier. He slid his hands around her neck to reach underneath and lift them so he could adjust the sweater to rest properly on her shoulders, but he pricked his index 'finger.'

"Ow!" Instinctively, he stuck it in his mouth. He'd had the xenoalteration for seven months and still the fur felt foreign against his lips, the pad rough against his tongue.

"Sorry," she said. She looked positively morose as she went to pick her leather jacket up off the bathroom floor. When she began shrugging into it, he asked, "What are you doing? That jacket's ruined. And it's still wet."

"I don't have a choice. It protects me from the quills."

"No, take it off. We'll think of something else."

She gave him a grateful look, almost a hero-worship kind of look. For the first time, he wondered how she was going to look at him when she found out the truth.

Chapter Thirty-three

While Scott was in the shower, Bryn explored the house. It was small and neat—and about as impersonal as a hotel suite. Each room had exactly one framed print on the wall; sober still-lifes from artists she didn't recognize. The furniture was utilitarian; a sectional in the living room with firm, unyielding cushions and a plain wooden table with four chairs in the kitchen. The cupboards were empty except for one, which had a four-piece dinner set in boring beige stoneware and eight clear drinking glasses. One drawer held an eight-piece set of silverware with no pattern whatsoever and another had three striped dish towels that looked as if they'd never been used.

She had just decided the house must belong to a man who brought his mistress here when she opened the refrigerator and revised that thought. Inside were one bottle each of ketchup and soy sauce, a squeeze bottle of mustard, a jar of mayonnaise and an unopened twelve-pack of bottled water. No way a cheating dog could properly entertain a woman here, not without alcohol.

She helped herself to a bottle of water, wishing the empty pantry had something in it, even a few crumbs to stave off the hunger pangs that had been gnawing at her for hours now. She was contemplating slurping down a couple spoonfuls of ketchup when someone knocked on the door, startling her so badly she almost dropped her water bottle. She scooted into the bedroom and, mostly because she still doubted they had a right to be in the house in the first place, opened the bathroom door and said in a loud whisper, "Scott! Scott!"

He looked around the shower curtain, wet hair dark and dripping. He'd shaved, the first time she'd seen him without his customary stubble. He looked much younger than she'd assumed him to be.

"Is the pizza here?" he asked. "Damn it."

The shower spray stopped, so she shut the bathroom door, but it opened again almost immediately. Scott was hastily tucking a bath towel around his hips as he brushed past her, leaving wet footprints in the carpet. She'd seen his body before, on the day he fought The Viscount, but the circumstances had been far from intimate then. Now she felt her quills respond to the sight of his lean frame. She vowed never to tell a soul what it meant when they went flat like that.

He'd neglected to tell her about the pizza, but she didn't chastise him when he came back into the room and set the box on the end of the bed. By the time he came back out of the bathroom again, dry and dressed in clean clothes, she'd tuned the holovision to a 24/7 cartoon channel and eaten an entire slice of pepperoni. He joined her on the bed, and in half an hour they consumed the whole thing between them.

After setting the box aside, he examined the tiny red quill prick on his finger-pad before giving her an assessing look.

"I have an idea," he said. He went into the bathroom and she heard the sound of the shower curtain rings being drawn across the rod. After a few minutes, he returned with a section of torn plastic in his hand; the pattern of shells and swirls told her he'd scavenged a piece right off the curtain.

He handed her a tiny pair of manicure scissors, wiggling his fingers and saying, "I can't use these."

With his guidance, she cut a circle the diameter of her shoulders out of the plastic, cut a slit to the center and made a smaller circle in the middle. He helped her place the bib around her neck and then made a dissatisfied face.

"It's fine," she said, pleased that he'd made an effort.

"Not going to stay on very well. Too bad we don't have any tape."

Bryn thought of the duct-taped guy they'd left in the sand. With more finality, she repeated, "It's fine."

She sat back on her pillow while he switched channels. They watched a news story about the gun battle between "unknown perpetrators" on Coney Island.

"We're famous," he commented.

"Infamous," she corrected.

After sports and the weather, her father appeared on screen standing next to Dr. Finnegan and a man dressed in a pressed, tailored suit. Instinctively, Bryn knew it was Manny, the 'marketing guy' her father had hired. Under the guise of making a public plea for her safe return, her father began his campaign to use her for his own purposes.

"My daughter is distraught after her traumatic kidnapping and mutilation," he said, voice cracking on the last word. If Bryn didn't know better, she'd swear Harry Vega was devastated by this new turn of events. Maybe he was, but not for the reasons he'd like everyone to think. "She's suicidal and making very poor decisions. If you see her, please contact the XIA at the special hotline they set up for us."

An 800-number scrolled across the holo of Bryn her father had taken at the kitchen table. She did, indeed, look traumatized and suicidal. Manny finished the press conference with a statement that sent frissons of alarm down her spine, "There is a ten-thousand-dollar reward for any information leading to the safe recovery of Bryn Vega."

Through gritted teeth, she said, "My father doesn't have ten-thousand dollars."

"Well, you're worth that much to someone."

His words were uttered casually, but she looked at him out of the sides of her eyes until he said defensively, "I'm not going to turn you in." Sounding like an afterthought, he added, "They'd arrest me if I tried."

Bryn felt the comfortable camaraderie fade away. Scott grabbed the holo control and switched channels, finally settling on an old action movie made before holovision was invented. The movie had been holoized, but there was something a little off about it; a fuzziness that normal holos didn't have. Still, it succeeded in distracting her. After a while she realized she was on the verge of dozing off, so she turned to ask if he planned on sleeping on the couch or what.

He was lying on his back, eyes closed, mouth partially open, breathing evenly. The top half of his dark hair spilled across his pillow; the bottom portion that had been shaved when she met him had grown to about half an inch. She didn't want to wake him, but she also didn't want to sleep on that stiff couch herself, so she climbed under the covers on her side.

Sleep must have come quickly, because when she woke sometime later, she didn't remember experiencing any of the host of discomforts and troubling thoughts that usually manifested in the intractable insomnia that had been plaguing her for weeks. The room wasn't dark; she'd shut off the holovision but left the bathroom light on. Something had awoken her, though—a noise maybe. She lay still and tried to listen past the pounding of her heart. After a while, when nothing happened, her pulse slowed. Scott said this was a safe house. She reached up to adjust her quills so she could roll to the side facing his direction and began to doze again.

Somewhere between sleep and waking, her drifting thoughts coalesced. Her eyes flew open and she saw him staring at her.

"You're a cop, aren't you?" she asked.

Chapter Thirty-four

He'd been thinking how beautiful she was, how much he wanted to get under the covers and touch her. In the lethargy of half-sleep, his body eagerly responded to the notion. It had been a very long time since he'd slept with a woman, with or without sex. His arousal subsided rapidly at her words.

It would be a risk asking how she'd come to that conclusion; if he allowed her to voice her suspicions, they might solidify in her mind. On the other hand, her insight might be valuable. Whatever he'd done to give himself away could get him killed. If he were to confirm the truth, tell her that, yeah, he was essentially a cop, he would put her in even further danger. Knowledge like that was worth more than gold to his competition—they wouldn't hesitate to hurt her to get it. And if she were forced to tell, or if she let something slip in the presence of another XBestia, he was a dead man. He could only hope this was idle speculation on her part, easily deflected.

He held up his hand and extended his claws. "You ever see a cop with these?"

"No, but-"

He rolled off the bed and pulled the covers aside, saying, "Would a cop do this?" He slid in next to her, very close.

"Um, I don't know. Maybe-"

He kissed her, ignoring the quills that poked his forehead. Her mouth opened in surprise under his, lips soft and pliable. He reached for her, finding that the sweater had worked its way up, giving him easy access to snake a hand under it. Her waist was firm and narrow, the skin silky even against his touch-dulled finger-pads. Her bra was lying on the bathroom floor with the other dirty clothes. The urge to touch her breast almost overwhelmed him. He barely managed to stop and rest his hand against her ribcage, which expanded against his fingers with her sharply indrawn breath.

He knew she liked him, knew he was taking advantage, but couldn't help himself. If she told him to stop, he would kill himself doing so, but she didn't. Instead, she pulled away briefly to take another quick, gasping breath and then found his mouth again, deepening the kiss. Her leg lifted, giving him ample opportunity to pull her closer and slip his knee between her thighs. She moaned in her throat and her hand found its way under his shirt. That moan, combined with the warm touch of her fingers, sparked a surge of intense pleasure; if this kept up, he wouldn't be able to stop.

There were innumerable reasons not to allow this to go any further, not the least of which was: no condom. He broke away from her mouth but almost gave in again at her little mew of protest.

With a monumental effort, he said, "We can't."

She rolled partially away, chest rising and falling. "I know."

"I want to…but…"

Her glistening green eyes looked huge, like the innocent anime characters his sister used to love. It occurred to him that Bryn was probably a virgin, and he was an enormous jerk for almost taking it from her like that. But she said, "We don't have to. I mean, we can just…"

She trailed off and his imagination vividly filled in the blanks and fired him up all over again. He let out a regretful groan and disentangled himself from her, trying not to linger with his hand on her thigh.

"Now I know you're a cop," she said.

She was trying to be funny, which made it that much harder to disabuse her. "Jesus. Stop saying shit like that unless you want to get us both killed, okay?"

"I would never tell." She sounded crushed, and painfully young.

"There's nothing to tell."

She nodded and said softly, "Okay."

He'd wanted to withdraw from the situation tactfully, but it seemed more prudent to feign an anger he just didn't feel. He grabbed his pillow and muttered, "I'm sleeping on the couch."

He felt her eyes follow him out of the room, hating himself for hurting her, but nursing a justification that couldn't be denied.

Chapter Thirty-five

Bryn had experienced a myriad of new emotions in her life lately; terror, horror, betrayal, despair—now shame added itself to the list. She wondered how many synonyms there were for the word 'shame.' She felt them all.

Tears leaked out of her eyes and trickled into her underfur. She didn't want to remember the last night she'd gone to sleep without crying, because it was the last night of her old life, before she'd been plunged into xenofreak hell. Maybe her dad was right; maybe she was suicidal. At least, after the humiliating scene that just occurred, she thought she understood why someone might resort to it.

She didn't know why she'd insisted Scott was a cop when it obviously pissed him off. Her observations of his character, his baffling willingness to help her, this convenient house…the solution to the equation was nothing if solving it pushed him away. And she was certain she had solved it. He'd just proved it to her by not taking what she was so eager to give.

Still, she'd never been so embarrassed. Facing him in the morning would be exquisite torture. For a while, she considered sneaking out and running away again, but she'd just be exchanging one uncertain future for another. If Scott was a cop, it meant he was undercover fighting against Fournier and the XBestias. It meant he was one of the good guys, and the thought put torch to the first flare of hope she'd felt in a long time.

Sleep eluded her. She'd never slept next to someone in her whole life, yet the empty spot where he'd lain left her bereft in ways she couldn't explain. She knew she was placing too much trust in him, but it was more than that. She couldn't help but compare the clumsy fumblings of her ex-boyfriend Paul with Scott's assured touch and…ah, his kiss. Every time her thoughts strayed into that territory, her body responded so forcefully she squirmed with the frustration of it. Her quills would tighten, a sensation she was quickly beginning to equate with lust, and when they finally relaxed it reminded her of what she was trying not to think of and off they'd go tightening up again.

She did fall asleep eventually. In the morning, she woke to the sound of the toilet flushing. She had a brief fantasy of him coming out of the bathroom, sitting on the side of the bed, kissing her with that scarred mouth of his and saying, "I'm sorry."

Instead, he flipped the overhead exhaust fan on and said, "Don't go in there for a while."

She tried to go back to sleep but kept recalling bits from the night before and reliving her mortification. Reluctantly, she dragged herself out of bed. Scott was sitting at the kitchen table, looking at something on his holophone.

"Laundry's almost done," he said matter-of-factly. "Where on Trill Street do you need to go?"

"It's West Trill. Provincial Mutual."

He typed something. "Yeah, okay, here it is. We'll have to take…three buses."

She bit her lip, nibbling at a bit of loose skin, halfway hoping he'd acknowledge the elephant in the room and halfway hoping he wouldn't.

He didn't.

The dryer buzzed and he disappeared through a door in the kitchen, returning a few minutes later with a basket of clothes.

"Found this in the garage." He handed her a battered old fishing hat. "Probably won't get stuck on your quills."

She was happy to put her own clothes on, but a little disturbed that he'd handled her undergarments in the course of washing them. The elastic in her old panties was stretched out and her bra was dingy and frayed around the edges. There'd been no one at home to ensure she had more than the barest of girly necessities, and since she didn't have a boyfriend and money was tight, she gave lingerie low priority.

She'd set her boots over the heating vent the night before and draped her jacket nearby so they would dry. The leather on both was stiff and damaged from saltwater. Standing in front of the mirror, she put the jacket on, set the faded green fishing hat over her quills and draped the scarf over the top. Crossing the ends under her chin to hang down her back effectively hid the quills poking out of the bottom of the hat, but the end result tromped all over any number of fashion laws.

"You look stupid," she told her reflection. But it didn't matter. So what if she looked ready to go ice fishing when the sun was shining outside in what would likely be another warm summer day? If she left her head uncovered, she'd get even more stares than this ridiculous get-up and would certainly be recognized.

She giggled to herself. "Now you've got a porcupine and a price on your head." Predictably, the mirth didn't last.

Scott had conjured himself a pair of Levi's that hung from his hips in such a way that she found it hard not to gawk at him in admiration. He also had on a pair of lightweight boots that looked like they fit him better than the last pair. Add to that a grey zip-up hoodie with a white t-shirt and some sunglasses, and he looked too normal to be in her company—when his hands were in his pockets anyway.

He was unusually talkative on the bus, asking probing questions about her father's motivation for having her mutilated. She didn't tell him much—talking about it would only depress her further. Scott also showed a sudden interest in Carla and seemed disappointed when Bryn told him, "I hadn't seen her in years before yesterday. She's a virtual stranger."

They picked up fast food for breakfast and ate while walking up West Trill, past a car dealership, a Walmart and a bicycle store. The Prudential Mutual building was a sprawling, one-story brick structure that looked like it had once housed a bank.

Scott leaned against the wall by the front doors and said, "I'll wait outside."

The receptionist raised her over-plucked eyebrows at Bryn and asked, "Can I help you?"

Bryn's heart fluttered, but she tried to appear calm. "M—my mother passed away several years ago. She had a life insurance policy with this company, and I was the beneficiary. I just turned eighteen and would like to know how to go about collecting."

The receptionist's long red fingernails hovered over her keyboard. "Name?"

Bryn's nervousness ratcheted up a notch. "Her name was Miranda Vega."

Tap tap tappity tap. "Her date of birth?"

Bryn told her, and answered several more questions after that. The receptionist remained expressionless throughout. She finally picked up a telephone handset and told Bryn to have a seat in the waiting area. Bryn sat on the edge of one of the chairs, wringing her hands, ready to bolt out the door if she got the slightest hint that she'd been recognized.

After about ten minutes, a man in a rumpled suit appeared from a side door. He had a chubby round face and a pleased smile. "Ms. Vega?" He held out his hand. "Stan Berry."

Bryn stood, relieved. So far, so good.

Berry's office was small, neat and smelled like vanilla air-freshener. The blinds were open on a large window spanning the west wall, revealing a patch of landscaping shaded with giant ferns. Beyond that was the parking lot. She saw Scott wandering around but doubted he could see in; the exterior glass on the building had been coated with a reflective surface.

Berry plunked himself down behind his desk and invited her to sit. She declined, choosing instead to stand behind one of two chrome side chairs, gripping the pleather backrest. His smile really did look pleased, almost smugly so, as if he lived to give out large insurance payments to clients. Bryn shrugged off a niggle of doubt.

"I'm so glad you came to see me," he said with a little chuckle. "I can really use the ten thousand."

For a brief, deluded moment, she thought he meant he would get a commission on the payment. Then she remembered the amount of the reward for information leading to her 'safe' return.

She swallowed and stiffened her spine. "I'll pay you twenty thousand once the insurance check clears."

"Ooo, tempting, but too late. Your father thought you might stop by, so he left his personal holo number with me. He's already on his way."

Bryn turned to the door and saw through the side glass that a security guard had come to stand outside it. There was no way to get a message to Scott—she'd have to get herself out of this one.

She unwrapped the scarf and removed the hat, setting it on Berry's desk. His brows rose as she felt her quills puff up like they had when she'd been in the tunnel of spiders. Perhaps that was a trace of fear she saw in his eyes?

"Ya got me, Stan," she said. Three steps took her to the door, where she reached out and twisted the lock.

"Uh, you know you just locked yourself in, right?" Something glinted in his hand; it was a thin metal letter opener. He ran the tip nonchalantly under a thumbnail.

"Yep," she said, moving to stand behind the side chair again. With no warning, and in one fluid movement, she hefted the chair and flung it through the plate glass window. The crash was deafening.

"What the hell are you doing?" Berry yelled. Outside, she saw Scott run in her direction.

Glass shards stuck up from the window frame, preventing her from making an easy exit. And Berry wasn't about to let his ten thousand dollars escape that easily. He came around the desk brandishing the letter opener. The security guard rattled the door handle. Bryn grabbed the other chair and swung it. Berry ducked, but she used it to knock the remaining glass from the frame before setting it under the window. Scott arrived, reaching in for her as she stepped up on the seat.

"Oh, no you don't," Berry said through gritted teeth. He wasn't smiling now. He attempted to jab her with the letter opener, but it struck her thigh on the thick seam of her jeans and bent under the pressure. Scott grasped one of her arms and Berry clutched at the other. Bryn kicked out, but the chubby insurance man clawed at her leg, hollering, "Get in here, Martinez!"

She heard the sound of more glass shattering and caught a glimpse of a blue-sleeved arm fumbling blindly for the door handle. Scott yanked so hard it felt like her shoulder was about to dislocate, but it dislodged the clinging Berry and pulled her hips onto the sill. She felt a sharp sting in her backside just as Berry got desperate, jumped up on the chair and threw an arm around her neck.

With a shrill scream, he let go and fell back, quills protruding from his face, shoulder and arm.

Chapter Thirty-six

As soon as Bryn's feet hit the dirt, Scott took her hand and said, "Run!" They tore through the parking lot into the neighboring lot. It was the bicycle shop they'd passed earlier, and Scott had already scoped it out. While he was waiting for Bryn, a man had ridden his bike alongside the shop and dismounted, propping it up against the wall before entering a side door.

The bike was still there, unchained. Scott quickly straddled it and took Bryn by the shoulders, guiding her to stand facing away from him with the front wheel between her legs. "Hands here," he said, thumping the hand grips. She didn't need any further direction. He held the bike steady as she hopped up and settled her butt on the handlebars.

It was not the first time Scott had stolen a bicycle. His only other attempt had been at age five when he made off with Hector Nunez's new Spiderman bike one hot August day. The little snot had seen him do it, however, and Scott's dad took away his video games for two weeks. His parents attributed it to sibling rivalry, because they'd just adopted a little girl.

This time, the owner of the bike didn't catch him, and they were three blocks away before he noticed the blood on his hand. Since he felt no pain, he assumed it was Bryn's.

"Are you hurt?" he asked, breathing hard with effort now that the sidewalk was slanting upwards.

"It's fine." He barely heard her response—she was concentrating on maintaining her balance and hadn't turned her head.

The blood began trailing down his wrist. He stepped up the pace, quadriceps burning. At the top of the incline was a field of grass with evenly spaced pine trees, stretching to an isolated building. Beyond the building on one side he saw a baseball field and on the other a basketball court. It was a school.

"Hang on." He turned onto the grass and cut across the field. There were two vehicles in the small parking lot; a silver car and a van with the words, 'We Clean 'Em Carpets and Floors.' Summer was winding down and the school must be preparing to open its doors by having the carpets in the offices cleaned. The other car would belong to the janitor, who would be on hand to open and lock up.

Scott stopped behind a copse of trees and helped Bryn down before dropping the bike into a patch of low shrubbery, which hid it pretty well. He turned Bryn to assess the damage. The denim fabric had a dark red blotch surrounding a tear in her jeans.

"Butt's cut," he informed her.

"No kidding." She twisted her torso in an attempt to see the damage as they walked to the school.

A thick corrugated hose ran from the back of the carpet cleaning van into one of the school's side doors, which was propped open with a rubber wedge. The engine was running, powering the steam cleaner. He smelled cigarette smoke. Gesturing for Bryn to wait by the side door, he walked along the wall and peered around the corner. A man, he presumed it was the janitor, was sitting on a bench, smoking and involved with his holoreader.

Scott ran back and looked in the side door. No one in sight. The humming hose stretched down a linoleum-floored corridor packed with displaced furniture. He waved for her to follow him inside. Heading in the opposite direction from the hose, he glanced through doorways until he found the teacher's lounge. It was empty of furniture and carpeted, but since the carpet was damp, he figured they'd be safe.

"Take your pants off," he said. "Rinse them in the sink." While she did that, he searched the cupboards until he found the first-aid kit. In the nearly empty refrigerator, he spotted the second item he needed: an open box of baking soda way in the back.

She was at the sink rinsing and wringing her jeans out, dressed from the waist down in white bobby socks and those unsexy panties he'd washed at the safe house, the left buttock soaked with blood.

He knelt down behind her and opened the first-aid kit. "Hang on, this may hurt."

He heard her mutter, "Oh, my God, how embarrassing," as he peeled her panties away from the wound and down so she could step out of them.

"Bare-assing is right." He couldn't resist the pun and was rewarded with a groan from Bryn. Her bottom was firm and pert, but under the circumstances, it wasn't hard to stay clinical. He blotted the two-inch long gash with paper towels. It hadn't stopped oozing blood, and he suspected there was still a glass splinter or two inside. He handed her the baking soda box, saying, "Add a little water and make a paste."

Once she'd done so, he gently spread the baking soda paste onto the wound before taping a large gauze pad in place over it. "That'll help draw out any shards of glass that might still be in there. It's the best I can do for now, but you'll need stitches soon."

He discarded the mess, including the ruined panties, and put everything away while she struggled back into her wet jeans, hissing in pain as she shimmied them over her hips.

He helped her into her boots, and she asked, "Now what?"

"You need a new disguise. They're going to be looking for a girl in a leather jacket and beige scarf."

They found last year's overflowing Lost and Found box in the main lobby—luckily the school hadn't donated the items to charity. Since it was a middle school, most of the coats were too small for her, but they did find a plain blue, lightweight nylon jacket that some largish boy had probably abandoned because it had a broken zipper. She left her leather jacket in the box with a disappointed pout.

The new jacket didn't have an attached hat, and the only hats in the box were the knit variety that wouldn't contain the quills—although he did note with a flicker of satisfaction that the insurance guy had thinned the quills out some. There was one scarf, but it was too thin, too pink and had a popular cartoon fairy emblazoned on it.

On the way out they passed the double doors to the auditorium. Bryn stopped him by touching his arm before slipping inside. She turned on the overhead lights and seemed familiar with the layout—went straight backstage to the costume closet—it was easy for him to imagine her as the lead in her high school musical.

Another box, this one full of hats that were wholly unsuitable to wear in public; tricorn soldier hats, ten-gallon cowboy hats, feathered and bejeweled hats, even a poorly constructed plastic fruit one.

"Aha!" she whispered theatrically, pulling out and brandishing a curly blonde wig. He helped her put it on, not an easy feat since the thing was designed to fit snugly against the skull and the quills made that just about impossible, but eventually they got it settled. Quills stuck out everywhere, but the curls fell past her shoulders and concealed them pretty well. If no one looked closely, she'd almost pass for normal.

There was a full-length wardrobe mirror by the curtain, probably for last-minute costume checks before the kids went onstage. Bryn approached it slowly and when her face came into view, reached out to touch her fingertips to the dusty glass. He hovered behind her, looking over her shoulder.

That this was some kind of momentous occasion for her was obvious. Her face was pale and desolate, and the harsh lighting slanting in from the auditorium reflected off unshed tears pooling in her eyes. Venturing an opinion might set her off, but he felt helpless, so he said, "Looks pretty good."

Even though he'd expected an adverse reaction, he was taken by surprise when her face crumpled, and she burst into tears. He stood there as she covered her face with her hands, watching her shoulders shake silently. The seconds ticked by; he didn't know what to do.

He thought of his sister, something he found himself doing more and more lately. Whenever May had cried, he would pull her into his lap and pat her on the back, murmuring, "There, there, little bear," until she began to giggle, even at the end when it was so hard to distract her from the pain.

He reached out to comfort Bryn, but as soon as he touched her, she whirled around and slapped his hand away.

"Why didn't you stop them?" she cried.

Her voice was way too loud. He held up his hands. "Sh-sh-shhh!"

She blanched, expression instantly contrite. With her knuckles, she swiped the tears from under her eyes. In a softer voice, she said, "You could have stopped them."

There were so many things he wanted to tell her, but all he could say was, "It wasn't my call."

Her shoulders drooped and she stared at the floor. "Whose call was it?"

She was probing again, asking if he answered to Fournier or not. "Let it go, Bryn."

Her eyes lifted and her voice dropped. "Let it go?"

"I mean…" he drew in a breath. She was deliberately misunderstanding him. "It's just, now's not the time."

"Will there be a time?"

He had no ready answer. By way of apology, he raised a hand to her cheek, halfway expecting her to slap him down again. Instead, her lips parted on a little hiccupping sob. His intention was to offer comfort, make her feel better, but before he knew it, she warm and yielding in his arms.

Chapter Thirty-seven

Bryn met him halfway, a flood of emotions propelling her forward, intense and indefinable. There was no thought, only feeling. His firm-soft mouth, his body pressed against her, his roaming hands pulling her closer until the clothing between them presented a frustrating barrier. She yanked his shirt up to reach under and trace the lines of his back. Her fingernails grazed his sides, bringing goosebumps alive under her fingertips. All the while she was drowning in his kiss.

He broke away, searching her eyes. If he was looking for permission to continue, she made sure it was plain on her face.

A man's voice echoed across the auditorium. "Is someone there?"

Bryn's breathing went from shallow and fast to frozen. She and Scott stood in place, listening. No footsteps sounded; no one discovered them. After about ten seconds, the lights went out and the door clicked shut.

"I think we better go," Scott whispered.

"Where?"

"I have an idea." He felt for her hand. The only light came from the green exit sign over the main entrance. They navigated the darkness across the stage, down the stairs and up the aisle. Once there, Scott quietly opened the door and they looked out. The sound of the generator powering the carpet cleaner had ceased, but the hose was still in the hallway and she heard voices. Scott waved for her to follow, tip-toeing to a door marked 'Boy's Restroom,' directly across from the propped-open side door. Once hidden inside the dark restroom, Scott cracked the door and they peeked out.

The hose made a thrumming sound against the door frame as the carpet guy began hauling it in. In the light from the door crack, she saw Scott wink and mouth the word, "Distraction." He darted into the hall and by the time he joined her back in the restroom, the fire alarm was blaring.

They didn't have long to wait before the janitor and the carpet guy ran in, looking for the source of the alarm.

"What the hell did you do?" The janitor yelled.

"Nothing!" The carpet guy threw his hands in the air. They ran down the hallway.

Scott grabbed Bryn's arm and drew her with him outside. "Get in!" She jumped into the back of the van and helped him push the hose spool out. It clattered on the tarmac, but the noise was dwarfed by the strident alarm.

Scott shut the van's back doors, vaulted into the driver's seat, and shifted the running vehicle into gear. Bryn, conscious of her injury, made her way more slowly into the passenger seat as he drove away. She watched out the window; neither the janitor nor the carpet guy appeared before they turned a corner and the school disappeared from view.

"Won't the fire department respond?" she asked.

"Probably."

"And the carpet guy will call the police as soon as he realizes the van is gone."

"Uh-huh."

"So…what if we get pulled over?"

"Hopefully we have enough of a lead to get where we're going and ditch," he said.

"Where are we going?"

He glanced over at her. "Bluto's."

"Is that up for discussion? Because I vote we go somewhere safer."

"There is no such place."

Instead of driving right up to Bluto's, Scott parked the van on the street behind the restaurant, a few blocks from the lair of Nosferatu.

"Oh, please tell me we're not taking that tunnel," she said.

"Can't. Crime scene."

She thought she caught him with information only a cop would have. "How do you know?"

She followed his pointing finger to the front of the boarded-up building, which was wrapped with distinctive yellow tape. "Oh," she said.

There was no one around—at least, not anyone they could see. It was too early for the restaurant to be open, so they tried knocking on the back door. After several minutes it opened, and a large black man leaned out. Bryn recoiled at the sight of the tusks protruding from his wide mouth.

"Phaco," Scott said.

"Lupus' lookin' fer ya," the man named Phaco said. He opened the door further to let them in, but Scott hesitated. "He's not here now, is he?"

"Nah. You comin' in or what?" As Bryn passed uncomfortably close to Phaco on the way into the kitchen, he looked at her with small, pig-like eyes that still managed to seem kind. "Mouse tol' me 'bout you. She was worried."

132

"Oh, yes, well, thank you. I'm—I'm fine, as you can see."

He laughed, a hearty ho-ho-ho like Santa Claus. "Yer not gonna be fine if you keep hangin' with Cougar, here. He about to get his ass-hat handed to him."

They followed Phaco through a door off the kitchen that led into a hallway. He opened another door and said, "Sorry, folks. I lied."

Scott tensed up and put an arm out to stop Bryn from entering the dark room. In an undertone, he said to Phaco, "Take her somewhere."

"Can't. She invited." Bryn didn't know what was going on. She looked into the room and realized it wasn't empty. There was a man standing in the shadows; a tall man with a beard. Sitting at the desk was a woman—Padme.

Scott stepped inside and Bryn stayed close, one hand holding onto his hoodie like an anchor. The door shut with an ominous click. Somehow, she doubted Padme would be overjoyed at the reunion. The Pakistani girl jumped up and came around the desk, displaying no surprise at seeing Bryn with Scott. She flipped on the overhead light.

"Let me see it."

Bryn didn't have to ask what 'it' was. The wig was much easier to remove than it was to put on. She waited for the verdict as Padme studied her quills.

"How does it feel?" Padme asked.

"I'm getting used to it."

Padme laughed, a short, barking sound. "An admirable attitude."

"Do I have a choice?"

Padme cocked her head to the side, considering. "No, you do not."

"Enough," the bearded man growled. Bryn looked at him in the light and her eyes grew wide. That was no beard she'd seen. A sickening bolt of fear shot through her as he moved across the room and stood in front of Scott.

"You and Dundee really screwed the pooch," the wolf-faced man said. "Disappointed a very powerful client. Tell me why I shouldn't kill you right now."

"Because I know where the Panda is," Scott replied. "And I can get it back for you."

This was news to Bryn.

"Where is it?" Lupus asked in a deceptively soft voice.

"At a farm upstate. The ARA took it. We were outgunned."

Lupus' seemed to relax somewhat, but Bryn was convinced he could burst into violence at any moment. "The Animal Rights Army," he said. "And you know this, how?"

"I told him," Bryn said.

Scott took a sharp breath as Lupus' big shaggy head swung her way.

"Please elaborate…Porky," Lupus said. His words were phrased as a polite invitation, but Bryn felt like she was wearing a red hood and he was considering whether to devour her. And 'Porky' was the name she'd given Dundee, which meant the Australian was still alive and had spoken to Lupus.

"I know Kareem, their leader," she said.

Lupus smiled, or at least she thought it was a smile. He leaned down almost to her level and showed his teeth, which looked disconcertingly human against the thin black of his canine lips. "And how did this Kareem know about the shipment?"

Scott rescued her. "I'll be sure to ask him when I take it back."

Lupus straightened up slowly. After a moment, he said, "Mouse told me how the two of you managed to hook up. Very Romeo and Juliet, complete with tragic ending. Cougar, you will accompany me to recover the panda. Porky, you have a date with your father, and Padme will escort you."

Chapter Thirty-eight

Before Scott could even shoot Bryn a warning look, she exclaimed, "What? No!"

Padme merely gestured to the door.

Bryn stood her ground and glared at her. "You're wanted for kidnapping and escape. I'd like to see you try to collect that ten-thousand-dollar reward."

Padme shook her head slightly, rolling her eyes. "I'm not interested in the reward. Who do you think offered it in the first place?"

"Who? You?" Bryn scoffed.

"Enough!" Lupus said again. "Get her out of here."

Bryn finally glanced at Scott. He expected to see fear and anger in her eyes, but why did he have the feeling it was directed at him? Perhaps because he led her here, and was passively allowing Lupus to deliver her to her father? Yet he couldn't help but feel that despite the gravity of Bryn's situation at home, she was safer there. Her father may be a humongous jerk, but he wouldn't kill her, something that was more and more likely to happen while she pretended to belong among the outcasts of the Xenofreak Nation.

Padme took Bryn's arm, but Bryn shrugged the smaller girl's hand off. Scott suppressed a pang of something, concern maybe, as she walked out the door, but was too relieved that she'd quit protesting to give it much thought. Padme tossed him a look over her shoulder that wasn't hard to read; satisfaction.

Lupus got right down to business, as if he'd already forgotten the two young women. "Where's the farm?"

Scott had memorized the coordinates Shasta sent him, and Lupus entered them into his holophone. "Two-hour drive if we don't hit traffic. How many ARA soldiers?"

"I don't know."

It was always hard to tell what Lupus was thinking by looking at his face, but he made up for it in the timbre of his voice and choice use of words. "You're not worth a god-damn, you know that?"

"Yes, sir."

"Don't sir me. We're not in the military anymore, boy. Get on the phone and find me a truck and some god-damned backup. And you better come up with a decent plan, with minimal carnage because we don't need the press on this one, or I'll hang you out by your furry thumbs."

Scott accepted a whack on the side of the head as he walked past Lupus on his way to Phaco's desk. Lupus muttered something about getting some lunch. Scott pretended not to notice that he used his sleeve to open the doorknob. It was a frustrating fact that Lupus never left prints on anything, or left any cups lying around with his DNA on it. Scott did catch what he'd said, "We're not in the military anymore," but it could have simply been his way of saying "you're," since Lupus knew Scott had been a Marine for a day.

'Minimal carnage' was not the XBestia way, but it made sense as far as this job was concerned. Under normal circumstances, the ARA would boast publicly about the panda rescue, but they hadn't because they knew the authorities would confiscate the animal and quite possibly put it in a zoo. The ARA vegan animal extremists would hate zoos almost as much as they hated human consumption of meat. Their goal would be to somehow get the panda back to its native habitat in China, a lofty objective that would take time and resources. This silence on their part worked in the XBestia's favor. As long as Lupus and company didn't leave a bunch of corpses for the cops to investigate, they should be able to retrieve the cargo with no one but the hapless ARA soldiers the wiser.

It took four hours to get to the outskirts of the rundown, thirteen-acre farm just outside of Poughkeepsie. They drove in a ten-foot long decommissioned U-Haul rental truck with Arizona plates. The truck looked unassuming, but it was armored, had honeycomb bullet-proof tires, and the cab had been opened up to connect to the back. The driver was an ex-NASCAR mechanic, a Native American xeno who called himself Chief Joe. He had a bulbous red nose that suggested alcoholism and wore a Mohawk, but instead of a strip of hair down his head, it was a rather raggedy band of feathers. In the passenger seat was his partner, a female xeno named Liz. She, too, had a partially shaved head, similar to the cut Scott was growing out. Her graft, some kind of reptile skin in the shape of an arrow pointing down, was situated at the base of her brain. The first time he looked at it, it appeared to be green, but the second time it looked brown. He wondered if it was chameleon skin.

Lupus sat with Scott in the back, slumped and dozing almost the entire way, while Scott familiarized himself with the arsenal on board: four long-range CO2 dart-gun rifles with thermal night vision scope capability, and a box of darts pre-filled with tranquillizer sufficient to knock out a 200-pound man, pressurized and ready for use. Two separate darts with a different anesthetic were designated for the panda in case they needed them.

Once they reached the farm's coordinates, Chief Joe slowed down as Scott leaned into the cab to look out the window and study the perimeter visible from the main road. A stand of old sugar maples completely concealed the farm. The main gate appeared to be reinforced, but the fencing on either side looked like standard agricultural barbed wire, and the land was level. Scott pointed to a section of fence to the right of the gate, an area thinly populated with saplings. Chief Joe nodded.

They drove a quarter mile further before Chief Joe pulled over at a place where the shoulder of the road widened into a lookout point. It was almost dark and there was no other traffic. The terrain was woodsy with green meadows, and the air coming in through the windows felt humid and warm, laden with the chirping of crickets and frogs.

Lupus sat up and stretched. "We here?"

Scott said, "Yep."

Lupus grunted and pulled out his holophone, switching it to conference. After one ring, Padme's face appeared. She began to talk without waiting for a prompt from Lupus. "These guys are dedicated, but small potatoes. Kareem's mother LaShonda Williams won a lottery jackpot in 2013 and managed to hang onto most of it until she died last year of lung cancer. Kareem, who graduated from NYU with a Bachelors in Liberal Studies, inherited several million and has been essentially building his army ever since."

"That's fascinating," Lupus said, sounding profoundly bored, "but would you mind please getting to the part about how many of these stooges we are up against?"

"I hacked into the ARA's email through their website. They have over one hundred active members, only a handful of whom reside in the area and are overtly involved in the day-to-day operations. Two hours ago, Kareem sent an email to a Miss Karen Lee inviting her over and telling her, in essence, that they would have the place to themselves tonight."

Scott tucked away the information that Padme had the ability to hack into someone's email. She'd never revealed that she was anything more than tech-savvy.

"So we brought all this firepower to take down a guy on a booty-call?" Liz asked.

"Not necessarily," Padme replied. "I sent a map of the farm—main house, barn, chicken coop and two outbuildings. It was originally an organic dairy and egg farm, but the livestock was sold off and the grazing fields are fallow. The structures were built a century ago. Barn is constructed of local stone a third of the way up and finished with timber. Fencing is not electrified. There is, however, a video surveillance alarm system with infrared capability."

"Can you shut it down?" Lupus asked.

"Not from here. The alarm company has an adequate firewall, though I was able to extract information from correspondence between Kareem and the company. An email dated two years ago had an attachment with the original schematic proposal for installation of the cameras. I sent it to you. The cameras use software analysis that will alert Kareem via holocall if it detects intruders, or if one or more of the cameras go offline. If he does not contact the company to give the all-clear within ten minutes, the system will alert police. As to how many people you may encounter, I can tell you that the previous owner converted one of the outbuildings to a housing unit in 1987. As we speak, the occupants are streaming a holo entitled, 'Mask of the Undertaker.'

"That's a good movie," Chief Joe said, earning a sidelong look from Lupus.

Padme continued, "In addition, there are three people using the postal address assigned to that unit. All male between the ages of twenty-five and thirty. None of them have military service records, but their arrest records suggest they are familiar with firearms."

Scott was dumbstruck that Padme had obtained all that information in the four hours they'd been driving. Although in point of fact, she would have had significantly less time to do so, since she'd had to take Bryn home. He hoped Lupus would ask her how that went.

But Lupus only said, "That it?"

"The local police provide live scanner audio feed on the Internet. I will monitor it and call you if they are notified and responding to a security breach in your area. That's all."

Lupus flipped his holophone closed over her image without so much as a goodbye.

He looked at Scott. "What we got?"

Scott handed each of them an earbug and waited while they were inserted. "Frequency confirm."

Lupus, Chief Joe and Liz all said, "Check" in turn, and Scott heard each of their voices in his right ear.

He held up one of the dart cases. "This holds your ammo. It's like a straw dispenser. Push this lever and a dart will drop into the tray. In the syringe is the fastest-acting tranquilizer on the market, but it will still take about 30 seconds for full effect. We got one shot at a time, so make 'em count. I can't emphasize enough: if you have a shot, say so. We want verbal confirmation on each target so we don't dart anyone twice, else we'll have to take 'em with us to monitor their heart rate and respiration."

He distributed body armor vests, saying, "From what I saw yesterday at the beach, these guys like rifles, but there were a lot of bullets flying with only one hit, and it was non-lethal. Doesn't mean they got no aim—could be they were trying not to kill anyone. Tonight we can assume they will do their best to stop us, and they won't be using darts. Try not to get shot in the head."

Liz snorted and nudged Chief Joe. "That means you, featherhead."

Scott held up one of the rifles and demonstrated how to load a dart. "This switch on the scope turns night vision on and off. Accuracy depends on distance. Distance depends on CO_2 pressure, so before you take your shot, adjust this dial accordingly, one notch per five meters. Don't even bother to shoot if you're further than 100 meters from the target. The guns are quiet, but not silent. Be sure to police your darts. And for God's sake, don't poke yourself."

"Meters?" Chief Joe said. "How about giving us that in English?"

Scott handed him a slip of paper that had been included in the gun case. "This breaks it down for you."

Lupus opened his holophone and increased the projection to maximum. After studying the documents Padme sent and coming up with a plan of action, each of them put on a vest and strapped on a reinforced nylon belt that held a dart case and a powerful miniature flashlight.

Lupus nodded to Chief Joe. "Shall we?"

Chapter Thirty-nine

The chair in Dr. Finnegan's office would have been comfortable if the anesthetic wasn't wearing off Bryn's left buttock, which had been poked and prodded for glass fragments before being closed with four stitches. She'd arrived at the Milton P. Osborne Psychiatric Center four hours ago. There'd been no point attempting to get away from Padme. Even if she managed to escape, Lupus would probably hunt her down. Scott hadn't even blinked when the horrible wolf-faced man separated them. Bryn felt sick to the bottom of her soul but wasn't about to fall apart. Something told her the less emotional she got, the better her chances of survival in her new environment.

Padme had been planning to drop her off at her father's house, but Bryn begged her not to.

"How would you like it if someone sent you back to Pakistan—gave you to your uncle?" she asked.

Padme appeared unmoved, but she said, "I'll take you to the mental hospital, then. What's your psychiatrist's name?"

She'd gone so far as to call Dr. Finnegan and put Bryn on the holo to tell her she was voluntarily coming in. Bryn's shrink, accompanied by an orderly, was waiting out front when Padme drove up. Bryn got out and Padme drove off without a word. Bryn had turned to Dr. Finnegan and feigned remorse, staying calm and collected through the last humiliating hours.

Now sitting in the chair in a hospital gown, she said, "I'm not suicidal. I never was."

"Bryn, I saw the note you left your father." Dr. Finnegan opened the file on her lap and handed Bryn a sheet of paper. On it was one typewritten, run-on sentence.

In heaven I will get my hair back, I will be me again and I'll be with Mom, so don't cry for me, Daddy, I love you more than words can say.

"Wow, that's touching." Bryn handed the sheet back. "I didn't write it."

"Sure looks like your signature."

"Yes, it does. I wonder how long it took him to get it right."

"Are you suggesting your father wrote it? Look," Dr. Finnegan sounded like she was losing patience. "Your father said you'd had what he considered a psychotic break. You told me yourself you felt there was no way out. That no one would ever love you. That you felt helpless and hopeless."

Bryn thought about the choices she'd faced; staying with the man who'd ruined her life or going rogue and becoming a criminal. "You have no idea."

Dr. Forrester leaned forward. "Tell me."

Bryn leaned forward too. "My father is the one who arranged for me to be kidnapped in the first place. If I told you why, I guarantee you wouldn't believe me."

"That's a serious accusation. Do you feel like everyone is out to get you?"

"What? Oh, you mean, am I paranoid? Um, no. Dr. Finnegan, you were there when my dad said he had my car towed. Would I have taken all my stuff with me if I was planning to kill myself?"

Dr. Finnegan's chin came up and her eyes narrowed slightly. "Your father says you-"

"I'm sorry," Bryn interrupted, "I don't mean any disrespect, but you're starting an awful lot of sentences with 'your father said.' He's a very persuasive person. He needed you to think I was suicidal."

"Alright, let's step back and take your father out of the picture. Where have you been the last 48 hours?"

"Surviving."

"Why did...okay, I said I wouldn't repeat what your father told me, but for the sake of accuracy let's clarify a few more things. He said you went out and found your kidnapper and have been with him this whole time. Is that true?"

Bryn stared at her, unblinking, desperately trying to think how her father knew. Then the obvious struck her: Stan Berry. The smug insurance salesman had probably gotten a good look at Scott's hands when they were playing tug-o-war with Bryn's arms. It would have been easy for her dad to figure out who she'd been with, and then he must have contacted Nurse Vonda. Bryn and Scott hadn't just run into Lupus at Bluto's—he'd been waiting for them. If her father could be believed, Fournier had a stake in getting Bryn to cooperate. Then something else occurred to her. She remembered that overheard holo call where her father told the person on the other end, 'You'll get your money after the check clears.' Was that about paying Fournier for his handiwork? Despite her father's deflecting statements about embezzling donations, it was much more likely the check in question had been her mother's life insurance.

Bryn was so intent upon putting the puzzle pieces in the right places she almost forgot Dr. Finnegan's question. The doctor was patiently waiting for a response, so Bryn said simply, "Yes."

"I hope you realize you've been engaged in extremely reckless behavior. There's a phrase for someone who begins to relate to her kidnappers-"

Bryn rolled her eyes briefly up at the ceiling tiles. "Yeah, Stockholm syndrome, I know."

"The XBestia are dangerous," Dr. Finnegan said. "Xenofreaks are unpredictable. You know this."

"That's prejudice talking. People with xenoalterations are just expressing themselves."

"In a way that's very offensive to many people."

"It's impossible not to offend someone. Your preconceived notions of how everyone should behave offend me."

"We're not talking about me, Bryn. This is about you."

"No," Bryn said, struggling to maintain her composure. "This? Right here, right now, me talking and you not listening? This is about my father wanting to commit me so he can take my mother's life insurance money."

"Your father warned me that you'd fixated on that delusion, so I contacted the insurance company you attempted to rob, and your mother never had a policy there."

"What?" Bryn burst out in disbelieving laughter. "I didn't try to rob them. This is insane. I assume you talked to Stan the man Berry? Dad knew I'd try to get that money, so he called Mr. Berry and offered the ten-thousand-dollar reward if I showed up. The only deluded one in this room is you."

Dr. Finnegan reached for her holophone. "I can call the corporate office, go over Mr. Berry's head and verify it."

"Please," Bryn said as all traces of belligerence vanished. "Please do that for me."

Dr. Finnegan hesitated, searching Bryn's face. She finally shrugged and turned her attention to the holophone. After a few minutes, she said, "Here's the number." She tapped and put it on conference. The torso of a pretty female automaton appeared. "Thank you for calling Provincial Mutual. Please enter your account number or stay on the line and an operator will be with you shortly."

"I don't suppose you have the account number," Dr. Finnegan said.

Bryn shook her head and bit her lip, worried now that Berry had somehow deleted the entire account.

A ring tone sounded and the holo of a live woman appeared. "Provincial Mutual customer service, this is Erica, how may I help you?"

Dr. Finnegan pushed the phone across to Bryn, who told Erica the same thing she'd told the receptionist at the office on West Trill. She answered a set of similar questions and waited nervously as the customer service rep entered the data.

"I'm sorry, Miss, but this case is closed," Erica said. "A check was issued...today, in the amount of $364,023.00."

Bryn's voice was barely audible. "Payable to?"

"Harold Vega."

Bryn met Dr. Finnegan's eyes. The psychiatrist said, "That son-of-a-bitch."

Chapter Forty

It was full dark by the time the truck's headlights illuminated their targeted section of fence next to the main gate. Chief Joe swerved into the empty oncoming lane, turned the truck 90-degrees to the right and slammed the accelerator down. Scott and Lupus braced for impact, but the heavy truck made short work of the old barbed wire fence, and the saplings beyond either bent or snapped beneath it as Chief Joe dodged the bigger trees to get to the gravel driveway. The truck barreled down the lane to a large clearing surrounded by the main house and outbuildings. Chief Joe veered sharply to the left towards the barn, and Scott determined from the lights in the windows which of the two outbuildings was occupied. Before the truck came to a full stop, Scott opened the back and he and Lupus were out and running.

Scott headed for cover behind the trunk of a tall maple, barely making it before the first ARA soldier burst out of the housing unit. The night vision on his scope was unnecessary since the clearing was well lit by lights mounted on high-mast poles, like a prison yard. He aimed, but heard Lupus in his ear, "Got 'im." A 'pfuft' sounded to his right and through his scope he saw the dart's red stabilizer puff seemingly bloom like a flower against the soldier's throat. The darted man stopped cold and threw his head back as his rifle slipped from his grasp. His knees buckled and he keeled forward just as a second man came more cautiously through the door.

ARA soldier number two didn't have a rifle. He saw his comrade lying prone and began firing into the trees with a semi-automatic handgun. Scott said, "He's mine," and darted him in the right leg. The guy swung his gun in Scott's direction, but couldn't get off a shot before the drug entered his blood stream and began to paralyze him.

"Two down," Lupus said for the benefit of Chief Joe and Liz, one of whom would be breaking into the barn to locate the panda, while the other covered the back of the main house.

If there was a third man in the housing unit, he was either not coming out or had exited from a back door and was circling around. The main house, between the barn and the outbuildings, had yet to produce Kareem.

Scott reloaded his dart rifle and said, "Report."

"House all quiet," Chief Joe said.

"Barn-" Liz began, but Scott heard a dull retort in his ear, as if Liz had clapped a hand to her own head, boxing the ear that had the bug in it. He began running back toward the barn, using the trees as cover. Just as he reached the closest maple, the barn door opened, and Liz stumbled out with her hands in the air. Scott lifted his dart rifle and looked through the scope. Liz had a dark smudge on her cheek that could have been blood. The barn was softly lit from inside. He saw the silhouette of a man in the doorway, one arm raised with a gun pointed at Liz's back.

"Testing, testing. Is this the xenofrequency?" Scott recognized the voice in his ear, which sounded amused at the pun. Kareem must have confiscated Liz's earbug.

"Roger that, Kareem," Scott said. "You are in my sights."

Scott saw Lupus in his peripheral vision, working his way tree by tree to the back of the barn.

Kareem raised his arm to place the barrel of the gun against Liz's head. "Xenobitch gets it in the back of the head if you don't drop your weapon."

"And as soon as she falls, you won't have a woman to hide behind," Scott said. He saw that Lupus was about to step out into the open to get to the barn. A shadowy figure just beyond him flitted from one tree to another; at first Scott thought it was Chief Joe, but then he caught sight of the Indian between the house and the barn. Scott dropped to one knee, dialed his dart rifle up to maximum, aimed high and fired. The lowest branches on the stand of maples grew well above a man's head, so there was nothing to hinder the flight of the dart through a break in the tree trunks. It struck the third ARA soldier in the thigh just as he was sighting on Lupus.

Scott loaded another dart into his rifle and adjusted the CO_2 pressure. "Third man down."

"I will do it." Now Kareem sounded significantly more stressed to Scott, which tended to confirm there'd only been three gunmen on the property. "One less xenoscum won't be missed!"

Scott saw Chief Joe come around the corner and flatten himself against the barn wall. He began inching closer to Liz. Lupus crossed the space between the trees and the barn and came up from the other side.

"You're surrounded," Scott said. "All we want is the panda." He was watching through the scope; he didn't have a clean shot, and Kareem held the gun steady against Liz' skull.

145

"Cops are going to be here any second," Kareem responded.

"You don't want 'em here anymore than we do. We haven't killed anyone and don't plan to. Let her go," Scott said. He needed the ARA leader to keep talking and stay distracted from his surroundings. Chief Joe had moved to within a couple of feet of Liz and even though she held still and faced forward, from her expression it was obvious to Scott she knew he was there. If Kareem leaned forward a few inches, he'd see him, too, but he clung to the partial protection of the barn door frame. Lupus reached the other corner of the barn. Chief Joe raised a hand and held it poised palm-up toward Kareem's gun, which told Scott he was about to make his move. Scott angled the barrel of his dart rifle until the crosshairs centered on Liz' midsection. He maintained silence, since any claim to the target would alert Kareem.

Chief Joe's hand shot out for the gun and Liz ducked simultaneously. The gun went off and the moment Liz dove out of the crosshairs, Scott fired. Unfortunately, Lupus leapt around the corner and also fired. Two darts hit Kareem, one in the belly and one in the side. Chief Joe grappled with Kareem until the gun flew out of his hand into the barn. Moments later the double dose of anesthetic toppled the ARA leader.

"Let's get that panda!" Lupus shouted, just as the holophone in his pocket, which he should have had on silent, rang.

Scott ran for the barn. Liz lay on the ground clutching her head, and as he got closer, he saw that she'd been grazed across the top of her scalp by Kareem's bullet. Chief Joe knelt down to help her. Lupus beat Scott to the barn door, where he slung the strap of his dart rifle over his shoulder and paused to flip open his holophone.

Scott heard Padme's voice through Lupus' earbug. She'd barely said, "Police are responding," when a scream came from within the barn, the kind of scream a warrior might produce when plunging into battle. A young black woman was rapidly advancing on Lupus, a gun—Kareem's gun—clenched in both of her hands. Scott's only weapon was the unloaded dart rifle. Still running forward, he depressed the lever on the dart case and a dart slipped into his hand. Lupus spun around, but the young woman fired point-blank at his torso, then turned the gun on Chief Joe as he threw himself on top of Liz. Scott's arm went back and with all the skill he'd developed during a childhood of playing darts in the garage with his father, he hurled the dart.

It struck her in the cheek and provided a sufficient distraction to stop her from shooting Chief Joe. She pointed the gun at Scott, and he worried that the hypodermic dart had penetrated the cheek and discharged its contents into her mouth. He had no idea what would happen if that were the case, whether the anesthetic would do its intended work as fast—or at all—if she swallowed it. But she staggered and fell.

Scott ran to Lupus, telling Chief Joe, "Get Liz in the truck!" Lupus was wearing his body armor, but as Scott had feared, when he'd turned away from the gun, he'd exposed his unprotected shoulder area. The bullet had penetrated at the underarm and entered his chest diagonally.

Lupus was conscious but breathing shallowly. "Get the…panda. I'm…fine."

Scott would have ignored the order if there was anything he could do for Lupus. The best thing would be to get him to a hospital as fast as possible, which was not going to happen.

The job hadn't gone well thus far, but by a great stroke of luck, the panda was not only in the barn in its crate, but it was also still loaded on the white van the ARA soldiers had stolen from them on the beach. Scott and Chief Joe deposited Lupus into the back of the U-haul next to Liz. Scott made sure to pick up Lupus' holophone and slip it into his pocket. Then they dragged Kareem and his girlfriend out of the way so the van could exit the barn.

Scott said, "You take the van, I'll take the truck."

They didn't have time to run around policing the darts after all, but before he got into the truck, Scott made sure to get Liz' earbug out of Kareem's ear. Then he placed his dart rifle in Kareem's girlfriend's hand and strapped his ammunition belt around her waist. Chief Joe chuckled and said, "That oughta confuse things," but Scott had done it mostly so the authorities would know what anesthetic was used. The dose was intended for a 200-pound man and the girlfriend weighed significantly less than that, not to mention Kareem's unintentional double-dose.

On the way out, Scott had to drive back over the downed barbed-wire fence and was concerned that the van behind him would pop a tire, but that didn't happen. He drove the speed limit down the dark country road until a police cruiser passed him. The cruiser wasn't going terribly fast and didn't have its lights flashing. Just a routine alarm check.

After the cruiser, Scott picked up speed and didn't relax until he'd gotten onto the highway. Technically, he didn't relax then, either. Liz was conscious and tending to Lupus, but he suspected she had a concussion. Lupus faded in and out. Whenever he was lucid, he growled in pain, asked questions and barked orders.

Liz and Chief Joe talked to each other through the earbugs.

"What the hell happened in that barn?" Chief Joe asked.

"Aw, I didn't even see them," she said sheepishly. "He had her in a horse stall and was about to get into her pants. I guess he brought her out to see the panda—musta been some kinda aphrodisiac."

The conversation got personal after that, and Scott took his earbug out to give them some privacy. He'd been driving for half an hour when Liz said, "My head hurts almost as much as childbirth did. What do you think would happen if I stuck myself with a dart?"

"Don't," Scott advised. "It's best to stay conscious with a head injury."

He heard the sound of an ammo case dispensing a dart. "But it's an anesthetic, right? What if I take just enough to take the edge off the pain?"

"It's not that kind of anesthetic. If you stick yourself, I swear I'll drive to the nearest hospital."

Lupus' voice was weak, but his words were strong as ever. "You do that, boy, and I will kill you. I would like some of that stuff myself."

"Well, sir, I'm going to have deny that request on the basis that the anesthetic in that syringe will knock you out but will not provide pain relief. Your vitals are iffy enough without you deliberately suppressing them."

It took Scott a moment to realize the grating sound he heard was Lupus laughing. Scott said, "And while you're conscious, I'd sure like to know where you want me to take you."

"You got my holophone?"

"Yes."

"Call Padme when you get to the city; she'll give you directions from there."

Even though Lupus and Liz couldn't see his expression, Scott kept his face neutral. Inside, he felt an excitement that grew stronger the closer they got to New York City. There was only one place Lupus could and would go. Scott only hoped he'd ingratiated himself enough to survive the knowledge.

Chapter Forty-one

Despite the revelation that Bryn's father had lied to Dr. Finnegan, the shrink had been reluctant to release her.

"There's still the matter of your continuing association with your XBestia kidnapper," she'd said. "And I don't have a choice but to honor the 72-hour hold because it was court-ordered. We'll talk more tomorrow and come up with a plan, but at least tonight you'll be safe here."

Bryn most decidedly did not feel safe surrounded by crazy people—not crazy like xenofreaks, but certifiably insane crazy. Still, she had a room to herself and they'd given her some anti-anxiety medication that took the edge off. She got the first good night's sleep she'd had in a long time.

In the morning, she ate a breakfast of scrambled eggs and hash browns with a very flimsy plastic spork. Not long after that, Dr. Finnegan met with her.

"I had a visit from an XIA agent first thing this morning," she said. "Apparently, they know your father was involved in your kidnapping and are very interested in clarifying his role. I'm sorry I didn't believe you."

They talked for a bit longer and later an orderly brought her a bag of clothes. The items were things that had been hidden at the back of her own closet, things she rarely or never wore and hadn't taken with her when she'd run away. Even before the orderly said, "Your father is here to see you," she knew.

She put on the too-short black polyester 'slacks' she'd been required to wear when she was fifteen working her first job at an ice cream parlor, and the pink acrylic sweater Grandmother Vega had knitted her when she was twelve. It was a tight fit and scratchier than ever, but she supposed she wasn't trying to impress anyone here.

The Psychiatric Center had a central room with tables and games just like in the movies. It smelled faintly like cooked cabbage. There weren't very many people in the room, but most of them turned to see the orderly lead in the new girl with the strange clothes and even stranger 'hair.' Bryn didn't know if it was a residual effect of the medication they'd given her the night before, but she didn't care.

Her father was sitting in an armchair by a window. On the other side of the glass were bars disguised as decorative iron scrollwork, painted light blue, as if the color would blend in with the sky and camouflage the scrollwork's true purpose. Today the sky was grey anyway, heavy with low-lying clouds; perfect for her mood.

"Brynnie," he said, standing and coming at her with outstretched arms. She allowed him to fold her into a hug but didn't return it. He stepped back and looked at her. "Well, I see I'm a bad judge of clothing."

In days gone by, she would have smiled; she always had when he tried to make a funny.

"You're a bad judge of a lot of things," she said.

She expected him to look wounded—to feign hurt feelings, but he nodded. "I deserve that."

Her father rarely admitted he was wrong. It had to be a ruse and put her even more deeply on the offensive. "What do you want, Dad?"

"To talk." He waved to the chair opposite the one he'd been sitting in.

She sat and watched him sit, too. He appeared to be gathering his thoughts, so she said, "Just spit it out."

"I told you about my plans because our relationship is important to me. I didn't want—don't want—to conceal the truth from you."

Several retorts elbowed each other for supremacy, but she went with, "I don't know if I can take any more of your truth."

He gestured to her head, "I didn't ask for that. I was horrified when I saw what he'd done. I never meant to put you in danger. Or scare you."

The medicine must still be fogging her brain. Under normal circumstances she would have laughed derisively, but she couldn't muster the energy it would require. "Dad, I've been in a constant state of fear and danger since this started."

He'd been calm and reasonable thus far, but now she thought she saw that old fervent glint in his eye. It really didn't take much to get him going.

"I know you think I'm the one who belongs in here, and I'm sure Carla fed you a line of bull, but my intentions were honorable. Sacrifice for the greater good."

"Then why didn't you sacrifice your own head?"

"Because no one would care! I'm just a middle-aged nobody with an ax to grind, but you—you could become a symbol for all that was once beautiful and good in the world that became tainted as a direct result of the indifference of our lawmakers."

"And that garbage about embezzling PHS money to pay for it?"

"Oh, that's happening. Everything I told you about the dirty politicians is true. They all have their hands out. But I needed the insurance money to pay for…" his eyes flicked upward to her head.

Bryn gulped back an angry response. She already knew why he'd stolen that money. "I still don't understand why Dr. Fournier would want to help you," she said. "You'd be shutting down his underground clinic."

"Let's just say that like me, he's got a big stake in legalizing human cloning. Once public tide turns against xenoalteration, the next to go is xenotransplantation."

"Which saves thousands of lives every year. It saved Mom."

"No, it killed her. A cloned heart wouldn't have failed on her."

Bryn shook her head. "You don't know that, and I don't know much about cloning, but I do know they've never been able to work out the kinks even with animals."

"And without government sanction and funding, they never will. Animal rights activists, pure humans, religious doctrine, political standpoints; none united, but all are factors on one side of the fence, and on the other, a vision of the future that can't be denied. As unacceptable as growing embryos is, cloning will never be able to transcend that stigma and develop other processes if human experimentation isn't allowed to happen. We are in an era capable of great medical advances but crippled by ethical debate."

Her father was using all his persuasive powers to convince her. Bryn couldn't help but think of some of the natural cosmetics she'd used over the years that claimed on the packaging, 'Never tested on animals,' as if they hadn't used the knowledge obtained from companies that had tested on animals to formulate their products.

"It sounds like a debate that can't be won, Dad."

"It can if there is a uniting factor urgent enough."

"What does that mean?"

A rather grim, unpleasant smile formed on Harry Vega's lips. "History has shown that despite their differences, people will band together under certain circumstances."

"Like what? War?"

"That. Or pandemic."

Bryn shifted on her chair again to combat twinges of pain in her backside. "Like a plague or something? Nobody united against the Black Death, more like they avoided each other."

"That's because they didn't understand it. But I've said too much. Suffice it to say you are protected in the event that…something happens."

A shadow fell over her father and they glanced up. Agent Yang and a tough-looking black woman stood over him. He laughed. "I know my rights. You can't use our private conversation against me in court."

Agent Yang said, "We can if one of you was wired."

There was nothing phony about the look her father gave her now—a reflection of her own betrayal. She pushed aside the quills covering her ear and pulled out an earbug, displaying it for him between forefinger and thumb. Instead of giving it back to Agent Yang, she flicked the switch to 'off' with her thumbnail and slipped it into her pocket. The agents didn't notice because at that moment, her father stood and made a move like he was going to bolt. A third agent rushed to cuff him. As her father was led away, he tried to catch her eye. A part of her acknowledged there was more she wanted to say to him, but the part that wanted revenge won out and she turned away, looking out the window at the grey day.

Chapter Forty-two

To Scott's disappointment, Padme directed him to the Warehouse, where he assumed he'd be met by one of the nondescript white vans.

"He's getting weaker," he said quietly to Padme's holo-image as he drove. "I don't know if he'll survive a transfer and another long drive."

She didn't comment on his estimation of Lupus' chances. "How far out are you?"

"A few minutes."

"Drop off Liz and tell her to go to Exam Room Two. You and Chief Joe take the ramp to the parking garage." She disconnected.

When he turned onto the street with the sprawling Warehouse in all its squalor, things seemed to have gotten back to normal: there were xenos crawling all up and down the block. It didn't surprise him that the local cops hadn't bothered to keep the XBestias from moving back in after the raid. There were neighborhoods more worthy of their time.

As instructed, Scott dropped Liz off, pulled up to the security gate and waved to the camera. He waited while the heavy-duty iron bars slowly lifted. Parking in the garage had been restricted to Abel, Lupus, and the vans transporting patients. Overhead halogen lights lit the steep, curving concrete tunnel that led to the underground lot. Scott had been down here before with Abel and it seemed like a huge waste to have built the underground lot with only four spaces. He imagined the previous owner must have cruised around in a luxury vehicle he didn't want his underpaid, overworked employees to have access to.

There were no other cars in the lot, but Padme was waiting with two men in scrubs Scott had never seen before. He stopped the truck, hurried to open the back doors and began moving dart guns and boxes out of the way to make room for the men to pull in a collapsed stretcher. One of the men, Scott figured they were at least nurses, but quite possibly actual doctors, briefly checked Lupus before they hefted him onto the stretcher and took him out.

Scott jumped down, wondering why the transport van wasn't here yet. Someone's head was going to roll for being late.

He and the other man helped Chief Joe move the crate with the panda onto a flatbed cart. As soon as it was done, Padme crooked her finger at Chief Joe and said, "You."

Besides the ramp, there was only one way out of the parking garage. A freight elevator with doors on either side was used to bring patients on their stretchers down to connect with the transport vehicles. Only someone who knew the code could activate it. Before the warehouse had been raided, Abel had shut it down. Padme entered the code and the doors opened.

Chief Joe clasped Scott's hand and said, "Nice workin' with ya."

"Same here."

The Indian xenofreak walked to the elevator like a man expecting a bullet in his back, and Scott didn't blame him. Once Chief Joe had gone up to the Warehouse, Scott moved to sit with his legs hanging from the back of the truck. Exhausted, he rubbed his eyes.

There was now a dark red intravenous bag hanging from a pole attached to the stretcher—blood. Liz had taken Lupus' body armor vest off earlier, and now the doctor cut his shirt off with scissors. Lupus sucked air in through his teeth when the doctor peeled the dried and stuck-on blood away from his wound. One of the doctors looked at Padme and asked, "Come on, what's the holdup?"

"Give me one of those," Padme said to Scott. She was pointing at one of the dart guns, so he handed it to her.

"Is it loaded?" she asked.

He nodded, distracted by the faded numbers painted on the ground for each of the four parking spots: 72, 73, 74 and 75.

"What's this dial?"

He looked up. "It's CO2 powered. You adjust that depending on how far away the target is."

"And each notch represents...?"

"Five meters."

As soon as he said it, he realized she wasn't displaying idle curiosity. She rotated the dial, stepped back and shot him in the leg. He felt the drug hit his system rapidly and didn't fight it. He knew why she'd done it: he'd passed muster and was about to be taken to Fournier's lair. But in a flash of insight, he also realized she hadn't darted him to keep him from seeing where the transport van was taking him. Scott's newly blurry gaze drifted towards the cement wall as he toppled to one side.

If the numbers on the parking spots were any indication, the original garage had been much bigger at one time. Fournier had sealed it off. If you knew the code, the elevator doors would open on the other side…

Chapter Forty-three

Bryn had done the XIA a favor and they followed suit.

The stern black agent's name was Shasta Fox. She told Bryn, "The court-order's been vacated. You are now free to go home. Keep in mind your father might be given bail, so if you have somewhere else to stay, I suggest you go there. But that won't happen for a few days. Provincial Mutual has cancelled the check and will be reissuing it payable to you by courier this afternoon."

The orderly led a stunned Bryn back to her room, but only so she could change into the clothes she'd arrived in. He left the door unlocked this time, so after she changed, she wandered back into the hallway without waiting for him to return. At the far end, she saw Agent Yang and Shasta Fox having a conversation. Impulsively, Bryn flicked the tiny switch on the earbug she'd pocketed and reinserted it.

Right off, she heard Agent Yang say, "-in deeper than we thought."

Bryn barely heard Shasta's reply; the older woman must have taken her earbug out and Bryn was hearing her voice through Agent Yang's. "He used the word 'pandemic.' Jesus, if he's talking about the typhoid…interview him—hard."

Bryn was standing by the door to her former room, pretending to be waiting for the orderly and trying not to look like she was watching the two XIA agents. From the corner of her eye, she saw Agent Yang look over at her. "What about the girl?"

Bryn strained to hear Shasta's response, but a noise from that end of the hall drowned it out. All she caught was the end, "-Harding's off grid, but we have to assume his cover's still intact."

Harding…Harding, Bryn thought. Where had she heard that name? She was concentrating so hard she didn't notice Dr. Forrester.

"Ready to go?" the psychiatrist asked.

Bryn jumped, suddenly aware that if she could hear Shasta through Agent Yang's earbug, then Agent Yang probably heard Dr. Finnegan. Sure enough, the agent's head whipped around and a hand flew to her ear. Bryn turned away when the two agents began marching in her direction so they couldn't see her take the earbug out and slip it back into her jeans pocket. Bryn smiled nervously when they reached her, but Agent Yang didn't look amused. She held her hand out and said, "Earbug."

"Oh, yeah." Bryn pulled it from her pocket and handed it over.

Agent Yang examined the earbug before turning it off and closing her fingers around it. "I had mine in the entire time, but I didn't hear you until just now."

"Was it on? Sorry. I guess it must have accidently switched on when I changed clothes." Bryn tried not to look as pleased as she felt with the lie.

Dr. Finnegan, ignorant of any undercurrents, said, "I'm sure you're anxious to get home, Bryn. I've arranged a ride for you. Again, please accept my apologies for…well, inconvenience seems like an inadequate word."

"Nightmare?" Bryn suggested. But even with a nightmare a person could wake up and go on with their life with only a residual bad feeling—and relief that it hadn't been real.

When she got home, her car was in the garage, still packed. She found her dead holophone inside and plugged it in to charge; now she'd be able to pay the past due bill and get it reconnected. She'd be able to do a lot more than that with her mother's insurance money. Go to college, for one. There had to be a way to get her quills under control so she could get a decent job after obtaining her teaching certificate.

She pulled her suitcases out of the back seat and went to take a shower. Under the hot spray she struggled to put her thoughts in order and make sense of her conflicting emotions. She was grimly pleased that her father had been caught, but a heavy guilt weighed her down. If it weren't for her actions, he wouldn't be in jail. And now that she was no longer on the run, she would probably never see Scott again. Had he really been a cop, or had his pull of attraction been so strong she'd unconsciously invented a more acceptable persona for him in order to justify her feelings? It was likely she'd never know, and the thought induced that awful squeezing sensation in the region of her heart. She didn't want to cry anymore, so she got out of the shower and briskly dried herself off.

The stitches on her backside hurt and were beginning to itch just like the ones Dr. Fournier had so lovingly placed in her scalp. The psychiatric center had given her a supply of large adhesive bandages. She placed one over the stitches, thinking of Scott's gentle touch when he'd patched her up in the school break room. The intern who'd given her the stitches had commented on the baking soda paste, saying, "That was smart. Made my job easier."

She dug through her suitcase until she'd sorted out her best pair of panties and her newest bra, which was still a few years old, but hadn't yet suffered the wear and tear of her other undergarments. She dressed in her most comfortable jeans and a stretchy black t-shirt she barely managed to drag over her quills.

She was sitting on the couch numbly watching holovision and eating sunflower seeds when the doorbell rang. It was the courier Shasta Fox told her to expect. Bryn showed him her ID, signed his holopad and accepted the envelope. With check in hand, she sat back down on the couch.

Being home gave her a disconcerting feeling of normalcy. Her body sank comfortably into her spot on the couch, the place where she'd done her homework, read trashy novels, and watched her favorite shows growing up. She should be rushing to the bank to deposit the check and making arrangements to move out, but all she wanted to do was sit and absorb the last vestiges of home. Once she left, she couldn't imagine the circumstances that might bring her back.

The talk show on the holo wrapped up and the local news came on. Bryn watched to see if there was any mention of Scott still being on the loose, but there wasn't. There was a report about a young woman outside of Poughkeepsie who authorities believe went on a jealous rampage and shot her boyfriend and his three friends with a dart gun before accidently shooting herself. Bryn started to laugh until the name of the boyfriend was released: Kareem Williams.

"Mr. Williams and his friends refused to press charges and refused to cooperate with police by releasing security tapes of the attack," the reporter said.

There was no mention of a panda, which told her Scott had removed it from the premises before police arrived. She felt ambivalent about the news. On the one hand, it meant Scott was probably back in Lupus' good graces and thus safe from retribution. On the other hand, the panda was now back in Fournier's clutches.

She thought about what Scott said, "What makes a panda different from any other animal?" She'd been quick to attribute a more acceptable meaning to his words, but what if he really didn't care? He'd denied being a cop and the more she thought about it, the more she realized how foolish she'd been to ever think he was. Both Carla and Dr. Finnegan suggested she was suffering from Stockholm syndrome. It occurred to her that she didn't really understand what that meant, so she decided to look it up.

She went into the spare room, with plastic storage bins stacked on one side and her father's desk and old computer setup on the other. He was not a tidy person. There were loose papers and sticky notes everywhere and the gloomy space smelled a bit like a locker room.

Once she got online, she read an article on Stockholm syndrome and had to admit she fit the criteria. Kidnap victims misinterpret a lack of abuse as kindness and become attached to their captor. Scott hadn't abused her, but now that she saw his behavior in a different light, she realized he'd never been kind, either. He'd seemed indifferent the majority of the time. He was doing a job, just like with the panda. The only emotion he'd shown was when he'd kissed her…or maybe that, too, was her own feelings reflected onto him.

She rubbed her eyes and sighed, wishing she could turn those feelings off.

The holophone rang and she went into the kitchen to squint at the unfamiliar holo ID. It was a little white mouse sitting on its haunches nibbling on something. Carla.

Bryn sat in front of the hololens and pressed the answer button.

"Bryn!" Carla practically shouted. "I'm so glad you're okay!"

The background of the holo seemed to be moving, so Bryn asked, "Are you mobile?"

"Yes! I'm on the bus. Phaco told me that awful Padme took you to the loony bin. I went to set them straight about your father, but they said you'd been released, and he'd been arrested. Huzzah!"

Bryn smiled, but it must not have been convincing because Carla said, "Oh, honey, I know it's been a crappy few days, but things will get better now. You can come stay with me for reals this time!"

Bryn looked around the empty kitchen, seeing only ghostly memories from the past. "I'd like that."

"Well, today's my day off, so there's no time like the present. Oh, wait, I need to hit the grocery store first so I can offer you more than Pop Tarts and beer, so come over any time after two, okay?"

"Sounds great. I'll see you this afternoon."

Bryn puttered around the house, looking for anything else she might want to take with her now that she wasn't packing stealthily in the middle of the night. She went back into her father's office to shut off his computer and found herself pulling up a search engine. She typed in her name and opened the most recent news article. She skimmed it, but it looked like a rehash of old news. There was no mention of her father's arrest, but that was sure to come. She wondered if the news vans would swarm the house again. The thought made her cringe, and she decided to leave right then. She reached out to shut down the computer, but something caught her eye and she stopped with her hand extended.

Halfway down the article, one sentence leapt out at her. "Two of the kidnappers, Scott Harding and Padme Lango…" she didn't even read the rest. Her eyes were frozen on Scott's last name.

An unrestrained grin formed on her face. "I knew it," she said.

Chapter Forty-four

Scott woke slowly and wondered why it felt like he had a mouthful of cotton. He was lying on a narrow hospital bed, fully clothed. Memory returned: he was in Dr. Fournier's secret facility, and it had been right under him the whole time. A turn of the head showed a sealed water bottle on the table next to him. He reached for it; even if he wasn't dying of thirst, hydration was important to flush out the residual effects of the drug.

He sat up and downed the entire bottle. Dizziness hit him in waves every time he moved, but he thought it might have more to do with the fact that he hadn't eaten since he'd grabbed a quick burrito at Bluto's the afternoon before.

The room he was in was nothing like the exam rooms in the Warehouse. Those were deceptively run-down, with dirty walls and beat-up equipment. Here, all looked sterile and hospital-like. There was no evidence that this place had once been a parking garage. The walls were painted grey and the ceiling was composed of white drop panels. The floor was polished linoleum. A tiny camera dome in the corner monitored his every move. Within minutes, the door opened.

He was halfway expecting nurse Vonda or Nancy, but it was Padme.

"Good morning." She came close to the bed as he swung his legs off the side. Her dark brown eyes gazed so steadily into his it unnerved him.

"How's Lupus?" he asked.

"Stable. The bullet missed any organs."

"Why'd you dart me?" As if he didn't know.

Padme stepped back, but she was still watching him closely. Was she trying to communicate something? He recognized the make of the camera in the corner; it would have a sensitive microphone with voice recognition software. Even a whisper would be picked up and analyzed. Scott took Padme's demeanor as another warning; probably, as she'd suggested often enough in the past, he still wasn't fully trusted.

"Dr. Fournier would like to speak with you," she said. "Come with me."

Scott slid off the bed and stood unsteadily. Padme offered him her arm. It was the first time she'd voluntarily allowed him to touch her, not that he'd ever tried. He needed the support, though, so he took it, grabbing her thin upper arm and trying not to lean too heavily on it as they walked out into a dimly lit, wide hallway. They took turn after turn, passing several sets of double doors like you'd see in a hospital. Scott felt like he was in a rat maze, a cold, underground warren.

"Where are we?" he asked, without expecting an answer.

"This is the Clinic."

He nodded. The place was bigger than he'd expected, but quiet. They saw no one on their trek. He wondered how Fournier got power, water, sewer and ventilation down here.

"It's huge," he commented.

Padme pulled him along. They finally passed someone, a man in doctor's scrubs. Scott thought he recognized him as one of the doctors who'd worked on Lupus.

"When I arrived," Padme said. "It looked nothing like this."

"How does he keep it secret?" Scott tried to sound only mildly curious.

"Loyalty."

There'd been builders down here, there would be doctors and nurses that came and went. Loyalty on such a scale seemed inconceivable, but it had to exist, because this place existed and after years of looking, the XIA hadn't a clue where to find it. Scott didn't have a chance to ask Padme what she meant by 'loyalty,' though, because they'd arrived at a wooden door, different from all the others, heavier and more official-looking. She knocked. Scott noted the presence of another security camera.

The door clicked and Padme opened it. Scott was feeling steadier, so he let go of her arm as they entered. The room wasn't large, but it was carpeted, and the lighting was brighter. A glass-topped desk guarded another door and sitting at the desk was a girl, maybe in her early to mid-teens. Scott stopped and stared. It wasn't her xenografts, fans of small, grey and white patterned feathers where her eyebrows should be that stopped him, but her face. She looked exactly like his sister May—if May had lived long enough to reach adolescence.

Padme placed a hand on his arm, as if in warning. "This is Nicola."

Pretty, blonde-haired Nicola stood. She smiled and said, "He's busy so it will be a few minutes. Are you hungry?"

Nicola's smile, so like his sister's, broke through Scott's carefully concocted impassivity—tears stung his eyes. He knew who she was, or rather, what she was. To hide his reaction, he ducked his head and said, "Starving."

Nicola walked to a paneled cabinet and opened it. Inside was a concealed refrigerator. By the time she brought him a plastic-wrapped sandwich and a soda, he'd gotten control of himself.

"Thanks." He sat with Padme on a leather couch and devoured the sandwich in less than five minutes, all the while trying not to drop crumbs on the pristine rug. The wait for Dr. Fournier stretched into half an hour before Nicola said, "He's ready for you."

Padme jumped up and smoothed her hands down the front of her shirt, movements jerky. Scott had never seen her nervous before, but it made sense that she was now. Fournier had control over Lupus, who had control over her.

He had no idea what to expect when he walked through the other door. He recognized the man sitting behind a typical administrator's desk from photographs, although the older Fournier's face had deeper lines around his eyes and his light brown hair was thinning on top. Fournier came around the desk, held out his hand and said, "Cougar. It's good to see you."

Scott had never actually met him since he'd been unconscious before, during and after his surgery. He shook Fournier's hand and then stood there as the doctor examined his fingers, squeezing each one to force the claw out. "Looks great. Having any problems?"

"No, sir."

"Excellent. Thank you for recovering the panda." He looked at Padme. "Any word on how they knew?"

"None, but it's unlikely to have come from our end."

Fournier shook his head. "Jacques swears it wasn't his people, but he's been clumsy in the past. Ah, well. Did you give Cougar the tour?"

Padme said, "No."

"Well, I think he's earned it." Fournier waved towards the door and Scott took that as a dismissal. He followed Padme back out to the reception area. Nicola smiled May's smile again and he tried to return it, tried to keep in mind the circumstances that brought the girl into the world weren't her fault. Just like they hadn't been May's.

Padme led him into the main hallway, and he found that Fournier had followed behind them. For the next twenty minutes, they toured the floor with Padme as their guide. It was much like what Scott was led to expect it would be, essentially a combination hospital and research facility, only perhaps on a larger scale than the XIA suspected. They had all the equipment on hand that you'd see in a regular hospital, including the newest non-rad body imager.

Scott met over a dozen personnel: scientists, doctors, nurses, bioengineers and technicians, none of whom seemed normal. They all had xenografts or alterations; some of them were twitchy, like they were on drugs or had a neurological deficit, and one refused to make eye contact or shake his hand. Most were abrupt and moved quickly on, like they didn't want to stand in Fournier's presence any longer than need be.

The floor space was divided into operating rooms, recovery rooms, various storage rooms, and laboratories. Well before they reached the section housing the bioengineered animals, Scott heard and smelled it. He wore his neutral face as they walked past cage after cage of furry and feathered creatures, most balled up in slumber, but some of them bawling or squawking for attention. There was an entire wall of glass cages filled with mice, rats, snakes, lizards and baby alligators and crocodiles. Padme led them past a room with a disturbing sign over the door that read, 'Vivisection.'

"The pigs and most larger animals are kept off-site," she said.

Scott didn't see the panda, and Fournier, as if he'd read his mind, said, "The panda has her own special accommodations through that door, but we won't disturb her after what she's been through. She wasn't bioengineered, so she's not a compatible donor, but her children and hopefully clones, will be. The client is a very powerful Chinese drug lord who is anxious to desecrate one of his country's national emblems."

Scott was relieved when they left the animal rooms behind. Next, Padme showed him the staff living quarters, small rooms with bunk beds that looked like they belonged on a submarine. Again, Fournier anticipated his questions.

"We have staff from all over the world," he said. "They understand the need for discretion, so are content to live on site. As incentive, they are paid extremely well. And they do get out on a regular rotation, but only a few know the Clinic's true location. Many of them are wanted for criminal offenses, so it's a mutually beneficial arrangement. The Clinic is a secure facility that allows them the leeway they desire to conduct experiments that their governments, and ours, have deemed…unacceptable. We are making huge strides in many areas. It's unfortunate that none of us will ever be published in the medical journals…unless the laws change."

They arrived at a heavy-duty door on the far side of the floor from Fournier's office. "I must go," Fournier said. "Padme will show you the control center."

Scott shook his proffered hand again. When Fournier was gone, Padme held her palm under a holobeam security scanner and the door to the control center clicked. He followed her into a room that looked like something out of NASA mission control only on a much smaller scale. There was one office chair, and Padme sat on it.

"We are safe to talk here," she said. "This is my territory and there are no bugs."

"So, the rest of the Clinic…"

"Is heavily monitored, as is the Warehouse. The slightest word or gesture out of place is compiled in a report that goes directly to Fournier every day. The loyalty I spoke of isn't voluntary."

Scott looked around. "This is some impressive equipment."

"It is state-of-the-art. One of the engineers you met invented the grease you enjoy playing with. Another is an autistic savant who worked with me to develop Fournier's nanoneuron program."

Scott had been keenly interested in everything he'd seen and heard thus far, but now he felt a curl of excitement in his gut. "Oh, yeah?"

"Yes. Our nanoneurons are not like the ones used elsewhere. Most function simply as the intermediary between the brain and the xenotransplant. Ours are a little more complicated."

Scott reached out to touch the controls on a holo projector, pretending to be listening with half an ear. Padme slapped his hand away and said, "Pay attention. This is important."

She already had his full attention, but now he looked at her so she'd know it. Her eyes had that intensity he'd been seeing all afternoon and she had streaks of pink high on her cheekbones. She said this was her territory. All the clues he'd picked up about her technical abilities led here.

She said, "You've probably been told that nanoneurons use the brain's electrical activity as a power source, similar to the microtransmitters I told you about, the ones that use gastric-acid as a battery. Like the microtransmitters, our nanoneurons use cell towers, but instead of sending signals to the towers, they receive them. In this way, we can change the programming at any time."

"I don't get it. Why change the programming? It's pretty specific to each person's xenoalteration, right?" He flexed the fingers on his left hand, extending his claws.

Padme pressed her lips together. "The cerebellum, which as you know controls motor function, is the only structure in the brain thus far that accepts nanoneuronal implants. No one has ever been able to influence higher functioning. But the cerebellum has other functions…cognitive functions."

Scott struggled to understand her meaning. "And—you can affect those?"

"To some extent. Nanoneurons are infinitesimally small, therefore they are limited as to how much programming they will accept."

Scott wished there was another chair for him to collapse into. As unbelievable as it was, Padme was talking about mind control. "What cognitive functions are you referring to?"

"It's how Fournier keeps his people loyal," she said. "We can manipulate the two most basic emotions housed in the cerebellum: pleasure and fear."

She turned to her holo keypad and typed something. Then she stood, grasped his shoulders and guided him to her chair. He obliged her by sitting, but as soon as he did, she shocked him by climbing onto his lap and straddling him. He said, "No," and his hands closed around her waist to lift her away, but she reached out and tapped a holo key.

He barely had time to register that she'd activated something in his brain before she kissed him, and his body responded against his will with a rush of desire.

Chapter Forty-five

Just as Bryn was pulling out of the garage, a black sedan parked itself at the end of the driveway, effectively blocking her from leaving. Agent Yang got out and strode up the walk. Bryn rolled down her window.

"I won't delay you for long," Yang said. "Just need to serve this warrant. We have to go through your father's things."

Bryn took the folded document and tossed it onto the dash. "Great. Feel free. Can I leave now?"

Yang waved to the driver of the sedan, who backed up. Bryn pulled out and headed straight for the bank, where she deposited the check. The funds wouldn't be available right away, but she'd planned for that by doing something unprecedented—taking her father's emergency credit card from its hiding place in his desk drawer.

She drove to the mall and bought four bra and panty sets, a hip-length leather jacket, a pair of low-heeled boots, sunglasses, and a great bomber hat that covered most of her quills. When she walked into the food court, she felt like a dark Amelia Earhart. She bought a freshly baked cinnamon bun, but after a couple of bites the gooey, overly sweet confection turned her stomach. She closed the box; maybe Carla would eat it.

Summer was ending and families crawled the mall searching for school clothes. Everything around her was normal, and yet she felt like she was on an alien planet. She halfway expected to run into one of her friends and thought about walking over to the public holophone by the information desk to call Maria. She decided against it; it would take too much energy to answer all the questions her best friend was sure to ask.

On the way out, she stopped by her holoprovider's booth to pay her past due bill and found herself exchanging her basic phone for a state-of-the-art holophonepad and full service Internet. Once her new holophone was up and working again, she found she had over two thousand texts and emails. She read the first ten or so before concluding that most of them were from strangers who'd seen her story on the news and somehow gotten her email and text information. She deleted them all.

When she got to the apartment complex, Carla came downstairs and showed her where to park.

"I know this place looks iffy," Carla said as she helped Bryn haul her suitcases and bags from the mall up three flights of stairs, "but there's a pretty aggressive neighborhood watch."

She unlocked her apartment door, and as they walked into the living room, asked, "By the way, do you have my gun?"

"No," Bryn replied, dropping the bag with her new lingerie on the couch and setting her suitcase upright next to it. "Scott took it."

"That's good to know," said a male voice from behind her.

Bryn spun around. So much for the neighborhood watch. Kareem stood in the doorway to Carla's bedroom. He wasn't holding a gun himself, but she suspected he had one on him. He looked at Carla. "Shut the door."

Carla slowly complied. "Who are you?"

"Bryn knows," he said. "I'm a very ticked off guy who's got some questions."

"I don't know where the panda is," Bryn said.

"Oh, I think you do." Kareem sauntered further into the room.

"How did you know I was here?" Bryn asked.

"Same way I knew the panda was coming in at Coney Island. Got an anonymous call."

That didn't make sense. Bryn hadn't told anyone where she was going. "I really don't know anything. Couldn't you tell I was practically a bystander? I had no idea we were even bringing a panda to shore. I thought it was drugs or something."

Carla had moved to stand next to her. "Since you've broken into my home," she said. "I think introductions are in order."

"This is Kareem Williams," Bryn said. "Commander of the ARA."

"Well, Mr. Williams, can I get you something to drink?" Carla made a move for the kitchen, but Kareem held up a hand.

"That's very hospitable of you, but I'd rather you stay where I can see you." He turned to Bryn. "Whoever left that message was right about the panda in the first place, so it's logical to assume they must be right about you knowing where it is now."

"I don't. I swear. Do you still have the message? Can I hear it?"

Kareem pulled out his holophone and tapped. A generic text-to-speech robotic male voice said, "If you want the panda back, you can find Bryn Vega at her godmother's house in Brooklyn at 1602 Saint Martindale Drive, Apartment 304."

"Godmother?" Bryn asked, turning to Carla.

"Well, yeah, of course I'm your godmother." She shrugged. "Don't you remember?"

Bryn shook her head; it had been so long ago. "How did the caller know, when I didn't even know?"

A look of dawning realization swept over Carla's face. "I told Lupus and Padme. I had no choice, Honey. I spilled the beans about everything that happened. About you coming to see me, about what your father did, about Cougar helping us escape from Nosferatu. Lupus was furious about the cops crawling all over the place."

"Yeah, but Lupus wouldn't have sent that message," Bryn said, "so it had to have been Padme. But how did she know I'd be here? She's the one that took me to the psychiatric center."

Carla snorted. "She knew they wouldn't hold you after the truth came out."

"None of this makes sense!" Bryn exclaimed. "Why sic Kareem on me?" She looked at him and said, "No offense."

"None taken." Kareem had sat on the arm of the couch and was listening intently as Bryn tried to figure out what was going on. "Maybe whoever called me," he said, "doesn't know that you and I are acquainted. Maybe they assumed I'd shoot first and ask questions later."

"What I don't get," Carla said, "is why Padme would call the ARA to steal the panda in the first place."

Bryn stared at Carla, thoughts spinning. Why had Padme done it? Bryn sat on the couch and dropped her face in her hands, rubbing her temples and wishing Scott was here. Chances were he'd know what the Pakistani girl was up to. But Bryn had overheard Shasta Fox say Scott was 'off the grid,' which she assumed meant the XIA couldn't contact him.

"I don't care why this Padme tipped me off," Kareem said. "And I believe you when you say you don't know where the panda is, because I don't see why they'd tell you something like that. I do think you know where I can find the sons-of-bitches who hit us last night, though. Security tapes were too grainy to make anyone out, but we got a description of one of them; my girlfriend shot him."

For a brief, panicked moment, Bryn thought he meant Scott. But Kareem scowled and said, "He had a wolf face."

Lupus had been shot. Bryn met Carla's eyes, pleading. "Scott wouldn't take him to a hospital, right?"

"Right," Carla said cautiously.

"What if Scott's in danger?" Bryn asked. "What if Padme is setting him up for something?"

"Oh, no," Carla said, throwing her hands in the air. "They'll kill me if I tell you where the clinic is."

Kareem had been so polite and mild thus far that it surprised Bryn when he pulled a gun from his waistband.

He said, "And I'll kill you if you don't."

Chapter Forty-six

The force of Padme's kiss pushed Scott's head against the back of the office chair. Her cow ears swung forward and brushed his cheeks. He tried to stop her, but the nanoneuron program was doing one hell of a job stimulating his brain into thinking he really, really enjoyed what she was doing. She pulled away briefly to yank her shirt over her head then grabbed his hands and placed them on her back, saying in a thick voice, "Scratch me."

Scott found himself obeying—his claws came out and he started to rake them down her exposed flesh—but an image intruded into his mind; that of Lupus hurting her that day on the couch.

He desperately did not want the pleasure to stop, but knew if it didn't, he'd be lost, so he did what he always did when a program was doing something he didn't want—reached out and hit the escape button on the holo keypad. Immediately the intensity lessened.

"No!" Padme tried to get to the keypad, but he lifted her up, squirming and kicking, and set her down a few feet away. He blocked her way as she stood there with her small chest rising and falling under a plain white sports bra.

"You bastard," she said, hands clenched in fury at her sides.

Scott did some very fast thinking. She was angry, but he could see that she was hurt, too. He took half a heartbeat's time to flagellate himself for not having picked up on it before. She'd hidden her regard pretty well, though, so the blame wasn't all on him. If he rejected her outright, there was no telling what the repercussions would be. All she had to do was lie and tell Lupus he'd jumped her, and Scott would join his predecessors in the river. He chose his line of attack carefully.

"I'm all for getting close to you, Padme, but do not mess with my brain."

The fury evaporated, and he saw a look of tentative hope cross her face. She bit her lip. "I'm sorry."

He picked up her shirt and handed it to her. She held it wadded up against her chest and said, "I guess I—I forgot how normal people do it."

He knew she didn't want his pity, but he had to keep her talking, get her mind off seducing him or he'd have to follow through. And he didn't want to.

"What happened just then, was that my nanoneurons?" he asked.

She gave him a wan smile and pulled her shirt back on.

He looked at her monitor. "So the programming can make someone feel pleasure out of nowhere?"

"Or fear."

"Is that what happened to Abel?" He was taking a chance bringing Abel's death up. He had inside knowledge from Shasta that Abel died from an apparently natural death. If Fournier had activated Abel's nanoneuron programming to flood him with fear, had that been what triggered the heart attack?

"Yes. Abel knew too much and since he hadn't gone through Fournier's loyalty conditioning, he was a liability."

"Loyalty conditioning?"

She nodded. "Pavlov rang a bell every time he fed his dogs. Eventually they drooled at the sound of the bell alone. Fournier induces pleasure or fear in a subject in tandem with a stimulus. Eventually, the stimulus itself begins to produce the pleasure or fear."

He thought about what she'd done to him and suddenly had no doubt that if he hadn't stopped her, he'd be well on his way to drooling every time she wanted him to ring her bell.

"As mind control goes, it's obviously not practical," she said. "He chooses his subjects carefully because it takes some time to train them."

Scott frowned. "Are you 'trained?'"

"No. If I were, I'd be debilitated with fear just for telling you this."

"Am I scheduled to undergo conditioning?"

Her face gave it away and he said, "So you tell all the subjects what's going to happen before you brainwash them?"

A shuddering sigh escaped her. "You're different. I care for you. I don't want to see you become like Lupus. He was Fournier's first subject. It took weeks to break him. He used to be a decent guy. Now his nanoneurons reward him every time he's cruel."

She'd once described Scott as a decent guy.

"And I'm the one responsible," she continued, "not just because of the program I helped create, but because I have this." She held her arms out to indicate the control room. "I can find out anything about anyone."

"Yeah, I was pretty impressed with the stuff you dug up on the ARA."

"I'm the one who exposed Lupus' true identity. He did not choose to wear that wolf face. I protested and Fournier gave me to him. Made him enjoy hurting me."

Lupus' true identity? With blinding insight he realized there was only one thing she could mean by that. Lupus was one of the XIA agents who'd gone undercover and disappeared without a trace.

She had that look in her eye again and before she even said it, he knew what she'd been trying to tell him all along.

"I know who you are, Scott Harding."

Chapter Forty-seven

For the second time in her life, and all within a few short months, Bryn had been kidnapped. After everything she'd been through, she found it strangely difficult to work up the proper amount of fear. She didn't doubt that Kareem was deadly serious about getting Carla to tell him where Fournier's secret facility was located. The weird thing was, he and Bryn had the same goal.

Kareem had taken them to a house not far from Carla's apartment complex. It was a one-story rambler with a stained shag carpet that smelled like dog. She knew because Kareem had taped her up; eyes, mouth, feet, and hands behind her back and left her lying on the rug facedown while he took Carla into a separate room to 'have a little chat.'

After a while, she heard footsteps and voices. Other people were arriving, and from the sound of it, there were quite a few of them. She caught snippets of conversation that told her the ARA was gearing up for some hard retribution. Then she heard the unmistakable sound of a woman's muffled screams.

Suddenly the fear found her. She'd been convinced Kareem was incapable of hurting her or Carla, but she'd been wrong.

Footsteps again; someone approached and grabbed a handful of her new leather jacket, hauling her to a kneeling position. The tape over her eyes was ripped painfully away. The man in front of her wasn't Kareem. This man was white, older, with thin lips and a piggish nose. He had purple surgical gloves on his hands, covered in blood. He held something small and red and floppy up in front of her face and said, "Recognize this?"

It was Carla's xenograft, the mouse. Tears leaked out of Bryn's eyes.

"I see that you do," the man said. He yanked the bomber cap from her head and said, "You're next if she doesn't talk."

He shoved her back down on the carpet and she saw him stalk through the dining area. With the tape gone, she could see the ARA soldiers now. They came in and out of a door that looked like it led to the garage. She couldn't tell how many there were because from her vantage-point on the ground, they all looked alike. They wore mostly black, with black bullet-proof vests—just like the three who'd helped Kareem take the panda.

Occasionally, she heard raised voices from the back room. A man's voice, deep and threatening, and Carla's, shrill and scared. Bryn knew the chances of escape were nonexistent, but she tried to loosen the duct tape on her wrists anyway. Kareem had taken her new holophone out of her pocket. He knew Bryn didn't know where Fournier was, but once they decided Carla wasn't going to tell, they'd start in on Bryn to see if that would induce Carla to talk. It was only a matter of time. Bryn had so desperately wanted her quills to be gone but having them forcibly torn from her head was not the way she'd imagined it would happen.

She started rehearsing her pleas for mercy in her head. She'd talk about everything that had happened to her, reminding Kareem that she had never asked for the quills in the first place. She'd tell him all she'd learned about the Warehouse, about the people there. She'd tell him about Coney Island and Bluto's and the tunnel…

The tunnel. A little while ago Carla had said Lupus wasn't happy about the cops crawling all over the place, but they hadn't been at Bluto's. The crime scene tape had been on the building Nosferatu had been squatting in, the one at the other end of Bluto's tunnel. But Carla had said Fournier put escape tunnels in all his buildings. Bryn tried to remember what else she'd said. First, she told Bryn her boyfriend Bluto owned the restaurant. Yes, she definitely said he'd put all his money into buying it, so when she'd mentioned Fournier's tunnels, she had to have been talking about the building adjacent to Bluto's. Did Fournier own it? If he did, the XIA, and Scott, would know about it. Unless he owned it under a different name or maybe a dummy corporation. And whatever name was on the deed of that building might also be on Fournier's other buildings.

Kareem came into the room and knelt down next to her. His dark skin was ashen. Softly, he said, "My colleague is almost done in there. Your godmother's not going to talk, but he thinks she'll break once he starts in on you. To be honest, Bryn, this is turning my stomach. I'm sorry. If it weren't so important…we're not going to kill you, though, I promise."

He started to get up, but she rolled to her back and tried to talk through the tape. For a second, she thought he was going to ignore her, but he stopped and bent down again. Once he gently peeled the tape away, she poured out her theory. He seemed relieved at being presented with an option other than torturing her.

He took her holophone from his pocket. "Alright. What's the building's address?"

Bryn had no idea. "Go to Holomaps." It was a comprehensive national map service that showed every road and structure in the US, where a person could find out who owned almost anything, in addition to finding schematics for most existing buildings. "Check Bluto's on Coney Island. It's the abandoned building directly behind it."

After a minute or so, he said, "This one?" He held the holophone out and she said, "Yes."

"Says it's owned by, huh, you may be onto something, 'Best Medical Services, Corp.' Like XBestia, only not as obvious."

Bryn closed her eyes in relief. "Can you cross-reference it?"

"Yeah, it's a link." He tapped at her holophone and waited. If her hands weren't duct-taped together, she would have crossed her fingers.

He let out short whistle. "The company owns real estate all over New York, but even if it is Fournier, there's no way to tell which building might be the clinic."

Tears started in her eyes. "Just—you can just—check each place out..."

He shook his head. "No, Bryn. If you haven't noticed, we're at war. I sent out a call to arms to every ARA member. We can't go traipsing all over the city with the kind of firepower we're bringing down on that son-of-a-bitch. We need to know exactly where he is, and before he butchers that poor panda. We should have gone public with it when we had the chance. This is our only opportunity to fix it. If we take Fournier down, we'll be heroes."

"Heroes don't torture innocent women."

"They do if there's enough at stake. Sacrifice for the greater good."

A hiccupping sob escaped her. "You sound like my father."

"Your father's a good man."

"My father's in jail."

Kareem straightened up. The man in the surgical gloves came back into the room. He shook his head at Kareem and then his unfeeling eyes dropped to Bryn. Kareem lifted her and carried her into the room with Carla. The only furniture was two chairs and a folding tray table with a toolbox on it. Bryn expected Carla to be battered and bloody, but other than a tear-streaked face and messy hair, she looked fine. They must have cleaned her up, bandaged the wound left from removing her xenograft, been nice to her after the brutality. Bryn knew that strategy from reading up on Stockholm syndrome.

Kareem set Bryn down into a chair facing the chair Carla was sitting in. There was plenty of room between them for the torturer to get to Bryn and still give Carla a good view.

"Please, don't," Carla said, voice weak and cracking. "I told you everything I know."

"At your apartment, you said you knew where Fournier was," Kareem said.

"I lied. All I know is what Bluto told me. He did some work for Fournier—they converted an underground parking garage. That's where the clinic is. It's all I know. Punish me for lying, but please don't hurt her."

"Kareem, please," Bryn said. "Look at the Best Medical Services building schematics on my holophone. Which ones have parking garages?"

Kareem hesitated. The man with the surgical gloves eyed her quills and pulled a pair of pliers out of the toolbox.

Bryn whispered, "Please."

He was clearly reluctant, but he took her holophone out of his pocket and tapped at it. Long, drawn out minutes later, he said slowly, "There's only one building with an underground parking structure. It's a huge building, but the schematic shows the parking garage is—strangely small." To Carla, he said, "This Bluto told you they converted it?"

Carla nodded. "Said it took a long time, years, and there was a lot of work involved. They were real careful, it was totally secret. They have a hacker that steals power and water from neighboring buildings somehow. Bluto said…it was right under everyone's noses."

"A hacker that could alter a Holomap schematic?" A vengeful smile stole over Kareem's face. He held the holophone out for Bryn to see. "You know where this is?"

Bryn looked at the map and suddenly everything made sense. "The Warehouse," she said. "Right under everyone's noses."

Chapter Forty-eight

Just in case Scott misunderstood what Padme meant when she said she knew who he was, he asked, "Who am I?"

"You're the youngest ever XIA agent."

"How long have you known?"

She laughed a little. "Not long."

"What gave me away?"

"Besides the fact that you're so damned nice? When we escaped from jail. The choreography was good: I was convinced when the guard came in and chose to taze Barney instead of you. Other than the fact that it was too easy, I wouldn't have suspected anything, except I saw the handcuff key under the conference room table.

"Even then, I wasn't sure," she said. "It could have been a key to something else. Maybe you really did pick the lock with your claw. But then the photos in the media made me suspicious; the ones that vaguely resembled us. I thought, what better way to aid our escape than to switch the mug shots so we wouldn't be hindered by public recognition? It seemed unlikely the XIA would be so inept.

"I'd already checked your background, but after the escape I dug deeper. I found out you had a sister who died. As soon as I saw her picture, I recognized her. It was a simple matter to hack into the adoption database and verify where she'd come from."

It was ironic that the reason he'd joined the XIA would be his downfall.

As far as the XIA knew, his sister May had been Fournier's first, and only, successful attempt at cloning a human. When investigators busted him, they found more than just a grisly collection of body parts in his apartment. They found a baby girl with no birth records who was not Fournier's biological child. After Fournier skipped bail and disappeared, they put her in the system for adoption by parents who would never know what she was. When May was five years old, she was diagnosed with kidney cancer. Wilm's tumor, stage three when they found it. On the night the XIA recruited Scott in that San Diego jail, they told him about gene imprinting errors and how the tumor was a direct result of Fournier's carelessness during the cloning process.

Nicola, the girl in Fournier's reception area, was obviously a clone made from the same genetic material that produced May. Nicholas Fournier had named the girl after himself, so it stood to reason he'd raised her as his daughter. Scott wondered how normal a life the girl had. Did she go to school, did she have friends, or had Fournier kept her here underground, on display for his amusement like all his other trophies?

"What's Lupus' real name?" he asked.

"Eduardo Quinones."

The first agent to have gone in. "What happened to the other agent?"

"Lupus killed him."

"Jesus. So I take it you haven't told Lupus about me?"

"Obviously not. I tried to keep you from getting this far. I'm the one who tipped off the ARA about the panda. I figured if you botched that job, Lupus wouldn't vouch for you, but then you went and saved his worthless life and recovered the panda. So now, the only way to keep you from becoming a monster like Lupus is to turn myself in."

Scott hadn't known where Padme's string of confessions was going, but he didn't expect her to sacrifice herself. She'd always seemed so self-sufficient, so standoffish. He'd suspected she didn't like 'belonging' to Lupus, but he never guessed the truth. How could he?

As much as he didn't want to encourage her affection for him, at this juncture it was the logical thing to do. She may have said she wanted to turn herself in, but they were still standing in the heart of Fournier's territory. He needed to keep her believing he had feelings for her.

He held out his hand and she rushed forward into his arms, letting out a little cry of relief. The hug was brief; a chime sounded from her holocomputer and she pulled away. "I need to check that. It's the Warehouse alarm system. Kareem Williams is pretty upset about last night's raid. I intercepted an email from him to his followers. He's using the panda as an excuse to fire them up against us."

She tapped her holo keyboard and the screen split into six views from cameras set up in what Scott recognized as areas in and around the Warehouse.

"Oh, no," Padme murmured.

There was no sound, but four of the views on screen showed chaos: xenos running from armed gunmen amid smoke and fire. Scott looked for telltale identification on the back of the invaders' vests, but there was nothing to indicate these were FBI, DEA or XIA agents.

Lupus' head appeared on the small monitor over the control room door and his voice blasted over the loudspeaker, "What the hell's going on outside?"

Padme buzzed him in. The sound of the alarm echoed in from the hallway; it was ringing throughout the facility. Lupus was fully dressed and other than the sling on his arm, the only thing to indicate he wasn't hale and hearty were the bleary red eyes blazing out of his wolf face.

Padme made room so Lupus could see the monitors. "You shouldn't be up."

"I'm supposed to sleep through that? Who are they?"

"ARA," Padme said. "Retribution for the panda."

The fifth view on the monitor was the parking garage entrance. An extended cab truck filled with soldiers pulled up some distance away. One of the men ran up and stuck a dark, oblong object the size of a baseball onto the security gate before hightailing it back to the truck.

"What is that?" Padme asked.

"Sticky breach bomb," Scott said.

A flash on the monitor was accompanied by a dull concussive thump felt in the control room. Dust trickled down from the ceiling. The truck crashed through the damaged security gate.

"Maybe they just don't know what's behind the gate," Padme suggested.

They watched that all-important sixth view on the holo monitor: that of the empty parking garage itself. If the ARA soldiers were just out to destroy everything in the warehouse, they'd see the empty garage and turn back around.

The truck appeared onscreen and stopped at the bottom of the ramp trailing smoke from the explosion behind it.

Padme laced her fingers together tightly and held her knuckles up to her mouth. "Do they know we're here?"

A man jumped out of the truck and stuck another bomb on the elevator doors.

"They know," Lupus growled. He looked at Scott. "Let's go."

Chapter Forty-nine

Kareem had brought Bryn along, "Just in case we need to negotiate a trade." She didn't think she'd be worth much if it came to that but wasn't about to point that out to him. The less valuable she was in his eyes, the more expendable.

She sat in the back seat of Kareem's white truck, jammed in between two men bristling with weaponry. Her quills bristled, too, and the men didn't conceal their disgust. "I'd rather chop my own head off than look like that," said one.

"You trying to be some kinda Medusa or something?" asked the other. Bryn hunched her shoulders and pressed her knees together to make herself as small as possible.

After they drove through the damaged security gate and entered the parking garage, one of the men plugged his nose. "Ugh, what is that smell? Is that you?" He looked at Bryn. Kareem, from the driver's seat, said, "Shut it!"

His lieutenant, the man in the passenger seat, jumped out and attached another bomb to the elevator doors. The blast filled the parking garage with smoke. Kareem and his men waited for it to dissipate a little before cautiously getting out of the truck. "Bring the girl," Kareem said.

The man who'd called her Medusa grabbed her arm and hauled her out of the truck without waiting for her to get her feet under her. She stumbled along behind until he jerked her arm and pushed her ahead of him as a human shield. If anyone came out of the elevator firing, she'd be the first to go down.

The men flattened themselves against the concrete wall. One of them saw a security camera and shot at it. His bullets ricocheted around the parking garage. "Leave it!" Kareem shouted.

He waved to the man holding Bryn's arm, who shoved her forward. "What do you see?" he asked. The elevator was big, the kind that hauled freight or could hold more than one stretcher in a hospital. The doors on the parking garage side were blown inward, and she flinched as she leaned over to look inside, expecting a hail of bullets, but the doors on the far side of the elevator were intact. She heard sirens and wasn't sure if it was coming from above them and outside, or from beyond the barrier of the elevator doors.

"It didn't go all the way through," she said.

Kareem's lieutenant took a quick look to verify. He waved everyone back as he readied another one of the little bombs and ran into the elevator and out again. Without the protection afforded by the truck, the blast was deafening. Bryn threw her hands over her ears instinctively and was rewarded with several pricks from her quills. She coughed as acrid smoke burned her nasal passages and lungs, but it cleared much more quickly this time, sucked into the void beyond the elevator.

The brave ARA soldiers pushed her forward again. The sound of the sirens was coming from within. She peeked and saw an empty corridor, but the interior of the elevator had been badly damaged. The floor had buckled and there was a yawning hole that would prevent anyone from walking through to the far side. She told Kareem what she saw and again the lieutenant verified it.

Bryn heard more sirens, but these were definitely coming from outside; the police were responding. Kareem looked over to the exit ramp. If he chose to stay and continue his assault on Fournier, he'd be trapped.

He punched his fist into his open palm and spun around. "There!" He pointed to the only objects in the garage other than the truck: the parking blocks in each parking space. The blocks were the solid black rubber kind with yellow reflective stripes, about six feet long, mounted to the concrete with metal spikes. One of Kareem's men got a pry bar from the truck and with a lot of kicking and swearing, they managed to get one loose.

It barely spanned the hole in the floor of the elevator. Bryn knew without being told that she'd be the guinea pig to test it. Her new boots hadn't been kind to her feet that day, and now she was asking them to take her across a narrow, unstable bridge over a yawning void with jagged edges that would tear her to pieces if she fell. She wobbled the first few steps, but when she rested her left hand against a portion of buckled paneling, she got her balance. When she reached the middle of the parking block, it began to sag a bit and with a secret smile, she knew it wouldn't hold the heavier men's weight. The corridor ahead was empty, but it ran perpendicular to the elevator, which meant there could be anyone waiting on either side. She doubted they'd stop to confirm her identity before shooting, so her only hope was to hit the ground flat. She placed her right foot on the very end of the parking block and, taking a deep breath, launched herself forward. The force of her leap pushed the parking block out from under her, so she didn't get as far as she'd intended, but two things happened: she dove to the ground without getting hit by any bullets, and the parking block clattered into the hole. A brief glance over her shoulder showed the angry face of Kareem's lieutenant. As he raised his rifle she rolled out of view.

"Get another parking block!" From the sound of Kareem's near-screaming voice, he'd lost any semblance of control. Bryn got to her feet and started down the long, wide corridor. It looked like she'd entered an abandoned hospital, but just as she was beginning to think the xenos that ran the place had all vacated, she turned the corner and found it full of men running in her direction. She closed her eyes, threw her hands into the air and braced for some kind of impact.

"What the hell are you doing here?" Lupus' gravelly voice sent shivers down her spine.

She looked up. Scott had stopped next to him and his surprised face sparked so many emotions she almost laughed aloud. Not only was he alive and well, but since he, Lupus, Dundee and two other men were all holding guns, it appeared his cover was still intact. Lupus and Dundee had matching slings on opposite arms and neither one looked all that healthy. They must have been recruited from their hospital beds to defend Fournier's facility. The odds were not in their favor.

"Long story," she said, "what's important is there are seven ARA soldiers in the parking garage. They have guns and grenades, but they damaged the elevator floor when they blew the doors, so they can't get across."

"Then how'd you get across, Darlin'?" It was Dundee who asked. "They throw you?"

She told them about the parking block. "They're getting another one now, but I don't think it'll hold any of their weight. Oh, and I'm pretty sure the cops are on the way, but Kareem is crazy mad. He's not going to leave."

"The cops'll box him in and keep him busy," Scott said in a low voice.

Lupus said, "Give them your weapons."

Scott and Dundee handed over their rifles to the other two men while Lupus issued instructions. "Hold them off. When the power goes out, you better be at the tunnel."

The two men trotted off. When they disappeared around the corner, Lupus looked at Bryn. His face was impossible to read, but she suspected he was more than annoyed at having to deal with her. "You and I are going to have a serious talk about how you ended up among the ARA, but now's not the time. Dundee. Take Porky here to Padme in the control room."

Bryn met Scott's gaze. His eyes were brimming with warning; he didn't have to tell her not to protest, not to ask that Scott be the one to escort her.

She knew no matter what, he'd stay in character and do as he was told. She'd been so relieved to see him, but his presence didn't make her any safer.

Dundee grabbed her arm, the one everyone had been hauling her around by lately. Before he could pull her along with him, she yanked it free. "I can walk, thank you."

His mouth quirked in a smile that wasn't reflected in his flat eyes. He swept an arm in front of him. "After you."

Chapter Fifty

Scott and Lupus wove their way through the maze of corridors. When they arrived at the door to Fournier's reception area, it immediately opened. Nicola looked flustered. "Thank goodness you're here. He's pretty upset."

Fournier chose that moment to burst out of his office, thin hair mussed and face red. "Where the—Lupus! Padme has informed me that the ARA are at our door. And now of course the police are here. How did this happen?"

"We'll figure that out when the smoke settles. Right now, I suggest you allow the staff to take one of the escape tunnels." Lupus spoke calmly, but Scott sensed the tightly coiled anger beneath the surface.

Fournier snapped, "Yes, yes, have Padme unseal the main tunnel, and tell her to turn the damned alarm off! I'll be right behind you; I have to wipe my holo drive. Cougar, I'm placing Nicola's safety in your hands. And Lupus— get the panda out! Those bastards won't get it a second time. Go!" His hands flapped as he vanished behind his office door.

"Wait, we're leaving?" Nicola pouted like May always used to before she was going to cry. "I need to get my stuff."

Lupus shot Scott a look that said, "Deal with it." As he ran out, Scott caught the door and held it for Nicola, saying, "There's no time. Come on."

To his consternation, she bolted in the opposite direction for a nondescript door on the far side of the room. With a groan of impatience, he tried to follow her inside, but found she'd locked it. He rattled the handle and said, "Nicola, there are men with guns who hate xenos outside. Come out."

"No! I have to pack!"

The door was the typical hollow particleboard found in houses everywhere. Scott stepped back and kicked a hole next to the knob. Getting in was a simple matter of reaching in and unlocking it. The room was large and more than a typical teen bedroom. Besides the customary small bed, dresser set and desk, there was a treadmill, a big holovision mounted on the wall and a bookcase with real books.

He expected her to be grabbing her clothes or music or games, but she stood next to the bookcase, shoving books into a knapsack.

"These were my mother's," she said. "It's all I have of her."

Scott knew he hadn't been wrong about Nicola being a clone since Padme had confirmed it. Was Nicola unaware of her origins, or did she consider her genetic donor her mother? Either way, her tearful determination to rescue the books meant she'd been told her 'mother' was dead.

"All of them?" There was no way they'd be able to carry the load between them.

"No, just these psychology books. And my bird. I can't leave her." She handed him the knapsack and darted across the room to grasp the handle on top of a cage containing a grey and white cockatiel. The bird let out a protesting squawk and flapped its wings as she lifted it. Scott took note of a patch on its breast where feathers were missing; feathers that matched the ones forming Nicola's eyebrows. The bird was her xenodonor, and the fact that it was still alive told him a lot about the girl's character—and about Fournier's indulgence of her.

"Okay." She stood for a moment in the middle of her room and took a deep breath. "I'm ready."

Scott briefly contemplated marching into Fournier's office to arrest him. The police were outside, the entrance to the clinic had been breached and it was only a matter of time before the XIA took over.

But Bryn had somehow managed to get herself in the thick of things again. No telling what Dundee would do with her if he got the chance. The Australian xeno may be injured, but he could not be discounted as a threat. Scott had the opportunity to make up for his past failure to protect her, and he was damned if he was going to let her get hurt again.

Chapter Fifty-one

The moment Bryn and Dundee rounded a corner that put them out of sight of the others, he grabbed her arm again, but instead of steering her down the hall, he pushed her through the nearest set of double doors. It was dark in the room, except for the light from the corridor shining through the rectangular windows in the doors. He shoved her up against a wall and his body followed. Crushed up against him, she cringed away in disgust.

"I think we've got enough time to get to know one another." His hips grinding against hers made his meaning clear. She tried to push him away, but even injured, he was significantly stronger.

His breath was moist and foul, but thankfully, the quills kept him from getting any closer. "Get those quills out of my face," he said.

Cooperation had gotten her out of a lot of scrapes lately. "I can't," she said, trying to sound reasonable. "They do that when I'm scared, and you're hurting me."

"The Dundee won't hurt you…much." He pulled away, but only to fumble at his belt with his good hand.

To hell with cooperation. Bryn made a break for the door, but his hand shot out and grasped her wrist. When he pulled her back towards him, she used the only weapon available to her: she head-butted him in the face with all her might. He screamed and released her wrist so suddenly she stumbled and fell to the floor. The top of her head was ringing from the blow, but she scrambled to all fours and crawled to door. She expected him to fall on her any second, but he was still screaming, and a quick glimpse showed at least a dozen quills protruding from his face, several of which had penetrated his eyes.

"Oh, my God." She surged to her feet and shot through the door, hand over her mouth because she was afraid she would vomit, not sure if she was more horrified at what he'd almost done to her or what she'd done to him. Nearly hysterical, she ran down the corridor back in Scott's direction, but he was nowhere in sight. She heard gunfire in the direction of the elevator, which spurred her to run the opposite way. After a few turns, she was hopelessly lost.

She kept moving, expecting at any moment to round a corner that would bring her back to a bloody-eyed, homicidal Dundee. Instead, she ran into Lupus.

"What the...?" he said. "Where's Dundee?"

"I—I..."

He grabbed her poor arm and hauled her after him with a frustrated grunt. She jogged next to him as he strode through a big room filled with animals. "Cutty!" he hollered.

A thin woman in a lab coat poked her head out of the door. "What's going on?"

"Get the panda in a portable with wheels and do it now! Meet by the main tunnel in five minutes."

"Five minutes?" the woman protested.

Lupus didn't stick around to hear her complaints. He dragged Bryn out, around another corner and stopped in front of a heavy white door. He slammed his hand on a button. "Padme!"

A buzz sounded and he opened the door. Inside was a room jam-packed with equipment and monitors. Padme was multi-tasking, rushing from place to place, tossing things into a black gym bag, tapping holokeys, and talking to someone. She held a hand up to stop Lupus from interrupting her and gave Bryn the briefest of glances. From the sound of the conversation, Padme was giving Fournier advice on how to destroy evidence.

Bryn looked at a holoscreen monitor with split views of the Warehouse, the parking garage and inside the facility. Padme hadn't expressed surprise at seeing Bryn because she would have noted her arrival, seen her run into Lupus and Scott. Had she seen what Bryn had done to Dundee? Bryn didn't see the Australian anywhere on the monitor and all the corridors looked the same. She kept her eyes glued to the holoscreen as Padme wound up her conversation and began making plans with Lupus.

"Turn off the alarm," Lupus said, and Padme hit a holokey. The constant ringing ceased. "Now unseal the main tunnel."

Padme tapped more keys. She paused to look around her, shaking her head. "I hate to see it all go up in flames," she said. "But we have ten minutes."

Bryn saw several things happening on the holoscreen. In the Warehouse, police had engaged the ARA soldiers. One corridor showed the woman from the animal room pushing what appeared to be a cage on wheels with the help of another white-coated figure. Scott and a young woman were running down another corridor. With a flash of trepidation, Bryn saw Dundee appear, feeling his way along the wall with his hands. From a view of the elevator from the clinic side, a battle had ensued. She said, "Um, we got incoming."

Lupus looked at the holoscreen, which now showed one of his men down and the other trying to hold off Kareem and three of his soldiers who'd managed to cross over the void in the elevator floor. One of the ARA guys tossed a grenade, and Lupus' man ran out of view to escape it. Bryn heard a dull boom and the walls shook. Lupus swore and grasped the rifle slung from his good shoulder. "Get out. Get everyone out."

He left, and without further ado, Bryn said to Padme, "I know what you did, and it backfired."

Padme stuffed one final item into the gym bag and zipped it up. "Not really. My goal was to get you out of the picture, and look where you are." She hefted the gym bag.

"I'm in the same place as you."

"Not for long." Without warning, Padme hurled the gym bag at Bryn. She caught it, but it was heavy and knocked her back, giving Padme enough time to slip out and slam the door. Bryn dropped the bag and tried to turn the handle, but it was a security door and Padme had done something to lock it from the inside.

Padme had said they had ten minutes before the place went up in flames.

Bryn was trapped.

Chapter Fifty-two

Nicola's bird was not happy and wanted everyone to know it. The alarm had shut off, but that only made the sound of gunfire and explosions more prominent—and the bird's piercing chirps no longer had competition. As they ran down the corridor, Scott hoped they wouldn't have to hide from the invaders; if so, the bird would quickly give their location away. On the heels of that thought, they came to a cross section that was filled with smoke. From the sound of it, the ARA had gotten through and were taking, and returning, fire.

Scott stopped in his tracks and asked Nicola, "Is there another way?"

She shook her head. "The tunnel is near the control room."

Footsteps coming from the direction of the gunfire alerted him. He pushed open one of the hospital double-doors and said, "This way!"

Nicola preceded him into the dark room, bird screeching madly.

"Can't you shut it up?" Through the narrow windows in the doors, Scott saw Kareem appear out of the smoke, headed in their direction.

"She's scared!" Nicola said.

"Shh! Hide!" Scott grabbed the cage and pulled it from her grasp, setting it on a counter near the doors before pushing Nicola into the corner behind a cupboard. He squatted in front of her, looking around for something he could use as a weapon. He had a choice between the books in the knapsack on his back, or one of the glass bottles on a shelf directly across from them. The bottles were filled with a clear liquid, and might just be heavy enough to take someone down if he threw it accurately. He leaned over and snatched one off the shelf before ducking back. The bird shrieked.

The light in the room darkened briefly and then got brighter. Scott risked a look and saw no one. Presumably, Kareem had glanced in through the window in the door, identified the source of the squawk and moved on.

"Let's go. Lupus said we'd better be at the tunnel when the power goes out." Scott wasn't sure what that meant exactly, but Lupus wasn't one to issue warnings without merit. He stood and moved out of the way for

Nicola. She crawled out from behind the cupboard and then exclaimed, "Gross!"

Scott shushed her again as she got up and held her hand out. "Is this…blood?"

It was too dark to tell for certain, but the smudge on her palm did look like blood. He saw something on the floor and with a sudden apprehension bent to pick it up. It was thin and about six inches long. He held it in the light coming through the window. He'd seen Bryn's quills enough to know which end was the root and which the point. Blood covered the point end, which didn't mean it wasn't Bryn's, but at least the quill hadn't been yanked from her head.

He'd had no choice but to let her go with Dundee, but that didn't ease his guilt. If that reptilian bastard had hurt her…but Scott didn't have time to imagine payback.

The bird had gone silent, but as soon as Nicola picked up its cage again, it produced another round of skull-splitting shrieks. She set the cage back down and removed her sweater. Once she'd tied it around the cage, the bird quieted down. Scott gave her a thumbs-up, and they cautiously went back into the corridor. In his left hand, he still held the bottle of liquid, just in case.

The way was clear in both directions. Scott took Nicola's hand and they began to run. A glance down the corridor where the smoke had cleared showed two bodies lying prone on the floor. They rounded a bend and up ahead, a man in a sling was walking slowly, dragging his hand along the wall.

"Who's there?" Dundee called. "Help me!"

Scott grinned at the sight of his blood-smeared face. Unfortunately, Nicola didn't find it as amusing. She screamed. Scott started to pull her past him, but Dundee threw his good arm out and attempted to grab her. Scott wanted to punch him in the face, but it was obvious Dundee couldn't see, and he'd never been one to hit a man when he was down. He got between Dundee and Nicola and took hold of Dundee's arm.

"Where's Bryn?" he asked. "I mean, Porky?"

"That bitch!" Dundee spat. "Look what she did to me! I'm going to kill her!"

It was obvious from Dundee's comment that he didn't know where Bryn was and the last time he'd seen her, she'd been alive. Whatever he'd done to get a face full of quills, leaving an injured man behind went against everything Scott had been trained for in the Marines. He tugged on Dundee's arm and said, "Come on. We'll get you to the tunnel."

It was much slower going after that, but eventually they reached the door to the control room. Nicola said, "It's not far from here."

He stopped in front of the camera over the door. "Padme? Are you still in there?"

No response. All he heard was a kind of banging noise, a muted, rhythmic sound that he dismissed as distant gunfire. They didn't have time to linger. He guided Dundee down the corridor. Nicola led the way.

Chapter Fifty-three

When Scott turned and followed the pretty blonde girl away from the control room door, Bryn stopped banging and screamed at the holomonitor, "No! Scott! I'm here!" It was bad enough he'd been five feet away and couldn't hear her through the security door, but he was helping her would-be rapist, Dundee.

Bryn sat in the office chair and pulled it up to Padme's holo computer, but found the computer locked and password protected. She yanked open the top drawer of the desk and began tossing things out. Pencils, pens, ruler, batteries—no password on a sticky note. She opened the next drawer down and found books and notepads with writing—in Arabic script. The bottom drawer had coffee mugs, dishes, boxes of tea and snack bars. She slammed it shut and looked frantically around the room. Padme was an uncommonly neat person, and the room didn't have any other cupboards or shelves.

Her eyes fell on the black gym bag Padme had thrown at her. Padme had been packing to take it with her; it stood to reason that the items in the bag were of value to her, but she'd sacrificed them to get away. Bryn unzipped it and dug through the contents. These were Padme's personal items, a scarf, sunglasses, books and, "Aha!" It was a holoreader, an older version, but still Internet capable. She turned it on and found that Padme had password protected it, too. Bryn started to throw it across the room, but the screensaver stopped her. It was a holograph of Scott.

What had Padme said? That she'd wanted Bryn out of the picture. It hadn't made sense at the time, and it still didn't. Even if Padme was madly in love with Scott, Bryn found it hard to believe she would kill for him. But then again, Bryn had met an awful lot of people lately who had contempt for life, especially if that life was not their own.

Padme also said they had only ten minutes before the place went up in flames. Bryn didn't know how much time had passed, but it couldn't be long now before whatever was going to happen…happened. She made another pass around the room. There were no hinges on the door to remove.

There was only one vent in the ceiling, but it was way too small. Bryn squinted at the ceiling itself. The rest of the facility had those drop-panel ceilings common in office-buildings, but this room appeared solid all around. The walls were painted cinderblock, but she could see nail pops all in a row down the middle of the ceiling where the sheetrock or drywall had come away from the stud. From the dust on the desk, it must have been recent; maybe due to all the explosions.

She knew about nail pops because three years ago a strong earthquake out of Quebec surprised New York residents unused to feeling the earth tremble under their feet. At the Vega household, several items had fallen from the mantel and a crack appeared in the drywall of the dining room. Bryn had helped her dad tear it down and put up a new wall. She'd had a sledgehammer and a pry bar then, but there were plenty of objects in the control room suitable for the job.

She rushed from one piece of equipment to another, selecting something long and heavy—she didn't know its function—and unplugging it. She climbed up on the desk, ducking down because the ceiling was so low. The nail-pops indicated where the two-by-four stud was, so she aimed for a spot a few inches away. The first blow barely made a dent and she worried the material used to construct the ceiling was tougher than she thought. After a half dozen more hits, though, she'd knocked out a hole as big as her fist. She dropped the makeshift sledgehammer and put her hand through the hole up to her elbow, thrilled when she encountered nothing in the space beyond the ceiling. She reached up with her other hand and curled her fingers around the edge. It was a simple matter of hanging her body weight from the sheetrock to break a large piece off. In less than a minute, she'd made a hole big enough to fit her body through.

She stuck her head inside and saw the control room framework, silver air ducts, pipes and wiring. Above that was concrete; beyond was nothing but black, but that didn't stop her from climbing up and crawling along the studs. The light from the control room faded the farther she got. Soon, she felt ahead of her and encountered something different. Instead of two-by-fours, the ceiling consisted of thin metal bars holding up panels. She sat on the last stud and kicked easily through the nearest panel. It fell to the ground, but the space below was black. Bryn turned onto her belly and dropped down, hanging by her hands and swinging before letting go. It was a short drop to the ground. She touched around her: shelves with mystery items on them. She felt her way around the perimeter of the place until her hand encountered a light switch. It was a storage room.

When the door handle turned under her hand with no resistance, she nearly cried aloud in relief.

Chapter Fifty-four

Scott expected a crowd of people to be waiting at the tunnel entrance, but the only one there was Padme. She was standing between a plain door and the caged panda.

"What happened to you?" she asked Dundee.

"I need to see the doc," he muttered.

"Can you see…at all?" She waved a hand in front of his face. Dundee kept his eyes closed, leaned against the wall and didn't answer.

"Oh, look!" Nicola said, leaning down to look at the panda. Someone must have sedated the animal, because it was lying on its side, face mashed against the mesh of the cage.

"It won't fit," Padme said. "The tunnel is too narrow for the cage. I let the others go ahead while I figure out how to get the panda out."

Dundee slid down the wall in a heap, but turned his face up when Scott asked, "Did Bryn get out?"

Padme nodded. "Everyone is accounted for, all the patients and staff, except two of the men, Lupus and Dr. Fournier."

Nicola gasped. "Where's my dad?"

"I spoke to him a few minutes ago. He is on his way."

"Lupus' men are dead," Scott said. "The ARA are roaming the corridors."

"All of you must go," Padme said. "In minutes, incendiary devices throughout the facility will be ignited."

"Did they get all the other animals out?" Nicola asked. Padme nodded again, but Scott knew this time it was a lie. It made him sick to think of all the bioengineered animals burning to death. If he could, he'd save them all, down to the smallest creature. But at least Bryn was okay; and Scott had been charged with Nicola's safety. He set the jar he'd been carrying down, noting that it was labeled 'Grease,' the chemical that burned cool fire. It seemed like forever since he'd been living up above in the Warehouse among the xenos, fighting his way into their good graces. His mission, to find the facility, had been accomplished. All he had to do now was wait for Fournier at the safe end of the tunnel and he could bring the Bestia Butcher to justice.

He urged a protesting Dundee to his feet as Padme opened the door. Inside was a broom closet. He wasn't surprised when Padme kicked the bottom corner of the back wall and a secret door opened. Mouse had been right: Fournier had tunnels in all his buildings.

Nicola took her birdcage in one hand and helped Dundee into the tunnel with the other, saying, "You poor man. Daddy will fix you up soon."

Scott started to follow, but Padme stopped him and said softly, "I meant what I said. When we get topside, will you help me cut a deal?"

"You know I'll do what I can."

He looked over her head and saw Lupus just as she placed her hand on his cheek. It must have looked like a lover's caress to Lupus, because anger narrowed his eyes to threatening slits. He didn't act on it, however, because he wasn't alone. Kareem Williams held Lupus, and now Scott and Padme as well, at gunpoint.

Chapter Fifty-five

All the corridors looked alike. Bryn tried to remember from the monitors where she might be, but she hadn't gotten a good idea of the floor plan even from the control room. Everywhere she turned she saw evidence of the fight between the ARA and the xenos. There were bullet-holes and blown out walls and…dead men. She ran down each corridor and stopped before she got to each intersection to look and make sure she wasn't about to run into anyone. The place seemed deserted. She couldn't go out the way she came, so her only hope was to find the escape tunnel and hope it was still open.

She reached a corner with an official-looking wooden door and tried the handle. It didn't turn, but whoever had come through it last hadn't shut it properly and it opened. Inside was a typical reception area. She heard a noise further in, behind another door. Was this where the tunnel was? The clock was ticking; she didn't have time to dawdle in uncertainty. She ran through the reception area and the empty office beyond. The rooms ended in what she instantly recognized as the bedroom of Dr. Fournier. There was no mistaking the shelves full of preserved body parts, lovingly displayed and lighted like precious works of art.

Bryn put the back of her hand to her mouth and looked away. The noise she'd heard was clearer now—an angry shout for help coming from what looked like a closet. She hurried over and looked in; a secret door at the back of the closet gaped ajar. The tunnel went straight down a set of metal stairs. Somewhere below, a light appeared, disappeared and appeared again.

"Padme!" A man yelled. "Lupus!"

The cry for help wasn't the motivating factor that spurred Bryn to take the vertical stairs two at a time; this was the escape tunnel, and she was thrilled to have found it. The walls were damp and close. At the bottom she had to duck down, just like at Bluto's, only here, the dirt walls weren't reinforced with concrete, they were shored up with the occasional wooden four-by-four. After walking only ten feet, she saw the problem: a cave-in had trapped someone. The grenade explosions must have made the dirt walls unstable. Out of a pile of rocks and earth protruded a head and shoulder. The man waved the flashlight in his one free hand and shouted, "Help!"

"I'm here," Bryn said.

The man tilted the flashlight in her direction and tried to look over his shoulder at her. Even filthy and badly lit, Bryn recognized him. She'd seen Dr. Fournier's holograph enough times during her recovery to know him anywhere.

"Get me out of here!" he bellowed.

She started to mindlessly obey but stopped. "No. Maybe this is a fitting end for you."

"Who is that?"

"Someone who hates you with all her heart."

"Well, I guess we'll die together then," he said. "Because you won't be getting out any other way."

Bryn bit her lip. He had a very valid point. There wasn't enough room for her to crawl along the pile of rubble and over his head, even if he didn't grab hold of her to prevent her leaving. She would have to help him, but there was one thing she could get out of him in exchange first: information.

In all the fantasies she'd had about confronting him, her main concern had been to find out why he'd ruined her life. She thought about asking him 'why?' now and realized the point was moot. His motivation, however complex and revealing, was unimportant. He was a screwed-up individual who liked to hurt people, period.

She thought about clarifying her father's role in all of this, but knew that too, was unimportant. He and Fournier obviously had history. They schemed together to do this for their own, possibly very different, reasons. If she got out of this alive, she wanted to give Scott something back for all he'd done for her. She wanted to make her part in this insanity mean something.

"Tell me about the pandemic," she said.

"Who is that?"

"It's Bryn Vega."

"No kidding?" he craned his neck in an attempt to see her again. "How the hell did you get here?"

"You want to waste time discussing the details, or do you want to tell me the truth so I can rescue you?"

"Your dad told you, I assume? What did he leave out?"

"All he said was he did this to me to protect me."

"Right, well, that was one of the reasons. Um, okay, it's simple really. Your father was the one who first noticed that your mom never got sick after she got the pig heart."

"You were her surgeon?" It should have occurred to her long ago.

"Of course. Don't you remember?"

"No." She'd been a kid at the time. The doctors talked to her dad and her dad told her what was happening. She hadn't had any interaction with the surgical team.

"Well, yes, I was. I investigated your father's concerns and discovered Miranda's xeno heart somehow activated her immune system against normal human ailments both viral and bacterial. I still don't know exactly how."

He was talking fast. The tunnel air was moist and cold enough to make her shiver even in her jacket.

He said, "One of my xenos went to South America and came back carrying typhoid. I don't know whether the bacteria he brought back was already mutated or if it somehow mutated after he'd contracted it, but yes, I do have a strain in my possession that has the potential to devastate humanity if it got out. There—is that what you wanted to know?"

A groaning noise from a wooden beam over his head alerted her to the fact that the walls and ceiling were still unstable. She began digging. He set the flashlight down so it shone in his direction and helped with his free hand as best he could. Bryn concentrated on his left shoulder in order to dig out his other arm. The wooden beam groaned again. She picked up the flashlight and stepped back, shining it above Fournier's head. With a suddenness that shocked her, the beam snapped. Earth from above forced it down so quickly she barely had time to jump away, and even so, her legs were buried up to her knees.

The air was clogged with dust. She coughed and kicked her legs free. When she shined the flashlight on the pile of debris, she didn't see Fournier at first. Then she saw his hand, clenching and unclenching.

He was still alive. And more importantly, the tunnel was still open. She swallowed her panic and climbed up the pile, digging frantically. She concentrated on the place where she'd last seen his head, the place now occupied by a shattered support beam. Luckily, the dirt was loose enough that she dug his face free within a few seconds. He gasped for breath in the murky air. The flashlight revealed a deep gash across his forehead. The dirt on his face had become bloody mud.

"Forget me," he said. "Get out!"

She hated this man with every cell in her body. Still, tears fell. "I'm sorry," she murmured, looking through the narrow hole that led to the intact tunnel beyond him; the way to freedom.

"Bryn." His voice was weak. "Your mother would be proud."

It was quite possibly the last thing she expected to hear coming from the Bestia Butcher.

"Tell your father...tell him Nicola is not for him. I made her for me." He was whispering now. "But she was never Miranda."

Bryn had no idea what he was talking about. She would have to crawl over his head to get out, and as repugnant as she found the idea, she would do it to survive. But the tunnel wasn't done collapsing. Clumps of dirt began to rain down on her and she was forced to back away again, toward the ladder. In one big rumble, the right wall completely gave way. Bryn climbed the ladder to the top, knowing she couldn't help him now. She stumbled out of the closet, horrified that she'd witnessed Fournier's death, and scared witless now that the tunnel was gone.

She'd have to risk the elevator. She started for the door to Fournier's office, but just then, the power went out.

"Great," she said, recalling Lupus' words, "When the power goes out, you better be at the tunnel."

She still had the flashlight, and by its light she crept past the grisly display of body parts, aware of a strange new sound coming from all around, sort of a whooshing. She went by the bed and tripped over something on the floor. In reaching out to steady herself, she knocked into a podium with one of the jars on it. It began to fall and instinctively, she caught it.

The flashlight illuminated the contents briefly. "Gross," she muttered, recognizing a heart when she saw one, but the label on the jar stopped her cold.

Miranda Vega.

Fournier had kept her mother's heart.

She set the jar back on the pedestal, mouth working with no sound coming out until finally: "Oh, Mom."

She ran. Through the office, through the lobby and out into the maze of corridors. Even with the flashlight, it seemed as if her eyes had adjusted to the dark. There must be a light source. She looked around as she ran. The whooshing was louder, and it was definitely getting brighter. She looked up. Several of the ceiling panels appeared to be glowing orange.

Fire.

And now she could smell it, noxious smoke from the synthetic material making up the panels. Shouldn't they be fire resistant? But Fournier had built this place with escape in mind and perhaps he'd chosen a product with an inadequate safety rating. A product that to her untrained eye seemed to be more flammable than it should.

Chapter Fifty-six

When the power went out, Scott shoved Padme into the closet, shouting into the dark, "If you shoot, Kareem, you'll hit the panda!"

Lupus had taken the opportunity to make his way closer, as Scott found out when the big man smashed him into the wall and said, "Stay away from my woman."

Scott wanted to tell him she was all his but wasn't sure if Padme was still standing in the entrance to the tunnel. He didn't want her to overhear and—well, not misinterpret exactly—he just wanted to keep her thinking he cared. He said nothing and Lupus backed off, but only because the Clinic's incendiary devices had ignited.

Scott made a move for the closet, but Kareem could see him now in the light from the fires all along the ceiling. "Stay where you are."

"Dude," Scott said, "This place is on fire. You want to burn to death, be my guest, but I'm headed out the escape tunnel here."

"Not without the panda!" Kareem shouted angrily.

Scott put his hands in the air. "It won't fit. The tunnel's too narrow."

"Then the two of you freaks will take it out of the cage and carry it." Kareem brushed a burning bit of ceiling out of his hair, but quickly got back behind the sight of his rifle. Lupus began coughing in the smoke.

"Lupus can't carry anything. Your girlfriend shot him, remember?"

"Then you do it!" From the pitch of his voice, Kareem was losing it. He might shoot them both out of spite if Scott didn't at least try to save the panda. He opened the cage and reached in. The panda's fur was coarse and thick; Scott struggled to get a grip, finally curling his clumsy fingers around its front legs and pulling. It rolled out onto the floor and uttered a weak, protesting cry. It got to its feet, though, and when Scott pushed it towards the closet, it took a few steps. It must have smelled the fresh, earthy air coming from the tunnel, because it staggered purposefully into the opening. Scott hoped there wasn't a precipitous drop ahead of it, or the panda would certainly fall.

"Now get away from that door," Kareem ordered.

Lupus stiffened next to him; Scott knew he was going to make a break for the tunnel. If that happened, Kareem would shoot, and Scott would be between Lupus and any bullets that came his way.

But then, in a bizarrely unexpected turn of events, footsteps heralded another player in the game. A figure ran around the corner at the end of the corridor, waving a flashlight through the smoky air. Kareem had to turn to see who was coming, and Scott's eyes dropped to the jar of grease on the floor. To his left and behind him, Lupus ducked into the closet. The figure running toward them through the burning embers let out a cry of happiness. "Scott!"

It was Bryn. Scott didn't pause to think about Padme's lie. He bent, picked up the jar of grease and hurled it. Kareem had swung his rifle in Bryn's direction, but rightly judged her as a non-threat. He was swinging back around toward Scott when the glass shattered at his feet. He jumped back but slipped on the grease and went down.

Bryn skirted the mess and ran towards Scott, who saw Kareem roll over and point his rifle, murderous intent in his eyes.

"Bryn, look out!" He yelled, but at that moment, a falling chunk of burning panel ignited the grease in a bright ball of cool fire. Engulfed in what he would assume to be flames, Kareem began screaming. Bryn didn't stop her headlong flight. She slammed into Scott, strangling him with her arms and poking him mercilessly with her quills. He quickly disentangled himself, pushing her into the tunnel. "Later!" he yelled. "Go!"

The fire surrounding Kareem had fizzled away to nothing, leaving a dazed and confused ARA leader. Scott rushed him before he got his senses back, snatching the rifle away. "You're fine! Go, go go!" Kareem did as he was told, coughing and wiping his eyes as he staggered to the closet. Scott followed him in, prodding him in the back with the gun. "Move!"

He shut the door behind him to keep out the smoke, but Bryn's flashlight up ahead illuminated the dirt-lined tunnel, which was just as narrow and low as the one at Bluto's. The ground slanted downward and then evened out. When they caught up to Bryn, she was kneeling over the panda. It was lying in a heap, growling with every exhale. Scott handed the rifle to Bryn and said to Kareem, "Help me." Between the two of them, they managed to heft the weakly struggling animal.

It was a long walk before the ground began to slant upward. Scott was sweating and shaking with effort. The panda had stopped struggling. After everything the xenos and the ARA had put the poor beast through, it was miracle it was still alive.

That was only one of Scott's worries. They finally reached the door at the end of the tunnel, but no matter what combination of kicks and thumps to its corners Bryn tried, it refused to open.

Chapter Fifty-seven

Bryn sat with her back against the door and coughed. The air in the tunnel was getting thicker with smoke. She'd seen Scott close the closet door at the clinic end, but it had probably caught fire and was no longer providing a barrier.

Scott and Kareem were coughing, too. The panda, which they'd set down in the dirt, had gone limp and suspiciously quiet.

Bryn felt tears trail down her cheeks as Scott sat next to her. "I thought you'd gotten out," he said. "Padme told me you had."

She lay down and felt a faint waft of fresh air coming from under the door. "She locked me in the control room. There's fresh air here."

Scott and Kareem joined her on the ground and all three pressed their faces to the door frame. Scott seemed to get strength from it, because he grabbed the rifle and said, "Get back."

Kareem coughed and said, "Don't bother. No bullets."

Scott fired anyway, but the gun only clicked. He doubled over with coughing and dropped to the ground again.

Bryn shined the flashlight in Kareem's face. "I don't suppose you still have my holophone?"

He reached into his pocket and pulled it out. Scott grabbed it and immediately dialed. Seconds later, he said, "Shasta! It's Scott. We're trapped in an escape tunnel. Air's going fast."

Even past the sound of Kareem coughing, Bryn heard Shasta's reply, "We're here at the Warehouse. What are your coordinates?"

"Sending," Scott said. He tapped at the phone.

"Got it. You're very close. On our way now. Can you report?"

Kareem asked, "What are you, a xenofreak cop?"

Scott ignored him and kept talking to Shasta. "Lupus and Padme got away. They may be in the building where we're trapped, but they aren't armed." He paused to cough long and deep. "Fournier is still in the building-"

"He's dead!" In the light from the flashlight, Bryn saw his surprise. "There was another tunnel," she said. "It collapsed on him."

To Shasta, Scott said, "Scratch that. Fournier is deceased." He coughed again. "What's your ETA?"

Shasta's voice came across sounding as if she were running and winded. "We're here. Where are you?"

Scott and Bryn shouted together, "Closet!"

Bryn went into a coughing fit, but she heard sounds on the other side of the tunnel door. Shasta grunted and said, "There's a printer here. Bastards. Hold on."

More noises, then a crash. This time, when Bryn banged her fist on the top right corner, the door swung outward. She forced it open as far as it would go and pushed her way through to the other side. The smoke from the tunnel followed her out. She expected Scott to be right behind her, but he and Kareem had stopped to get the panda. After they'd all gone through, Shasta shut the door against the smoke.

Scott fell to his knees coughing but gestured to Kareem. All he could say was, "Bad guy," but it was enough for the agent with Shasta to immediately cuff the ARA commander.

Bryn saw that they were in a building but was coughing and choking too hard in between sucking in fresh air to notice much about it. Shasta shepherded them outside where an ambulance was waiting at the curb. Two EMTs rushed over with oxygen. Bryn confronted Kareem, angrily pulling her mask away. "Where's Carla?"

He acted like he couldn't hear her as she gave Shasta a condensed version of her second kidnapping, focusing on what the ARA had done to Carla to obtain information. She glared at Kareem. "He knows where the house is."

Kareem's hands were bound behind his back and his mask prevented him from speaking, so he only stared at her with hostile brown eyes. Shasta nodded to the agent holding Kareem's arm, who removed the mask and handed it to the nearest EMT.

"Where's the house, Kareem?" Shasta asked in a soft voice.

"I'll tell you as soon as someone with the authority to cut me a deal gets here."

Scott made a move like he was going to punch him, but Shasta stopped him. "I have the authority to negotiate a deal," she said. "But I'm not going to."

Bryn started to protest, but Shasta told her, "Don't forget: all holophones save their location each time they're used. If you accessed holomaps like you said while you were at that house, the coordinates are on your phone."

Kareem was quick to volunteer the address after that. Shasta dispatched a team to the house, telling him, "She'd better be alive."

"She's fine," he muttered.

This time Bryn went after him. No one stopped her as she thumped him in the chest with the heels of her hands and exclaimed, "She's not fine, you son-of-a-bitch! You tortured her!"

Kareem yelled back, "We fixed her! She's not a xenofreak anymore."

The agent yanked him by his arm and dragged him to a squad car. Shasta asked Scott in an undertone, "Did he have contact with Dundee?"

"I don't know," Scott said. "Maybe. Did the lab identify the blood from the Wavecruiser? Is Dundee the carrier?"

Shasta nodded grimly. "We'll have to isolate Williams from the general population until we're sure he wasn't infected. Until we're sure how this thing spreads."

Bryn remembered what Fournier said about one of his xenos contracting typhoid in South America. Dundee was more dangerous than she'd imagined. She looked over at Kareem and almost felt sorry for him. Scott must have misinterpreted the look. He slipped his arm around her waist. "He'll get his. There's a lot of xenos in prison."

Chapter Fifty-eight

The column of smoke from the conflagration went from black to grey to white as the water from several fire hoses added steam to the mix. The wind blew it away from their location, which made Scott suspect the smoke he smelled was actually coming from his own clothes and hair.

The street was clogged with vehicles. Ambulances vied for space with police cars that made way for fire trucks. Animal Control officers were called to the scene. The poor panda was in bad shape. The officers scooped it up for transport it to the zoo, where experts would hopefully revive it.

Scott stood off discussing events with Shasta, keeping half an eye on Bryn, who was still getting oxygen in one of the ambulances. Shasta's boss, the Deputy Director of the XIA, arrived in all his pompous importance. Mark Unger was a silver-haired man in his late sixties who came to the XIA from the FBI, where rumor had it he was forced to transfer out due to a threatened sexual harassment claim. From Unger's fastidious demeanor, Scott was pretty sure the claim hadn't come from a woman.

Unger's personality made Shasta seem warm and fuzzy. He headed straight for them and barked, "Report!" from across the street. Scott dreaded telling him what he'd learned, but when he got close enough, he said, "Lupus' real identity is Eduardo Quinones."

Unger sneered and looked off into the distance. "What about Friedman?"

The other agent. "Deceased. Quinones killed him."

"How did you obtain this information?"

Scott gave him a brief rundown on what Padme told him about the nanoneuron program.

"Did you get a copy of it?" Unger asked.

"No, sir."

Before he could describe the circumstances under which he'd obtained the intel, Unger said, "Fat lot of good that does us."

He directed small, rheumy eyes Shasta's way. "Find out where Fournier's body is. I want it located the instant the fire is out even if your people have to go in there wearing oven mitts."

Scott accompanied her to the ambulance where Bryn sat looking stunned and exhausted. Shasta immediately began grilling her about the location of the collapsed tunnel. Bryn tried to explain that she'd been hopelessly lost down there, but Shasta fired question after question at her until she obtained an approximate location. Soon after that, the fire was out, and Shasta went off to find Fournier's remains.

Bryn got kicked out of the ambulance when a severely injured xeno was pulled from the Warehouse alive. She sat next to Scott on the curb, where they shared a bottle of water and a protein bar the ambulance driver had offered them and watched emergency personnel scurry around.

"You're lopsided," Scott said, looking at her quills. "You really did a number on Dundee."

"He tried to…" she trailed off as her shoulders shook in a disgusted shudder.

Scott had suspected the Australian xeno had tried something and gotten schooled by Bryn. "He didn't hurt you, did he?"

"No."

"And Fournier? Did he say anything before the tunnel collapsed?"

"He said he had a mutated form of typhoid that could devastate humanity."

"Those were his words?" Shasta would appreciate the confirmation, but even with Bryn's testimony, he doubted the sluggish, bureaucrat-bloated CDC would jump on it. Bryn's words were hearsay; hardly damning evidence of a bioweapon, even combined with the bacterial samples they already had. They just didn't know enough about it.

Bryn rubbed her face, smudging the tearstained soot on her cheeks. "He said xenos were immune. That's one of the reasons my dad did this to me."

"To protect you. Huh." Scott looked over at the remains of the Warehouse and flexed his claws. He would always be a xeno, but he no longer had to pretend to be a xenofreak. Would his decision to mutilate himself to avenge his sister and parents ultimately save him? The irony struck him as funny somehow, but he didn't laugh. "Is that all he said?"

Bryn's brows dropped in a perplexed frown. "It was weird. I mean, everything's been weird, but he said something particularly strange about my mother. He gave me a message for my father that some girl—I don't remember the name—but he said this girl was not for my father. He said he made her for himself. The weird thing is that my dad's been talking about cloning. Human cloning; how he wants to legalize it."

"Was the girl's name Nicola?" Scott asked. He remembered the knapsack on his back and pulled it into his lap.

"Yes! How did you know? I don't understand what he meant, but he said she wasn't Miranda, and he was talking about my mom. I guess he was her surgeon all those years ago. He had all these gross body parts in jars just like everyone always said he had, and I saw…I saw my mom's heart…" Bryn's eyes shut tight on the memory.

Scott moved closer and put his hand on her back, rubbing up and down. "Look. I don't want to freak you out, but do you have any pictures of your mom when she was a teenager?"

"At home, yeah, why?"

"Because the cloning thing is real. I know for a fact Nicola is a clone."

"Okay." She sounded skeptical. "How do you know?"

"Because my sister was a clone. She was Fournier's first successful attempt. Well, successful to a point. She died because he made mistakes."

"I'm so sorry. But how did your sister…?"

"She was adopted. After he got busted, they found her and put her in the system and my parents adopted her without knowing what she was. Nicola looks just like her."

Bryn said slowly, "And you think my mom might look like…both of them?"

"These are Nicola's books." He unzipped the knapsack and took out one of the psychology textbooks. Inscribed on the inside front cover was the name he'd expected to see. Bryn looked at the words 'This book belongs to Miranda McKim.'

"You see?" he asked. "It makes sense."

"No, it doesn't! None of this makes sense. I want to see her. Nicola."

Scott took a breath and exhaled in frustration. "She's with Lupus and Padme."

"And Dundee? That's great. You want me to believe Fournier cloned my mother and now that he's dead, she's on the run with a bunch of psychotic killers, one of whom can kill people just by sneezing on them?"

From behind them, Shasta broke into the conversation. "She's not your mother. And Fournier isn't dead. They excavated the collapsed tunnel. No body. Looks like that last cave in shook him loose on the far side of the rubble and he managed to escape after all."

Chapter Fifty-nine

Two weeks later.

Bryn sat at a table and waited for the guard to arrive, scratching nervously at her head. Since she was the first ever recipient of a porcupine xenograft, there'd been no one to warn her that newly sprouted quills itch like the dickens. Scott sat on one side of her and Carla on the other. They'd come along as moral support, but she suspected Carla was also itching—to tell her father off.

When Harry Vega was finally led into the room, he wore an ill-fitting orange jumpsuit. His cuffed hands were secured to his waist and he shuffled to his chair with shackled ankles. Bryn steeled herself against any sympathy as he sat across from her and stared into her face unblinking. He had puffy under-eye circles and his skin looked sallow in the artificial light.

"Hi, honey," he said. His entire demeanor was somber, as if he'd been beaten down. Scott's words came back to haunt her, "There's a lot of xenos in prison."

The first thing she said to him, the only thing she really wanted to discuss, was, "Did you have Mom cloned?"

His gaze dropped to the table as he took a deep breath and released it slowly. "Not long after your mother received the pig heart, Fournier told me it wouldn't last. He said he wouldn't be able to convince the corporation that funded his research to pay for another xenotransplant attempt until he worked out the kinks. Said it was only a matter of time before the xeno heart would begin to fail and she would have to be put on the human heart donor list, which at the time was practically a death sentence since healthy hearts were so scarce."

Her father lifted his eyes. "He told me there was another way. If he could keep her alive long enough for a clone to grow up, for its heart to become big enough for transplant…"

"Its heart? A clone is still a person, Dad." Just like a xeno is still a person. "Mom would never agree to kill someone to save herself."

His head went back. "Of course she wouldn't. And neither did I. I told him no, but Vonda said he did it anyway. He was in love with your mother. You know she and I were having problems. I think she only stayed with me because of you, but I loved her with all my heart. Towards the end, if it had been up to me, I might have chosen to sacrifice the clone after all to save her. But that wasn't an option. It…she…was just a baby when Fournier was arrested. I don't know what happened to her after that, but I like to think there's another Miranda in the world somewhere. A Miranda whose heart is healthy."

Bryn felt Scott shift in his chair next to her, but he said nothing. She folded her arms on the table and leaned forward. "Dad, legalizing cloning won't change the fact that you'd be essentially raising human beings to harvest their organs."

That old fervent glint appeared in his eye. "Nonsense. Eventually, individual cloned organs will be grown in host bodies just like surrogate mothers grow babies. If you can bioengineer animal parts that are invisible to the human immune system, you can bioengineer human parts."

She didn't come here to give him a platform to air his ideals. He hadn't cooperated with the XIA, and they thought he might open up to Bryn if she asked him outright about the typhoid.

"You told me before that you thought a pandemic was coming. How did you know?"

He let out a short laugh. "After the surgery, your mom never got sick, even though you were a typical germ-filled kid who kept bringing home whatever was going around at school. You and me would get symptoms, but she never caught anything. I told Fournier I thought the xeno heart might have something to do with it; it intrigued him. After he went underground, Vonda and I occasionally talked. She's not allowed to speak to anyone about what Fournier does, but she considers me the exception because I know so much already. She told me about a xeno who's infected with a mutated form of typhoid and how Fournier was looking into ways to capitalize on it. It frightened her."

He tried to lift his hands and the chain rattled. "Not only did I not want to scare you with the truth, but it would have been dangerous to tell you. Vonda told me those people who died after the bank robbery were exposed. Anyone who came into contact with the carrier would die—unless they were a xenofreak."

Carla spoke up. "It's rude to refer to all xenos as xenofreaks."

He blinked. "Potato potahto. You think anyone cares at this point if I pretend to be reformed? I'm the enemy Grand Poobah. The only person more unpopular than me in this jail is Kareem Williams."

Scott drummed his furred fingers on the table, drawing her father's disapproving eye. "Protection is only a little cooperation away," he said.

Her father frowned and shook his head. "The XBestia have a long reach. They can get to xenofr—xenos in solitary confinement. They can get to me."

"Actually, they can only get to other xenos that have nanoneurons," Scott said. "I guarantee they won't touch you if you help us. We need to know where Fournier might be right now. Vonda's in hiding. How do you contact her? Help us stop him before any more pure humans die."

A veil dropped over her father's eyes. He sat back in his seat. "No. I've said enough. Bryn is safe and that's what's important." He stood so abruptly the legs of his chair scraped against the painted cement floor. "Guard!"

He shuffled to the door, looking resigned and defeated. Despite everything he'd done, Bryn suddenly found she believed his intentions were good. "I love you, Daddy."

His reply came softly. "I love you, too, Brynnie."

The door clanged shut behind him.

Chapter Sixty

Scott's usefulness as an undercover agent had run its course. If Fournier reestablished himself in the area, word would get out that Scott was a plant. He'd done his best to convince Shasta that Bryn needed a team to protect her, but Shasta demurred.

"She's not a threat to him. We already know everything she knows, so there's no point in his going after her."

"I'm not as worried about him as I am about Padme," Scott had pointed out.

It was moot; Shasta would have given in, but Unger was inflexible on the subject. Bryn was on her own.

Scott had been assigned a training position teaching recruits to fight dirty. He'd spent his free time over the last two weeks with Bryn, hoping someday he'd get to teach her some dirty things, too. But they'd taken it slow. What she needed right now was a friend, not a complicated romantic entanglement.

Today's visit with her father had been XIA-sanctioned, so he was technically on the clock when he drove Bryn and Mouse to the zoo. Mouse had quit Bluto's and gotten a job managing a concession stand there. When she tucked her hair into the forties-style hair net and plopped the little paper boat hat on her head, she became all business. Scott was hoping to get a break, but she made him pay full price for his and Bryn's lunch; hotdogs with all the fixin's that reminded him of Coney Island.

With a full mouth, Bryn said, "Remember Nosferatu?"

He nodded. Nosferatu's real name was Gordon Amador, a sex-offender out of California who hadn't bothered to register in New York. Coney Island attracted drifters like him looking for a lawless place to hunker down.

Scott and Bryn strolled in the direction of the new zoo exhibit. He saw a long line of people waiting to get in. It was a warm day, but Bryn didn't have to wear her leather jacket anymore. As a surprise, he'd had a local leather artisan construct a special collar for her. It was made out of soft-but-tough kidskin dyed to approximate her skin tone. It fit around her neck and flared out over her shoulders and down her back only as far as the quills reached. The artisan made it to be as unobtrusive as possible, and when Scott had given it to her, she'd been so touched she almost cried. Almost. After everything she'd been through, tears had become scarce in her new life.

They joined the back of the line, which stretched along a row of trimmed hedges. The people in front of them stared at Bryn, who smiled at them until they turned away. He caught the hurt look in her eyes, but she avoided his gaze and finished her hot dog in silence. The line moved slowly. They finished their lunch and he broke out of line to toss the wrappings in the trash. When he stood back next to her, it seemed natural to reach for her hand. She looked startled when he took it and ducked her head to hide a smile.

They were almost to the entrance of the exhibit. A freshly painted black and white mural decorated the outside of the brick building. Scott caught a glimpse of tall bamboo plants inside the glass enclosure. He automatically looked around him just before they entered. Other than the usual looks of contempt or interest, no one seemed to be watching them. In the distance, he saw the top of a cell tower on a hill.

The end.